My dear Readers,

Last month, I introduced you to Jesse McKettrick and his intrepid Cheyenne in *McKettrick's Luck*. This month, in *McKettrick's Pride,* you'll meet Rance McKettrick and the mysterious new bookstore owner Echo Wells. If ever there were two people who *weren't* meant for each other...

Rance is stubborn, handsome, practical and every bit as proud as his ancestor Rafe McKettrick. A widower with two small daughters and a consuming interest in the family conglomerate, McKettrickCo, Rance is all business. Echo, on the other hand, is a dreamer, with a heart as big as Arizona itself. She rescues a stray dog, drives a hot-pink Volkswagen and secretly runs an online love-spell business. Folks around Indian Rock start feeling the heat right away!

I also wanted to write today to tell you about a special group of people with whom I've recently become involved. It is The Humane Society of the United States (HSUS), specifically their Pets for Life program.

The Pets for Life program is one of the best ways to help your local shelter: that is to help keep animals out of shelters in the first place. Something as basic as keeping a collar and tag on your pet all the time, so if he gets out and gets lost, he can be returned home. Being a responsible pet owner. Spaying or neutering your pet. And not giving up when things don't go perfectly. If your dog digs in the yard, or your cat scratches the furniture, know that these are problems that can be addressed. You can find all the information about these—and many other common problems—at www.petsforlife.org. This campaign is focused on keeping pets and their people together for a lifetime.

As many of you know, my own household includes two dogs, two cats and four horses, so this is a cause that is near and dear to my heart. I hope you'll get involved along with me.

With love,

Linda Lael Miller

LINDA LAEL MILLER

McKETTRICK'S
Pride

HQN™

ISBN-13: 978-0-373-77190-5
ISBN-10:   0-373-77190-8

McKETTRICK'S PRIDE

To Sally and Jim Lang, with love

M^cKETTRICK'S
Pride

CHAPTER 1

THE DOG, FUR SOAKED, MATTED and muddy, sat for-
lornly on the rain-slicked pavement, next to Echo
Wells's custom-painted hot-pink Volkswagen bug.
Echo, rushing from the truck-stop restaurant with
the remains of her supper in a take-out box, in hopes
of not getting *too* wet before she reached her car,
stopped cold.

"I do not need a dog," she told the universe,
tilting back her head and letting the drizzle wash
away the last tired traces of her makeup.

The dog whimpered. It was a large creature, of
indeterminate color and breed. A slight indentation
around its neck revealed that it had once worn a

collar, and its ribs showed. One forepaw bore the brownish stain of old blood.

"Oh, hell," Echo said. She glanced around the parking lot, empty except for a few semitrucks and an ancient RV, but there was no one in sight, no one conveniently searching for a missing pet.

The dog had obviously been on its own for days, if not weeks—or even months.

Just imagining the loneliness, fear and deprivation the poor thing must have experienced made Echo shudder and opened a gaping chasm of sympathy within her.

The canine wayfarer had either been dropped off—there was a special place in hell, in Echo's opinion, for people who abandoned helpless animals—or it had gotten away somehow, while its owners were gassing up at the pumps or inside the restaurant having a meal.

"I just had this car detailed," Echo told the dog. The bug was her only vanity, a reckless indulgence with psychological implications she didn't care to examine too closely.

The animal whimpered again, and looked up at her with such sad hope in its soulful brown eyes that Echo's heart melted all over again.

Resigned, she rounded the car and opened the passenger door with one hand, balancing the take-out box in the other. The dog slunk along with her, half crouched, limping a little.

"Go ahead," she said gently. "Get in."

The dog hesitated, then made the leap into the seat—mud, rainwater and all.

Echo sighed, opened the take-out box and stood in the rain, hand-feeding the animal the last of her meat loaf special. So much for staying within her travel budget by stretching every meal into at least two more.

Ravenous, the poor critter gulped down its supper and looked up at Echo with such pathetic gratitude that tears came into her eyes.

"Don't worry," she said, to herself as much as the dog. "Everything's going to be okay."

She closed the car door, let the rain wash her hands clean, holding them out palms up as if in supplication, and rubbed them semidry on her ancient tan Burberry coat before settling behind the wheel once more.

The dog, dripping onto Echo's formerly clean leather seat, eyed her with weary adoration.

Echo started the car, and the combination of wet dog and her own soggy raincoat instantly fogged up the windows.

"This is Arizona," she complained to her new traveling companion. "It's supposed to be *dry.*"

The dog sighed, as if to concur that nothing was as it should be.

"You really *are* wet," Echo remarked matter-of-factly. She switched on the defroster, pulled the lever to open the trunk and braved the elements again to get out the quilt she'd carried around with her since childhood. After bundling the dog, she peeled off her raincoat and tossed it over the seat before getting back in the car and buckling up.

Cocooned in faded colors, the dog sighed again, lay down as best it could given the disparity between its size and that of the seat, and was snoring by the time Echo pulled out onto Highway 10.

Two and a half hours later, on the outskirts of Phoenix, she turned into the lot of a medium-priced chain hotel. The rain had stopped, and there was a muggy warmth in the night air.

The dog sat up, yawning, the quilt falling away in damp folds.

Echo assessed the creature again. "I was hoping to make it to Indian Rock tonight," she told her bedraggled passenger, "but I'm tired and, frankly, you stink. So I'm going to spring for a room, and we'll hit the road again in the morning. Wait here."

The dog looked alarmed at the prospect of her departure, and made a low, whining sound in its throat.

Echo patted its filthy head. "Not to worry, Muttzo," she said. "It's you and me until we find your people."

Grabbing her hobo bag, she got out of the car slowly, leaving a window cracked, and headed for the main entrance, hoping she didn't smell like the dog.

"Good news," she said when she returned after fifteen minutes, clutching a key card in hand. "We're in." The dog was so glad to see her that it leaned across and laved her face with its rough, meatloaf-scented tongue. "Of course, I *did* tell them you were a toy poodle."

Echo drove around to the back and parked under a light. The dog politely paused to do its business in the shrubbery while Echo wrestled one of her suitcases out of the Volks. Inside, they slogged along a carpeted hallway to room 117 and entered.

"You get the first bath," Echo told her canine friend, leading the way to the bathroom. As soon as she turned on the faucet in the tub, the dog leaped over the side and lapped thirstily at the flow.

The showerhead was on a long metal tube, one of those detachable jobs, so Echo took it down from its hook and knelt beside the tub. Finished slurping, the dog sat down, watching her, its eyes luminous with trust.

"What do you know?" Echo asked, after considerable spraying. Ten pounds of dirt rolled down to the bottom of the tub and swirled around the drain. "You're a white Lab. And female, too."

The dog gazed at her soulfully, enduring. One more trial in a long sequence of them.

Echo opened a tiny packet of soap and lathered the dog's coat. Rinsed. Lathered again. The soap bar wore away to a nubbin, so she fetched a bottle of shampoo from her cosmetic bag.

More lathering. More rinsing.

"You need a name," Echo said as she towel-dried the dog. "Since there's something faintly mystical and Lady-of-the-Lakeish about you—it's the eyes, I think—" She paused, pondered and decided. "I hereby dub you Avalon."

Avalon, apparently understanding that the bath was over, leaped out of the tub and stood uncertainly on the mat for a few moments, as though awaiting a cue. When Echo didn't issue any orders, the animal shook herself gloriously, dousing her human companion, and padded out into the main part of the hotel room.

Echo laughed, found the blow-dryer and plugged it into a wall socket. Avalon's snow-white fur curled endearingly under the onslaught of heat. Once the dog was thoroughly dry, Echo filled the ice bucket with water, set it on the floor and dodged into the bathroom for a badly needed shower of her own.

When she came out, bundled in a robe, with her curly, shoulder-length blond hair standing out around her head like an aureole, Avalon had curled up on the floor, at the foot of the bed. The dog opened one brown eye and lifted her head slightly, and there was a certain stalwart wariness in her manner now, as if she expected to be chased away.

Echo's throat tightened. She knew what it was like to feel that way, to hover on the fringes of things, hoping not to be noticed and, at the same time, yearning desperately to belong.

Her old life, in Chicago, had been all about waiting on the sidelines.

"Hey," she said, crouching to stroke Avalon's soft, gleaming coat. "I'm a woman of my word. We'll stick together, as long as necessary. Share and share alike." She put out her hand and, to her surprise, Avalon placed a paw in her palm. They shook on the deal.

After blow-drying her hair and winding it into a French braid to keep it from frizzing out, Echo pulled on a cotton nightshirt, brushed her teeth and climbed into bed, leaning to switch off the bedside lamp.

Avalon gave a soft, pitiful whine, as though she were crying.

Echo's eyes burned again. "Come on, then," she said. "There's room enough up here for both of us."

Avalon jumped onto the bed, nested at Echo's feet and fell asleep.

Echo, exhausted after days on the road, wasn't far behind.

CORA TELLINGTON GREETED HER granddaughters, Rianna and Maeve, with exuberant hugs, on the sidewalk in front of Cora's Curl and Twirl. The day was new-penny bright, and the only cloud on the horizon was the scowl on her son-in-law's face as he got out of the gigantic SUV he drove whenever he came back to Indian Rock.

Rance McKettrick eyed the storefront next to Cora's combination beauty salon and baton-twirling school, apparently noting that the For Sale sign was gone from the dusty display window.

"Finally unloaded the place, did you?" he asked. "Who's the sucker?"

Cora took in her late daughter's handsome

husband with a patient sigh. He stood six feet tall, and even in that expensive suit he was wearing, he managed to look like a rugged cowboy, just off the range. His hair was dark—Cora's fingers itched to give it a trim—and his blue eyes were dusky with his private sorrow. Since Julie's death, nearly five years ago now, though it didn't seem possible she'd been gone that long, Rance had been living a half life, going through the motions. Phoning it in.

Cora missed Julie as much as he did, if not more, because there are few losses more poignantly painful than burying one's only child, but she'd come to terms with the grief for the sake of her granddaughters. They were so young, only six and ten, and they needed her. Of course, they needed Rance, too, and he loved them, in his own harried, distracted way, but he seemed to be able to push them onto an emotional back burner whenever he went away on business—which was all too often.

"It's going to be a bookstore," Cora said of the storefront, as the girls rushed into her shop to raid the candy jar on the counter and be greeted by Cora's three employees, who always fawned over them. "This town needs one of those."

Rance assessed the place, looking skeptical. "It's going to take a lot of work," he warned. "And things are tough for independent bookstores these days. Everybody shops at big-box chains or online."

Cora ignored that. "I got a decent price," she said, studying him, with her hands on her still-slender hips. Thanks to years of baton twirling, Cora was still petite, even in her sixties, and she liked to dress flashy; hence her stylish jeans, silk blouse and rhinestone-trimmed denim vest. She changed the color of her hair often; that week, it was auburn, and pinned up into a do reminiscent of a Gibson girl's. "What's going on, Rance? You look like a thunderhead, rolling over the horizon and fixing to drop a *shitload* of rain."

Rance sighed, continuing to stand on the sidewalk, and for a moment, Cora felt sorry for him, even though she wanted to snatch him bald-headed most of the time, out of pure frustration.

"I was wondering if you could keep Rianna and Maeve for a few days," he said, having a hard time meeting her eyes. "There's a big meeting in San Antonio, at the head office. Even Jesse's going, which ought to tell you that it's critical."

McKettrickCo, the conglomerate that had made Rance's family rich, along with the largesse from their legendary Triple M Ranch, was on the verge of going public. There was a lot of dissension among the McKettricks over the move, and if they were converging on San Antonio, Cora realized, the meeting was indeed big. Jesse, Rance's cousin, was notoriously indifferent to company operations, but maybe now that he was planning to marry up with that Bridges girl, he'd decided to become more responsible.

To Cora's way of thinking, Rance and his other

cousin, Keegan, would have been better off to adopt Jesse's original attitude—cash the dividend checks and celebrate every new sunrise.

"Rance," Cora said carefully, "Rianna's birthday is coming up on Saturday. She was counting on a party. And Maeve's getting her braces on bright and early Monday morning, in case you've forgotten."

"Cora," Rance replied, looking grave and a little guilty, "this is important."

"Rianna and Maeve," Cora countered, "are *more* important."

"We're talking about their future," Rance argued, keeping his tone low. Folks were passing on the street, so he spared a rigid smile or two, but his overall expression went from grave to grim.

"Come on," Cora jibed. "They've already got trust funds that would choke a mule." She leaned in a little, to make her point. "What they *need* is a *father.*"

Rance bristled, as Cora could have predicted he'd do. "They've got one," he growled.

"Do they?" Cora asked. "Jesse pays more attention to them than you do. He's the one who came to their baton recital last week, when you were in Hong Kong or Paris or wherever the hell you were."

"Do we have to have this conversation on the goddamned sidewalk?" Rance demanded, in a furious undertone.

"We're not having it inside, where your *daughters* can hear."

Rance spread his hands. "Rianna and Maeve are

okay with this," he insisted. "We can reschedule the orthodontic thing, and Sierra's going to throw a little do for Rianna's birthday, on the ranch."

Cora folded her arms. She didn't like playing her trump card, but she was about to, because Rance McKettrick needed to wake the heck up and get it through his hard head that his girls were growing up. He couldn't keep on treating them like appointments to be shifted around to suit his crazy schedule. "What do you think Julie would say if she could see what's happened to her children, Rance? And to you?"

For a moment, he looked as though she'd struck him. Then he shoved one of his big rancher's hands through his hair and huffed out an exasperated breath. "Damn it, Cora, that was below the belt!"

"Call it whatever you want," Cora replied, hurting for him and determined not to let it show. "You and those little girls meant more to Julie than anyone or anything on earth. She gave up a career to make a home for all of you, out there on the Triple M, and now you treat the place like a hotel with express checkout!"

Rance was silent for a long time.

Cora waited it out, holding her breath.

"Will you look after Rianna and Maeve or not?" Rance finally asked.

Bitter disappointment swept through Cora like a harsh wind scouring a lonely canyon, even though she'd expected the conversation to end just this way. After all, it always did.

"You know I will," she said.

Rance took a conciliatory step toward her—raised his hands as if to lay them on her shoulders—then decided against the gesture and stood his ground. "I didn't pack any of their things," he said. "I figured you might want to stay in the ranch house, instead of here in town."

"You wouldn't know where any of their things *were*," Cora told him, defeated. *Julie, Julie,* she thought. *I try, but this man of yours is a McKettrick, and that means he's bone-stubborn. Might as well try to move one of these mesas as change his mind.* "You do what you've got to do. I'll take care of Rianna and Maeve."

"I appreciate it," Rance said, and Cora knew he was sincere. Trouble was, sincere fell a long way short of enough.

FEELING AS THOUGH HE'D JUST been dragged bare-ass naked over ten miles of bad road, Rance watched as his mother-in-law sashayed into the Curl and Twirl and slammed the door behind her. Squeezing the bridge of his nose between a thumb and forefinger in hopes of circumventing another tension headache, he turned and stepped off the curb just as a Pepto-Bismol-pink Volkswagen whizzed into the next parking space and nearly took off all ten of his toes.

It was a relief to have somewhere to focus his irritation.

"What the hell…?" he rasped, and stormed around to the driver's side of that bug, intending to open a can of verbal whup-ass on whoever was at the wheel.

The window went down, and a blonde with wide-set hazel eyes and a braid blinked up at him, cheeks flushing pink.

"I'm sorry," she said.

Rance leaned to glare in at her. A white dog, buckled into the seat belt on the passenger side, growled an eloquent warning. "I don't know where you come from, lady," Rance said, "but around here, people don't expect to get maimed for life trying to get into their own cars."

Her eyelashes fluttered, and her small, clearly defined mouth tightened a little. Her nose was delicate, and spattered with the faintest sprinkling of freckles. "Is that SUV yours?" she asked, after glancing into the rearview mirror.

"Yes," Rance answered, wondering what the hell his rig had to do with the price of rice in China.

"Well," she replied pertly, "if *you* drove a reasonable vehicle, instead of that enormous gas-hog, you would have seen me coming and the whole *non-incident* could have been avoided!"

Rance was so taken aback by her audacity that he laughed, but it was a short, gruff sound that made the dog growl again.

She blinked again, but then she stuck out a slender hand, startling him as much as she had by almost running him down. "Echo Wells," she said.

"What?"

"My name?" she prompted.

Rance took her hand. It felt cool and soft. The dog snarled and strained at the seat belt.

"Hush, Avalon," said Echo Wells. "We're in no danger. Are we—Mr....?"

"McKettrick," he supplied belatedly, holding on to her hand a moment longer than absolutely necessary. "Rance McKettrick."

She smiled suddenly, and Rance felt ambushed, as though he'd been dazzled by a sun-struck mirror popping up out of nowhere.

"No harm done," she said.

Rance wasn't so sure of that. He felt oddly shaken. Maybe she *had* run over him, with all four wheels, and he'd somehow survived and gotten to his feet in some kind of altered state. "What kind of name is Echo Wells?" he heard himself ask.

The smile faded, and it was something of a relief to Rance. The flash was still pulsing at the edges of his vision, but his knees felt a little steadier.

"What kind of name is Rance McKettrick?" she shot back.

Avalon bared her teeth and snarled again.

"What's with the dog?" Rance asked, mildly insulted. "I've always gotten along just fine with animals."

"You *did* come on a bit strong," said the redoubtable Ms. Wells. "Dogs are sensitive to energy fields, you know. And yours, if you don't mind my saying so, is a *mess*."

"I guess almost getting killed does that to a person," Rance said, after a moment or two of baffled recovery. "Messes up their—*energy field,* I mean."

Echo's cheeks went even pinker. The effect was similar to the smile, and Rance stubbornly resisted an impulse to back up a step or two. "Are you making fun of me, Mr. McKettrick?"

"No," he said, glancing at the crystal swinging from her rearview mirror. "But if you're into energy fields, then you're probably looking for Sedona, not Indian Rock."

She reached over, still staring defiantly into Rance's face through the open car window, and gave the dog a few reassuring strokes with her right hand. Momentarily, Rance wished he could sprout fur, so she'd touch him like that. A practical man, he quickly shook off the fanciful thought.

"Would you mind moving?" Echo asked, with acidic sweetness. "It's been a long drive, and I'd like to get out of the car."

Wondering what he was doing carrying on this conversation in the first place, Rance retreated.

Echo Wells opened the car door, unbuckled her seat belt and swung two shapely legs out to stand. The top of her head came just shy of his chin, and that skimpy little pink-and-white sundress of hers was about a size-nothing. Instead of the high-heeled shoes he'd have expected with an outfit like that, she was wearing pink high-top sneakers with gold ribbons for laces.

Smiling dreamily, as though Rance had turned transparent and she could see right through him to the feed-and-grain across the street, she drew a deep breath and expelled it from the diaphragm.

Rance frowned. He took up his share of space, and he wasn't used to being invisible—especially to women.

"Welcome to Indian Rock," he said, mainly to get her attention. His tone could have been a mite on the grudging side.

She went around to the sidewalk, opened the door on the other side, and let the mutt out. Avalon—silly name for a dog, just the kind of airy-fairy thing he'd expect from somebody with a crystal on her mirror, wearing pink high-tops and driving a car to match—pranced straight over and squatted next to his truck tire.

He glowered at the dog.

The dog obviously didn't give a rip what he thought. If she'd had a pecker, her look said, she would have lifted a leg against his shiny black paint job, or maybe christened the running board.

Echo Wells came back to her car, got her handbag, which was roughly the equivalent of a piece of carry-on luggage, and fished inside for a key. Then she pranced right over and stuck that key in the lock of the door of the empty shop next to Cora's place.

Rance was jarred. *This* was the new owner?

He realized he'd been expecting someone different. Someone like Cora, maybe. But definitely not this woman.

"Most folks drive to one of the big chain stores in Flagstaff for their books," Rance called, and considered biting off his tongue. Since it still came in handy once in a while, he pressed it to the roof of his mouth instead.

"Do they?" Echo chimed, sounding merrily unconcerned. Then she and the dog went inside, and she shut the door, hard.

Rance had half a mind to storm in there after her and tell her a thing or two, but since he couldn't imagine what those things would be, he stood on the sidewalk instead.

Before he could turn away, the door of Cora's shop sprang open and his daughters barreled out. Both of them were dark-haired, like he was, but they had Julie's green eyes.

It had been a full year after Julie's accident before he could look into those eyes without flinching on the inside. Still happened, sometimes.

"We almost forgot to say goodbye!" Rianna, the youngest, lisped, clinging to his right leg with both arms. She would be seven on Saturday.

Maeve, tall for ten, clutched him around the middle.

His heart softened into one big bruise, and his eyes stung a little. He embraced the girls and bent to kiss them both on top of the head.

"I'll be back in a few days," he said.

They let go of him, stepped back, craning their necks to look up at his face. Their expressions were solemnly skeptical.

"Unless you decide to go someplace else after you leave San Antonio," Maeve said sagely, folding her arms.

Rianna's attention had already shifted to the pink Volkswagen. She approached and touched one fender with reverence, as though it were an enchanted coach, drawn by six white horses, instead of a car.

"It's like a Barbie car," she said wondrously. "Only bigger."

Maeve rolled her eyes. The young sophisticate.

"Yeah," Rance agreed, though he didn't have the faintest idea what a Barbie car was.

The door of the soon-to-be-bookstore opened again, and Rance heard bells ring. He was confused, until he remembered the little brass tinkler Cora had hung above the entrance to the Curl and Twirl, so she'd know when a customer came in. Echo's shop must have one, too.

Echo stood in the gap, leaning one bare and delectable shoulder against the splintery framework and smiling at the girls. "Hi," she said, taking in both Rianna and Maeve in the sweeping, sparkling approval of her glance, and leaving Rance firmly outside the she-circle. "My name is Echo. What's yours?"

"Echo," Rianna sighed, spellbound.

"You made that up," Maeve accused, being the proverbial chip off the old block, but she sounded intrigued, just the same.

"You're right, I did—sort of," Echo said. "It suits me, don't you think?"

"What's your *real* name?" Maeve asked.

Rance should have been on his way to the airstrip outside of town, where the McKettrickCo jet was waiting, with Keegan and Jesse already onboard, checking their watches every few seconds, but he was as curious to hear the lady's answer as Maeve was.

"That's a secret," Echo said mysteriously, and put a finger to her lips as if to say, *Shush.* "Maybe when we've known each other for a while, I'll tell you."

"My name is Maeve," said Rance's eldest daughter, stoically charmed.

"I'm Rianna," said the younger.

"Well, if my real name were as beautiful as yours are, I'd have kept it," Echo confided.

Rance could almost hear the engines revving on the company jet.

"I'd better go," he told his daughters, who seemed to have forgotten he existed.

The white dog slipped past Echo, trotted over to Rianna and licked her face.

Rance, poised to lunge to his daughter's defense, was confounded by this display of canine affection.

Rianna giggled, stroked the dog with both hands

and looked back at Rance over one tiny shoulder. "Can we get a puppy, Daddy?"

"No," he said. "I travel too much."

"You can say that again," Maeve quipped. Sometimes she was more like a very short adult than a kid.

Echo raised one perfect eyebrow.

"Goodbye," Rance told his daughters.

Rianna was busy snuggling with the dog. Maeve gave him a look.

He got into his *enormous* gas-hog of an SUV and drove off.

"I LIKE YOUR PINK CAR," Maeve said, but only after she'd watched her father's SUV go out of sight. The look on her face reminded Echo of Avalon, sitting next to the Volkswagen the night before, hoping to hitch a ride and fully expecting to be refused.

"I like your *dog*," said Rianna.

"Dad won't let us get one," Maeve announced.

"So I gathered," Echo answered carefully. These were well-cared-for children. Their long dark hair was neatly brushed and clipped back with perky little barrettes, and their denim shorts and colorful sun-tops looked as though they came from some rich-kid boutique.

So why did she want to kneel on the sidewalk and gather them both into her arms? They probably had a mother.

"He's gone a lot," Rianna said.

"We stay with Granny all the time," Maeve added.

"Does your mom travel, too?" Echo asked.

"She died," Maeve said.

Echo felt bereft. "Oh," she replied, lacking a better response.

The door of Cora's Curl and Twirl opened, and a woman stuck her elaborately coiffed auburn head out. "Maeve, Rianna—" She paused, noticing the dog, then the car, and finally Echo herself, and broke into a big smile. "You must be Miss Wells," she said.

"Echo."

"Echo, then," the woman said pleasantly. "I'm Cora Tellington, and I presume you've met my granddaughters."

"I have," Echo said softly.

"Well, land sakes," Cora enthused, coming over to pump her hand. "I wasn't expecting you for a few more days yet. I would have dusted a little, inside the shop, and aired out the apartment upstairs if I'd known you were going to be here so soon."

"That's kind of you," Echo replied, already liking the woman. She'd purchased the shop sight unseen, and the whole transaction had been conducted via fax and overnight delivery services. She'd wondered what kind of person Cora Tellington was, selling property over the Internet for next to nothing. Cora had probably speculated about her as well. "Actually, I'm looking forward to getting the place in shape."

"Don't you have any furniture?" Maeve asked,

peering through the display window, which needed scrubbing.

Rianna and Avalon drew up beside Maeve, taking ganders of their own.

"How can you have a bookstore without any books?" Rianna asked.

"My things are coming in a truck," Echo explained. "And I've got a lot of work to do before I can stock the shelves."

Maeve whistled through her teeth in a way that shouldn't have reminded Echo of Rance McKettrick but did. "I'll say you do," she agreed.

Rianna turned and looked up at her worriedly. "Where will you sleep?"

"Right here," Echo answered. "Avalon and I stopped by a discount store this morning and bought an air mattress and some sheets."

"It'll be like camping," Rianna said, reassured.

"No, it won't, you doofus," Maeve said, with all the disdain of an elder sibling. "Camping is *outside.*"

"Enough," Cora interrupted gently, but she looked as worried as Rianna had as she studied Echo's face. "There's plenty of room at my place," she said. "Dog's welcome, too, of course."

Echo's heart warmed. "We'll be fine right here, won't we, Avalon?" Even as she said the words, though, she thought of Rance McKettrick, and wondered if she shouldn't have taken his suggestion and gone on to Sedona instead, started her new life there.

No, she decided, just as quickly.

When it came to starting over, Indian Rock, Arizona, was as good a place as any.

CHAPTER 2

EXPLORING THE INSIDE OF the shop with Avalon padding alongside for company, Echo had the inevitable second thoughts. Bringing the place up to her modest standards would take a considerable chunk of her cash reserves, which had been dwindling steadily since she'd made the decision to relocate.

She'd had a good job in the Windy City, planning and staging fund-raisers for an art gallery, a tiny apartment with a view of the lake, and a growing online business that had filled her lonely evenings, though she still wasn't making a profit.

Now she ran her fingertips across a dusty shelf, toward the back of the very small store. Her reasons for leaving Chicago—a nasty breakup she couldn't seem to get over, and the fact that her life had become sterile, without any discernible dimensions—seemed downright reckless in retrospect.

Had she made a mistake?

Avalon gazed up at her with that singular and unquestioning devotion only dogs can manage.

Pets hadn't been allowed in her building. The management didn't want stains on the carpets, or scratch marks on the doors. Not to mention barking, though the flight attendants in 4-B had made enough noise to rival an animal shelter at feeding time.

"Sterile," Echo mused aloud, feeling a little better. "Real life is *supposed* to be messy."

Avalon made a sound Echo took as full agreement.

They trekked upstairs, woman and dog, for a look at their new living quarters. The area consisted of two rooms, counting the miniscule bath, but the place had a certain run-down charm, with its uneven hardwood floors and big windows overlooking the street at one end and the alley at the other.

Avalon's toenails clicked on the floor as she explored, sniffing the stove, checking out the clawfoot bathtub, standing on her hind legs, forepaws resting on the sill, to look out the front windows.

"A little soap and water," Echo said, hoisting up one of the rear windows to let in some fresh air, "and we're golden."

Again, Avalon seemed to agree.

They spent the next ten minutes hauling things

in from the car—suitcases, the air mattress and accompanying bedding, Echo's laptop, and the various accoutrements of dog-care she'd purchased that morning at the discount store.

"We need cleaning supplies," Echo told Avalon. It worried her a little, this new habit of conversing with a dog, but the truth was, she'd been alone so long, she'd stored up a lot of words. "And food."

She filled Avalon's new water bowl at the sink—thankfully, Cora hadn't shut off the services—and set it on the floor. While the dog lapped, she poured kibble into a second bowl and put that down, too.

While Avalon crunched industriously at her bowl, Echo dumped the folded air bed out of the box, plugged in the attached pump and watched as the thing inflated.

"Definitely like camping," she said, remembering Rianna's words with a little smile.

But thoughts of Rianna led straight to Rianna's father, and Echo's smile dissolved. There was something distinctly unsettling about Rance McKettrick—besides his surly temperament. His good looks were almost overpowering, and everything about him, including his car, said *money*.

Echo had nothing against money, but in her experience, people who had it were used to getting what they wanted, and if somebody got in their way, too bad.

She thrust out a sigh. She was being unfair.

She knew nothing about Rance McKettrick,

really, except that he was a widower with two beautiful children, to whom he did not pay enough attention. He was wealthy, and way too handsome and he exuded the kind of uncompromising masculinity that both attracted Echo and made her want to run the other way.

Rance McKettrick was *not* Justin St. John.

He was not the man who had betrayed her and broken her heart.

Best she remember that, and at the same time keep her distance.

She had her shop now. She had a plan for the future, and her Web site was getting more hits every day. She had Avalon, even though the arrangement was probably temporary.

For now, today, she was doing just fine.

"Do you know what it *costs* to keep a Lear jet idling on a runway?" Keegan snapped as Rance boarded the sleek company plane.

Jesse, wearing his usual jeans, boots and western shirt, just smirked and took a sip of whatever he was drinking. He'd always been laid-back, Jesse had, but now that he'd hooked up with the lovely Cheyenne Bridges, and put a big, glittering diamond on her finger, he gave new meaning to the term.

He was getting regular sex, and it showed in his eyes and the easy way he wore his skin.

Rance felt a twinge of envy. There had been plenty of women since he'd got over the worst of mourning Julie, but he couldn't recall one of their faces in that moment, let alone any of their names.

Echo Wells floated into his mind, all gossamer and smooth. He recalled the tendrils of fair hair escaping from her braid, especially around her temples, and the way she'd smelled of some faint, flowery perfume.

He shook the recollection off.

No sense heading down *that* trail.

If ever a woman was wrong for him, it was Echo Wells, with her pink obsession and her grouchy dog and that dumb crystal hanging from her rearview mirror.

She probably read tarot cards and danced naked under the moon.

He smiled a little. Not an entirely unpleasant thought, if you left out the tarot cards.

"I don't give a damn what it costs to keep a jet idling on a runway," he told Keegan, settling into one of the plush leather seats and buckling up. "I'm rich, remember?"

"What else is new?" Jesse asked, and he seemed a little wistful as he turned to look out the plane window. Probably missing his lady, Rance reflected, with an utter lack of sympathy.

"Well," Rance said, as the pilot appeared in the doorway of the cockpit, looking for a nod to take off, which Keegan promptly gave, "I'll tell you what's new, cousin. A hippie woman bought the shop next to Cora's. She drives a neon-pink car and wears sneakers to match."

Both Jesse and Keegan looked at him with interest, Keegan frowning, Jesse smiling a little.

"I like my women a little broad in the beam," Jesse said.

"Oh, right," Keegan countered irritably. Somebody had sure pissed on his parade that morning. It pleased Rance to think it might have been him. "Like Cheyenne. The woman has a body that won't quit."

The engines revved, and the jet taxied down the strip, picking up speed.

Jesse grinned. "Eat your heart out," he said.

"You do need a woman," Rance told Keegan. "A little nookie might mellow you out."

Keegan glowered. "The kind you're getting?" he retorted.

"Boys, boys," Jesse put in, grinning that Jesse-grin that often made Rance want to put a fist down his throat, "you've both got perpetual hard-ons. That's your problem."

Both Rance and Keegan glared at Jesse.

He laughed.

"I do *not* have a hard-on," Keegan said.

"Not where it shows," Jesse countered.

Rance's thoughts strayed back to Echo, and he started imagining what might be under that soft, almost see-through dress of hers.

He shifted in the seat and crossed his legs.

"This meeting had better be good," he said, desperate to change the subject, along with his developing thought trend. "I'm missing Rianna's birthday for it."

"Tell me you remembered to get her a present," Jesse said. He looked serious now, and Rance recalled what Cora had said, about how Jesse paid more attention to the girls than he did, and it rankled.

"Of course I did," he lied. He'd call Myrna Terp, back in the Indian Rock office, first chance he got, and ask her to order something, have it delivered in time for the party at Sierra and Travis's place, out on the ranch. A pony, maybe. Or one of those kid-size cars that ran on a battery pack.

Preferably pink.

He felt better, and unaccountably disturbed.

He'd never bought anything pink in his life.

"How's Devon?" Jesse asked, turning to Keegan. Devon was Keegan's ten-year-old daughter, and since the divorce, he didn't see much of her. She lived in Flagstaff, with the ex, who was threatening to move to Europe with a boyfriend and take the kid with her.

Rance ached a little, thinking what that would be like.

Keegan let out a long sigh, and his broad shoulders, a McKettrick family trait, seemed to sag a little. He shoved a hand through his chestnut-colored hair and gazed down at the tastefully carpeted floor of the jet.

"Travis is picking her up Saturday afternoon, so she can go to Rianna's party," Keegan answered, and when he looked up, his face was glum. Travis, now their cousin Sierra's husband, was a lawyer for

McKettrickCo and a childhood friend to all of them, though he was closest to Jesse. "Do you ever wonder if it's worth it, missing all the stuff we do?" Keegan asked.

"Duh," Jesse said. He'd never held down a real job in his life. He was a trust fund baby, like the rest of the McKettrick men, and up until he'd run into Cheyenne Bridges again, he'd spent most of his time playing Texas Hold 'Em, chasing women and riding horses. Keegan and Rance had worked since they graduated from college, because it seemed like the right and responsible thing to do. Still, Rance sometimes wondered if Jesse didn't have the best of it, and he suspected that Keegan asked himself the same question he'd just voiced, in the dark hours of a lonely night.

"Cora gave me hell for leaving," Rance admitted. "There's Rianna's birthday, and Maeve was supposed to get braces put on her teeth on Monday morning." He paused, shook his head. "I can see why missing the party is a problem, but I'll be damned if I understand why I ought to be in the orthodontist's office instead of my own."

Jesse shook his head. "Because," he said, "kids are scared of dentists."

"Maeve isn't scared of anything," Rance replied, with some pride.

"That's what you think," Jesse said.

Rance studied him, alarmed. "Is there something going on with my daughter that I ought to know about?" he asked, putting a slight emphasis on the words *my daughter.*

"Why don't you ask her?" Jesse replied.

"Listen, if she told you something was troubling her, I want to know about it."

"Do you?" Jesse asked.

"Hell, yes, I do!"

Jesse relented. "You missed her recital. Everybody else's dad was there—except you."

"I've watched that kid twirl batons for hours on end," Rance protested. "That's about all she ever does."

"Not the same," Jesse argued coolly. "She had a special outfit for the shindig, and she won a ribbon. She wanted you *there,* Rance."

"Well, *you* were obviously there," Rance growled.

Jesse nodded, showing no signs of backing down. "Cheyenne and I both went. Took her and Rianna to the Roadhouse afterward, for ice cream. Do you know what the worst part was, Rance? Watching that kid try to pretend it didn't matter that you couldn't be bothered to show up."

The pressurized air seemed to crackle.

"Hold it, both of you," Keegan said.

"I don't need some poker-playing, bronc-riding womanizer telling me how to raise my daughter," Rance bit out.

"You sure as hell need somebody," Jesse replied, "because you're not getting it on your own."

"Enough," Keegan insisted. "We're on a jet, not out behind the barn."

Rance sighed angrily and thrust himself back in his seat.

Jesse turned to look out the window again.

They were landing outside San Antonio before anybody said another word.

ON SATURDAY MORNING, three days after her daddy had left town with her uncles, Keegan and Jesse, Rianna McKettrick opened her eyes and lay very still in her twin-size canopy bed at Granny's place on Zane Gray Road.

In the bed across from hers, Maeve went on sleeping, breathing softly.

"I'm seven," Rianna wanted to say, right out loud. "Last night, when I went to bed, I was only six. Now, this morning, I'm *seven.*"

It seemed a wonderful thing, a thing people ought to be told.

She knew Maeve would just roll her eyes and look at her like she was stupid. It made Rianna sad. The bigger Maeve got, the less she seemed to like her little sister, and try though she might, Rianna couldn't catch up.

It took some of the fun out of being seven.

With a sigh, she sat up, tossed back her covers and slid out of bed. She padded into the bathroom she and Maeve shared when they were at Granny's, which was just about all the time. She'd heard her daddy say that they all ought to stay out at the ranch house, but Granny didn't like to be that far from the Curl and Twirl.

Granny was a businesswoman. She had things to do.

All grown-up people did, it seemed to Rianna. All the time.

She washed her hands and headed for the stairs.

Granny would be down there in the kitchen, listening to the radio and waiting for the coffee to brew. Rianna could smell the familiar aroma already, and that made her sad, too. It reminded her of her daddy. The first thing he did, every morning when they were at home on the ranch, was make coffee.

Last night, after Granny had tucked her and Maeve in, listened to their prayers and left the room, Rianna had whispered to her sister that she thought Daddy might come to the party, after all. He had that jet to travel in, didn't he?

"Forget it," Maeve had said. "He won't be there. He's *busy*."

Remembering, Rianna paused on the stairway, doing her McKettrick-best not to cry. She wished she had a mommy, like the other kids at school.

She thought of Echo—Miss Wells, Granny said to call her—with her sparkly smile and pretty hair. It would be a fine thing to have a mother like Miss Wells, driving a pink Barbie car, pulling up in front of the elementary school and waiting to see Rianna and Maeve come out the door. Taping their drawings and arithmetic papers to the front of the fridge.

Rianna's throat ached, and her eyes burned so bad she couldn't see for a moment.

"Rianna, honey?" It was Granny, standing at the bottom of the stairs with the newspaper in one hand, looking up at her. "Happy birthday, sweetheart."

Rianna swallowed hard, summoned up a smile and went the rest of the way down the steps. "I'm seven," she announced.

Granny smiled, leaned down and kissed the top of her head. Patted her lightly on one shoulder. "You surely are," she agreed. "You're getting to be such a big girl."

"Maeve says I'm a dweeb," Rianna confided solemnly.

Granny bent a little more and hugged her tight. She smelled of lilacs, just like always. "Don't you pay too much attention to the things Maeve says," Granny told her. "She's growing up, just like you are, and sometimes that's hard. It makes a person crabby."

"Was my mommy ever crabby when she was growing up?" Rianna, unlike Maeve, had no memory of her mother. She wished she had, because then there might not have been a big hole opening up in the middle of her chest when she saw moms hugging their little girls, gathering them up like chicks, loading them into minivans.

Granny's face softened. "Oh, yes," she answered, and her voice sounded kind of funny, like she'd swallowed something and couldn't quite get it to go all the way down. "Sometimes she was. Mostly, though, she was happy. She was smart and beautiful, too, just like you and Maeve."

Rianna had heard those things before, many times, but she never got tired of listening. "How come Daddy isn't happy?" she asked.

Granny's face changed again, but it was different from before. It made Rianna wish she hadn't asked. Maybe Maeve was right. Maybe she asked too many questions. But how else was she supposed to find things out? It wasn't as if people told a kid anything much—beyond "Brush your teeth" and "Do your homework—" without a lot of prodding.

"He works too hard," Granny said. "And he misses your mama something fierce."

"I miss her, too," Rianna said. Maeve might have mocked her, said she couldn't miss Mommy because she'd been too young when she died, but Granny seemed to understand.

"She'd want you to have a real happy birthday," Granny said.

Maeve appeared at the top of the stairs, still in her pajamas, rubbing her eyes with the back of one hand. She yawned. "Is breakfast ready?"

"I'm seven," Rianna burst out, unable to contain the stupendous news.

"Big deal," Maeve said.

"Maeve McKettrick," Granny scolded, "if you're

going to be snotty, go back to bed." She turned to Rianna again and smiled. "Meanwhile," she went on, "there just might be a pile of presents waiting for you in the kitchen."

Rianna's spirits rose. She liked presents.

Maeve came grudgingly down the stairs.

"You think you're a teenager," Rianna whispered, waiting until Granny went on into the kitchen, to pay Maeve back a little for thinking it wasn't important to be seven. For one thing, Rianna reasoned, it was the only way to get from six to eight. "Just because you're getting braces."

"At least I'm not a baby," Maeve sniffed. "Like *you*."

Rianna clenched her fists at her sides. "I'm *not* a baby!"

Granny doubled back. She said she had eyes in the back of her head, and sometimes Rianna believed her. Imagined them peering out through the hard-sprayed fluff of hair.

"That will be quite enough," Granny said. "This is a beautiful day, and we're all going to be nice to one another."

There was a big stack of presents by Rianna's plate, all of them tied up with ribbon, and that took her mind off mean Maeve calling her a baby. She wondered out loud if any of them were from her daddy.

Granny's mouth pulled in tight again, but only for a second. "He had something sent to the ranch," she said. "Myrna Terp called me and told me so."

Mrs. Terp worked at McKettrickCo, and always slipped Maeve and Rianna cookies and hard candy in little twisty wrappers when they visited, while their daddy pretended not to notice.

"I hope it's a dog," Rianna said.

"As *if,*" Maeve said.

"Maeve," Granny finished.

Maeve rolled her eyes. She did that a lot. Rianna figured one of these days they'd pop right out of her head, like in a cartoon, and roll around on the floor.

"Maybe it's a mommy," Rianna said.

"You can't buy a mother, stupid," Maeve answered, but at another look from Granny, she bit her lower lip, pulled back a chair at the table and sank into it hard.

"Land sakes, Maeve," Granny muttered, "I can hardly wait until you're sixteen." She didn't sound like she meant it, though. That was another thing about grown-ups; they were always saying one thing when they meant something else entirely.

Rianna inspected the present on top of the pile. "Can I open it?"

"Eat your breakfast first," Granny said. She dished up Rianna's favorite, French toast, with blueberries and whipped cream on top. There was milk, too, and orange juice. Rianna was afraid she'd be eight before she got to open her presents.

After breakfast, she ripped in.

A coloring book.

A small plastic pony with a lavender mane and tail.

"That's from me," Maeve said.

There was some Barbie stuff from Granny and, finally, a gold locket in a red velvet box.

Rianna drew in her breath. Maeve had gotten one just like it when she turned ten. Rianna had thought she'd have to wait three more years to be grown up enough to wear anything but plastic pop beads.

Her fingers were shaky as she opened the tiny heart. Her mommy's picture was inside, and there was one of her daddy, too. Both of them were smiling.

Rianna scrunched up her face, trying to remember the pretty woman in the photo, wishing she'd come to life, like pictures did in the Harry Potter movies, and say, "Happy birthday, Rianna."

Or maybe, "I love you."

"You'd better not lose that," Maeve said.

Granny gave Maeve another look, helped Rianna get the necklace out of the box and fastened it around her neck, even though she was still wearing her pajamas.

The thin gold chain glittered magically as Rianna looked down at it.

Granny sniffled and turned away, standing at the sink for a long time.

"She misses Mom," Maeve confided in a whisper.

So do I, Rianna wanted to say, but she knew she'd get shot down, so she didn't.

Maeve patted her hand. Smiled like the old Maeve, the one who'd liked her. "Happy birthday, kid," she said.

THE SHOP WAS COMING together nicely.

Echo and Avalon were outside, on the sidewalk, admiring the gold lettering on the display window—Echo's Books and Gifts—when Cora pulled up in her old pickup truck. Rianna and Maeve tumbled out of the passenger-side door almost before their grandmother got the vehicle stopped.

"Look!" Rianna crowed, practically dancing in her delight. "I've got a locket, and my mommy's picture is inside it!"

Echo smiled, attributing the slight sting she felt, just behind her heart, to missing her own mother, who had died, along with her father, when she was four. She'd been raised by an aunt and uncle who had three children of their own, didn't need the irritation of an extra one, and frequently said so.

"Let's see," she said softly.

Proudly, Rianna opened the locket.

Echo bent to look.

Rance, a few years younger, heart-stoppingly handsome, and plainly happy. The woman in the adjoining photo had chin-length brown hair with a touch of red, a mischievous smile and large, expressive eyes.

"That's my mommy," Rianna explained reverently.

Echo nodded. "She's very pretty. And you look just like her." She raised her eyes, took in both Rianna and Maeve.

"I think we look more like Dad," Maeve said.

"Well, you do resemble him, too," Echo told her, exchanging glances with Cora.

"Did your furniture ever come?" Rianna asked.

Echo nodded. "Yesterday," she said. "Avalon likes the air bed, so she slept on that."

"You still don't have any books," Maeve remarked, approaching the display window. Avalon followed, licked the child's hand tentatively.

"Next week," Echo told her. "In the meantime, I've got a handyman coming to put up new shelves."

"You girls come on inside now and don't bother Miss Wells," Cora said, sounding distracted. It was only eight-thirty, but the Curl and Twirl was already full.

Obediently, Rianna and Maeve went into their grandmother's shop.

Cora lingered, looking a little flustered. "I didn't mean to sound abrupt," she said. "It's just that, well, days like this, I miss Julie—that's my daughter— even more than usual."

Echo nodded. "Birthdays and holidays are harder," she said quietly.

Cora brightened, making a visible effort. "It helps to keep busy," she said. She gave an anxious little laugh. "*Tell* me I remembered to invite you to the party tonight," she pleaded. "It's on the ranch, at Travis and Sierra's place." Cora had already explained, during other sidewalk visits, that Sierra was Rance's cousin and Travis was her husband.

Travis had grown up with Rance, Jesse and Keegan, but Sierra was a relative newcomer to the family.

"You did," Echo said. "And I told you I thought I'd be intruding."

"Nonsense," Cora said. "How else are you going to get to know people if you don't come to parties? You can bring the dog, too, if you don't mind letting her ride in the back of my truck. You could squeeze in up front with the girls and me."

"I guess I could follow in my car," Echo said. Cora was right. She was opening a business in Indian Rock, and she would have to get over her shyness and be a part of the community if she wanted this new chapter of her life to be a successful one.

Cora gave an approving nod. "We'll leave here around six o'clock," she said. Then she opened the door of the Curl and Twirl and vanished inside.

Echo ran damp palms down the thighs of her jeans. Rance wouldn't be at the party, she reminded herself, and there was no reason to believe the rest of the McKettrick tribe wasn't nice. Rianna and Maeve were sweet, and Cora was proving to be a good friend.

"We can do this," she said.

Avalon cocked her head to one side, perked up her ears and let her tongue loll, looking just like the digital picture Echo had taken the day before and posted to every lost-pet Web site she could find.

All of a sudden, Echo wanted to break down and cry, right there on the sidewalk. Because little girls lost their mothers. Because their fathers were too busy to attend birthday parties. Because maybe no one cared enough about this dog to search the Internet and then come to take her home, and because someone might do just exactly that.

CHAPTER 3

WHEN AVALON STAUNCHLY refused to get into the Volkswagen that evening at six sharp, Echo led the way back into the shop and up the stairs to her apartment on the second floor. Cora and the girls, about to drive off in Cora's pickup truck, trailed after them.

With a sigh, Avalon settled onto the air mattress she'd appropriated after the furniture arrived, scorning Echo's brass bed, an estate-sale find she prized very highly.

"Do you think she's sick?" Echo asked worriedly, turning to Cora.

Cora smiled, approached the dog and crouched,

gently patting the dog's belly. "No," she answered. "I think she's pregnant."

"You mean she's going to have puppies?" Rianna cried exuberantly, before Echo could present the same question—not so exuberantly.

"What else would she have, dingbat?" Maeve asked her sister.

"Puppies?" Echo repeated.

Cora straightened, smiling. She looked festive in her red jeans, matching boots and silk shirt, causing Echo to wonder, even in the midst of rising panic, if her soft blue broomstick skirt-sweater combo and open-toed sandals were the proper attire for a party on a ranch.

"I'm no veterinarian," Cora replied, "but I'll stand by my diagnosis just the same."

"Yikes," Echo said.

Cora bent and gave Avalon a long, affectionate stroke with one hand. "You just rest, girl," she told the animal. "I promise we won't keep your mistress out late."

"Shouldn't I take her to an emergency clinic or something?" Echo fretted.

Cora chuckled. "No," she said. "She's not in any apparent distress. Just a case of the oogies, I figure." She smiled fondly down at Avalon. "Right, girl?"

Avalon sighed, rested her muzzle on her forepaws and closed her eyes.

Meanwhile, Cora linked arms with Echo. "Come

along, now," she urged. "You're all dressed up and you've got someplace to go. Avalon will be just fine."

"Puppies," Echo reiterated, but she let herself be pulled out of the apartment and down the stairs, casting anxious glances backward every few steps.

"That's life for you," Cora said, out on the sidewalk again, watching as Echo fumbled to lock up the shop. "Do you want to ride with us?"

"I'll take my own car," Echo decided. Cora's truck would be crowded with her stuffed in there. Besides, she'd probably want to leave early. "I'll follow you."

Cora nodded, ushered the girls into the pickup and climbed aboard herself.

Echo, offering a silent prayer that Avalon would be okay in her absence, pulled out behind Cora and followed her the length of Main Street, then onto a series of country roads. After about fifteen minutes of travel, they passed beneath a huge, old-fashioned sign marking the entrance to the Triple M Ranch.

Echo knew little about the spread, just the basic facts she'd been able to scrounge up on the Internet, but passing under that arched wooden sign felt like slipping through a wrinkle in time.

The Triple M was the fourth largest ranch in the United States, and it had been founded by one Angus McKettrick, in the nineteenth century. Once primarily a cattle operation, the place was now dedicated to historical preservation. The family fortune, apparently considerable, was generated by McKettrickCo, an international corporation. Four houses remained from Wild West days, including the main ranch house, which Angus had built with his own hands, along with the original barns and other outbuildings.

Barreling along in a cloud of dust from Cora's pickup, Echo simultaneously worried about her dog and wondered what it would be like to be part of something as vast as the Triple M. According to her brief research, McKettricks had been living on this land for well in excess of a century. Echo, who had never lived in one place for more than a few years, could barely imagine having roots in a piece of ground that had seen so many generations come and go.

Presently, after many twists and turns, one of the ranch houses came into sight, a huge, sturdy wooden structure as at home on the land as a venerable oak or ancient ponderosa pine.

Children and dogs chased one another noisily across an expansive front yard, and colored lanterns hung from virtually every tree limb in sight, glowing red and yellow and blue, even though it was still daylight.

There were cars and trucks slant-parked at every possible angle.

Feeling self-conscious amid such practical, well-used vehicles, Echo found a place to tuck her pink bug, gathered her forces and got out. She reached behind the seat for the large stuffed pony she'd bought at the drugstore in town, as a birthday gift for Rianna.

While the girls ran ahead to join the festivities, Cora wended her way from her own distant parking spot to walk with Echo. From the other woman's expression, Echo gathered she'd half expected Indian Rock's newest arrival to bolt for town without saying howdy to anybody.

Since she'd been tempted to do exactly that, Echo blushed slightly and bit her lower lip.

"They're all good people," Cora assured her. Evidently, mind reading numbered among her other skills, like fixing hair and teaching little girls to twirl batons. "If that pony's for Rianna, you picked a real winner. She'll love it."

Echo straightened the big red bow tied around the toy's middle. She'd done that herself, in lieu of wrapping paper. "I'm never going to remember everyone's name," she confided. Despite the public nature of her job at the museum in Chicago, and the similar ones that had preceded it, she was naturally something of a loner.

"Not to worry," Cora assured her. "It takes time to get to know folks. Showing up, that's the important thing."

"Half the town must be here," Echo observed as she and Cora walked toward the house.

"Everybody except Rance McKettrick," Cora said ruefully.

Sadness whispered against Echo's heart, made it quiver slightly. She didn't speak, because she had no right to offer an opinion, though she certainly had one.

"My Julie would give that man what-for if she could," Cora added, before putting on a party smile and marching into the happy fray.

Echo had little choice but to go along, since Cora had once again hooked an arm through hers.

A tall woman with short, shining brown hair and thoughtful blue eyes approached, smiling. Cora introduced her as Sierra McKettrick, Rance's cousin.

"She's descended from Holt and Lorelei," Cora informed Echo.

Seeing that Echo was at a loss, Sierra smiled warmly. "We McKettricks are big on family trees," she explained. "Holt was the firstborn son of Angus, the patriarch. Lorelei was Holt's wife. The house was theirs."

Echo nodded, struck, once again, by a poignant sense of history.

"Echo owns the new bookstore next to my place," Cora told Sierra.

"The whole town's waiting for your shop to open," Sierra said, eyes twinkling. "*I'll* certainly be a regular customer."

Echo thanked her, and Sierra moved away, graciously greeting other guests. After placing the beribboned pony with a mountain of gaily wrapped gifts, she did her best to mingle. Cora came and went, making occasional introductions, bringing her a glass of punch, tacitly encouraging her to work the crowd.

Echo smiled a lot, scrambling to link names with

faces, and soon lost track. Sitting on the porch steps, taking a social breather, she watched as Travis Reid, Sierra's husband, strung an enormous piñata from a tree branch. Rianna and Maeve and a bevy of young friends and cousins waited eagerly below, while the adults looked on, enjoying the scene.

Cora plopped down beside Echo with a little sigh.

"Lordy," she said, "I'm getting old."

"Never," Echo replied.

Rianna, being the birthday girl, was to have the first whack at the piñata, now suspended by a rope. Travis tossed the other end to a handsome young man in a wheelchair, who caught it ably.

Sticks were handed out to all the children, who waited, anxiously polite, while Rianna swung, giggling, at the bobbing piñata.

A free-for-all followed, and the plaster bird, covered in colorful crepe-paper feathers, finally burst. Candy and small toys rained down, and the kids scrambled for their share of the booty.

It was a golden, glimmering keepsake of a moment, one Echo tucked away in a quiet corner of her heart.

A distant flapping sound distracted her, though, and everyone else at the party. As it drew nearer, they all looked up, shading their eyes against the last of the daylight.

"I'll be darned," Cora breathed, a smile breaking over her face, as a helicopter hovered above the field sloping away from the barn, setting the deep grass rippling in waves of green.

"They invited the president?" Echo asked, only half joking.

"Better than that," Cora said, getting to her feet and dusting off the back of her jeans. "That's Rance, unless I miss my guess, come to do right by his little girl!"

Echo caught her breath.

Adults restrained children wanting to dash across the field to the helicopter as it landed.

The blades blurred, then slowed.

The door of the copter swung open and, sure enough, out spilled Rance McKettrick like a conquering hero. Stooping until he was clear of the updraft, he grinned as Rianna climbed between two rails of the fence and ran toward him.

He wore jeans, a white shirt open at the throat, and a brown leather jacket that had seen better days, and the vision of him scooping up his young daughter and spinning her around and around in his arms imprinted itself on Echo's memory like a living photograph.

"Just when I'm ready to wring his fool neck," Cora marveled, with a hint of tears in her voice, "he comes through."

Two other men got out of the helicopter, grinning. Another child broke free of the crowd and dashed to meet one of them.

"The blond one's Jesse," Cora explained, "and the other is Keegan. That's Keegan's daughter, Devon, hugging his neck." She paused, smiling and shaking her head. "These McKettricks sure do know how to make an entrance."

While Echo was glad, for Rianna's sake, that Rance had arrived in time for the party, she was also strangely unsettled by his presence.

It wasn't just that they'd had words the day she'd arrived—that had been a silly misunderstanding, the kind of thing reasonable adults quickly forget. No, it was the way he made her feel—suddenly and wildly disoriented, as though he'd breached her innermost boundaries, blithely unaware that he was trespassing.

"I think I'll go back to town and check on Avalon," she said to Cora, but she was staring at Rance as he hoisted Rianna over the fence, then climbed nimbly over after her.

Cora clasped her hand. "You stay right here," she said.

It wasn't as if she could move, anyway. Echo stayed put.

Rance swung Rianna up onto his shoulders, while Maeve walked alongside, beaming up at her dad. He reached out, put an arm around Maeve's shoulders and pulled her close.

Jesse and Keegan followed, Devon leaping fawnlike at Keegan's side.

A beautiful dark-haired woman threw her arms around Jesse's neck as soon as he'd cleared the fence.

"That's Cheyenne Bridges," Cora said, ever helpful. "She and Jesse are getting married next month, up on the ridge."

Echo watched as Jesse and Cheyenne kissed, feeling peculiarly alone, like the sole survivor of a shipwreck riding in a rapidly sinking lifeboat.

She was so caught up in the romantic exchange that she didn't register Rance's approach until he was standing directly in front of her. Lifting Rianna down from his shoulders, he grinned.

Out of all the people at that party, he had to walk right up to *her?*

"Hello, Echo Wells," he said.

She swallowed. "That was quite an entrance," she remarked, stealing Cora's line because nothing else came to mind.

The grin widened.

Echo wondered helplessly if it was registered somewhere, that smile, as a lethal weapon and an unfair advantage of cosmic significance.

"The jet could only bring us as far as Flagstaff," he told her. "We chartered the helicopter there."

Echo, still recovering from the grin, floundered in choppy conversational seas. "Impressive," she said, because it *was* impressive, watching a copter land in a field during a little girl's birthday party.

Rance's face changed almost imperceptibly.

Rianna tugged at his hand. "It's time for birthday cake, Daddy!" she chimed. "It's time to blow out my candles and open my presents!"

Rance nodded, but the expression in his eyes was still serious, and a little perplexed. "You go ahead," he told the child. "I'll catch up."

Rianna hurried away, toward the cake and the presents, skipping as she went.

"I live to impress you, Ms. Wells," Rance said icily.

"I didn't mean—"

He walked away.

"Numbskull," Cora put in.

Echo, having forgotten all about Cora, turned to her with a questioning look.

"Him, not you," Cora said, putting one arm around Echo's shoulders and giving her a squeeze. "Come on. Let's get some of that cake."

Echo wanted nothing so much as to go home to her little apartment above the bookstore, and her dog. There, she could brew herself a cup of tea and put Rance McKettrick right out of her mind.

Alas, Cora wasn't about to let her leave and, besides, she didn't want to give Rance the satisfaction of sending her scuttling for cover. Assuming he'd notice her absence in the first place, which didn't seem very likely.

"IS THAT HER?" KEEGAN ASKED, holding a plate of cake in one hand and a glass of punch in the other. "The woman who bought that storefront next to Cora's shop?"

Rance followed his cousin's gaze to where Echo stood, chatting with Cheyenne. His jaw tightened and he wanted to sigh, but he didn't, because Keegan might read things into that that just weren't there.

Or shouldn't be.

"That's her."

Keegan grinned. "She's easy on the eyes," he said.

"Forget it," Rance replied, too quickly. "She's one of those New Age types. Drives a pink car."

Keegan's gaze sliced straight to his cousin's face. "Oh, well, then. A pink car? That changes everything."

Rance rubbed his chin. He hadn't taken time to shave before catching the jet to Flagstaff, and he was getting a stubble. "Not your type," he said, still watching Echo. She looked like a fairy princess, straight out of a storybook, with her hair pinned up and wispy around her neck, and he wouldn't have been surprised if she'd whipped out a wand with a twinkling star on one end. "That's all I meant."

"Not my type—or not yours?" Keegan asked.

Rance shoved a hand through his hair. "Look, if you want to put the moves on the lady, go right ahead. Just don't say I didn't warn you."

"Why do I get the feeling you're trying to fool yourself, as well as me?"

"What the hell do you mean by that?"

Keegan chuckled. "Hot damn," he said. "You're smitten."

"Smitten?" Rance scoffed. "Keeg, old buddy, you're spending way too much time with the lonely hearts club, if you're using words like that."

"I think I'll ask her out," Keegan mused.

Rance's spine stiffened. "Have at it," he said, and went to watch Rianna tear into her presents.

Myrna had come through for him, he saw, when Rianna got to the biggest gift in the bunch, wrapped in shiny paper and tied with a gigantic silver bow. She tore open the package and struggled with the cardboard box inside.

Even as he helped his daughter with the carton, Rance was aware of Echo, watching from a discreet distance. He wondered if Keegan really intended to ask her out, and what she'd say if he did.

Rianna let out a shriek of joy when the miniature car was revealed. It was a pink Volkswagen, with its own motor, working headlights and a horn.

"It's just like Echo's!" Rianna shouted, climbing into the little rig and tooting the horn. "It's just like Echo's!"

"I thought it belonged to somebody named Barbie," Rance said.

Rianna looked up at him. "Thanks, Daddy," she whispered, her eyes glowing in the gathering dusk.

Rance's voice came out hoarse when he spoke. "Guess you'd better take it for a spin," he said.

Rianna quickly found the ignition button, pushed it and drove right out of the carton. She did a few figure-eights, like a little clown in a circus parade, and flashed her headlights.

Laughing, people jumped out of her way.

Rance laughed, too, once he got over wanting to cry.

To think he'd almost missed this.

AVALON HAD PERKED UP by the time Echo got home, around nine that night. Hooking a leash onto the dog's collar, Echo took her down the stairs and outside.

Since almost everybody in town was apparently still at Rianna's party on the Triple M, the streets were empty. The sky was clear, speckled with stars, and there was a soft breeze, scented with newly mown grass, lilacs and roses in full bloom. Somewhere nearby, the faint *whoosh-whoosh* of a lawn sprinkler sounded.

"This is why I wanted to live in a small town," Echo told Avalon, who squatted dutifully. Using a plastic bag she'd brought for the purpose, Echo disposed of the evidence, dropping it into a trash can at the end of somebody's driveway. "It's so peaceful."

They came to a park, with a bandstand in the center, and lots of swing sets and trees. Since there was no one around, Echo decided to let Avalon off her leash to run, and was alarmed when the dog suddenly bolted across the grass toward an RV parked on the far side.

She was breathless when she caught up.

Avalon stood on her hind legs, yelping and scratching frantically at the door of the RV.

A light came on inside, and a woman stuck her head out. "Well, what's this?" she asked.

"I'm sorry," Echo said quickly. "I hope she didn't leave any marks on the paint."

Suddenly deflated, Avalon turned and slunk back to Echo, her head down.

"I'm sure she didn't do any harm," the woman said. "What a nice dog."

Echo reattached the leash, then crouched to rub Avalon's ears, trying to comfort her. The dog slouched against her, actually rested her head against Echo's shoulder, and gave a deep, shuddery sigh.

"Did your people drive a motor home like that one?" Echo whispered sadly, almost expecting the dog to answer.

Avalon gave a soft, despairing whimper.

"We'll find them," Echo told her, even as her eyes filled at the prospect of parting with her wayfaring friend. "I promise, we'll find them."

That night, Avalon foreswore the air bed and slept with Echo, curled despondently against her side and chasing something in her dreams. Echo, meanwhile, lay awake, wondering about Rance McKettrick.

What made him tick?

And why did she give a damn?

"OF ALL THE DERN FOOL THINGS to give a seven-year-old child," Cora scolded affectionately the next morning, as she made breakfast in the sunny kitchen of Rance's house. She'd spent the night in a guest room, since the girls had been too exhausted from all the excitement to make the trip back to town. "She must have run over my toes half a dozen times."

Rance, sipping fresh coffee and leaning against the counter, gazed out the window at the creek flowing by, shining in the sun. Keegan's house, the first one on the place, loomed augustly on the other side of the stream. "I told Myrna to get a Barbie car," he said, by way of explanation. He hadn't actually remembered what he'd told Myrna, until he asked her at the party, but Cora didn't need to know that.

He crossed to the window, squinting a little, trying to see if Keegan's Jag was parked in its usual place. The homestead, a log structure like Rance's own house, was old, and it didn't have a garage.

"Did you happen to see Keegan drive off this morning?" he asked, and then could have kicked himself. Cora possessed uncanny abilities of perception—women's intuition, she called it—and he wouldn't be a damn bit surprised if she guessed what he was really worried about.

"It's not my day to watch Keegan McKettrick," Cora said. "But since Devon's there, I imagine he's probably at home. If he's got a lick of sense, he'll take a few days off, instead of putting in twelve hours at McKettrickCo like he usually does."

Rance didn't dare turn around and look at his mother-in-law. He was afraid she'd see something in his face if he did. Not that there was anything to see—he just didn't want her misunderstanding his concern about where Keegan might have passed the night, that was all.

He was a little startled when Cora's hand came to rest on his shoulder; he hadn't heard her approaching. "That was a fine thing you did, Rance," she said quietly. "Getting back here for Rianna's party, I mean."

He looked down at her, not used to her praise. Once, they'd been close, he and Cora, but Julie had been the link between them, and things had changed after she died. The girls might have bridged the gap; instead, they were cause for argument, most of the time.

"I shouldn't have left in the first place," he said, to himself as much as to Cora. "I don't know what the hell I was thinking."

Cora's hand still rested against his shoulder. "Maeve and Rianna remind you of Julie," she said gently. "It's been five years, Rance. You need to let her go and concentrate on raising your daughters. Start seeing them for themselves."

Rance's throat closed. He set his coffee cup down on the wide sill of the window. Rafe McKettrick, his ancestor and Angus's second son, had hewn that sill himself and hammered it into place. Rafe had had two daughters, too, with his wife, Emmeline. Rance wondered if he'd ever felt as confounded, raising girls, as he did.

Fortunately, before he had to say anything, Rianna and Maeve erupted into the kitchen like a couple of bullets.

"Can I drive my car all the way to town, Daddy?" Rianna demanded.

Rance turned, grinning down at his daughter, trying his best to see the child behind the overlay of Julie that always clouded his vision where Maeve and Rianna were concerned.

"No," he said.

"It's thirty miles to town, you dummy," Maeve remarked.

"No name-calling," Rance told his eldest daughter. The truth was, all of a sudden he saw two individuals standing there, in baby-doll pajamas and bare feet, with only a trace of Julie showing around their eyes.

"I'll be careful," Rianna said, "and I won't speed. Cross my heart."

Rance laughed. "Your rig tops out at about two miles an hour, kiddo," he answered. "Take you a couple of days to get to Indian Rock, and your battery would die before you got to the main road."

Rianna looked gravely disappointed. "Well, what's the use of having a car if you can't take it anywhere?"

"End of the driveway and back," Rance decreed. "No farther."

"Across the bridge to Uncle Keegan's house?" Rianna tried. The kid had a future with the company, as a contract negotiator, if McKettrickCo didn't go public in the meantime. The fight was still on where that decision was concerned. The meeting in San Antonio had gone on for the better part of three days, with nothing settled.

"No way," Rance said.

Rianna plopped onto one of the benches lining the long table. It was a copy of the one across the creek, on the homestead. "I wanted to give Devon a ride," she lamented.

"Devon can't fit," Maeve said. "It's a *baby* car."

"Leave your sister alone, Maeve," Rance told his elder daughter.

Maeve subsided, but there was McKettrick thunder in her eyes.

"Babies don't drive cars," Rianna told Maeve.

"Enough," Rance interceded.

"How am I supposed to show Echo that my car is just like hers?" Rianna persisted.

Rance closed his eyes, remembering how he'd gotten his back up the night before, when Echo had called his arrival by helicopter "impressive." He'd been ultra touchy, stressed out because the meetings in San Antonio had done nothing but raise more trouble in the McKettrick ranks. He'd felt compelled to leave early so he could be home for Rianna's party, and when the company jet landed in Flagstaff, there was a delay chartering the chopper. He'd been flat-out wrong to take those things out on Echo by snapping at her the way he had.

"Echo *saw* your stupid car last night," Maeve pointed out.

"Maybe Avalon could fit," Rianna speculated.

Rance sighed.

Cora stepped in. "Eat your breakfast, both of you."

Rance gave her a grateful look.

"You, too," she said.

He took his place at the head of the table—a seat

he occupied all too infrequently—and let Cora serve him a plate mounded with fried potatoes, eggs and sausage links. He'd employed a variety of house-keepers and nannies over the years since Julie died, but none of them had lasted. Too much respon-sibility had fallen on Cora.

"Looks like a heart attack waiting to happen," he said appreciatively, and dug into the food.

Cora laughed. "Well, that's a fine how-do-you-do," she replied. "I cook you a meal, and you accuse me of trying to kill you."

Maeve's eyes widened. Her lower lip wobbled and, suddenly, she looked a lot younger than her usual ten-going-on-forty. "You wouldn't *really* have a heart attack, would you, Dad?" she asked.

Rance reached out, ruffled her hair. "No," he said quietly. "I plan on living to be a hundred and causing you all kinds of trouble in my old age."

Maeve relaxed visibly, and her eyes danced. For a moment, he saw Julie again. "Just keep in mind," she said, "that I'll have a say in picking out your nursing home."

Rance threw back his head and shouted with laughter.

"I get to help," Rianna said. "What's a nursing home?"

"Never mind," Cora told her, bending to kiss both her granddaughters on top of the head. "Nobody's going into a nursing home. Not in the immediate future, anyway."

A silence fell, and Rance looked up at his mother-in-law, suddenly realizing that she was getting older. She'd lost weight since Julie died, and there were wrinkles around her eyes and at the corners of her mouth. Her husband had passed away years ago, and she had no family other than Maeve and Rianna—and him.

"What's a nursing home?" Rianna repeated.

"It's like a hospital," Maeve explained. "Old people go there."

Cora, her gaze locked with Rance's, suddenly looked away.

He pushed back his chair, stood and followed his mother-in-law to the sink, where she stood with her back to the room. He laid a hand on her shoulder, just as she had done earlier, when he was at the window.

"Are you feeling okay, Cora?" he asked quietly. "You're not sick, are you?"

She shook her head, tried to smile. "No, Rance—I'm fine."

But as she turned from him to tackle the breakfast dishes, it was clear something was on her mind.

Maybe he ought to tell her he thought he knew what it was.

CHAPTER 4

ECHO SAT CROSS-LEGGED IN the middle of her feather-bed, awash in sunlight from the big windows opening onto the alley behind the shop, laptop open, Avalon snoozing peacefully beside her.

Four different people, in four different and far-flung parts of the country, had e-mailed offers to adopt Avalon, but no one claimed ownership. Both relieved and discouraged, Echo dispatched electronic thank-you notes and went to her own Web site.

Seeing it always made her smile.

It was her delicious little secret.

And the orders were piling up—more than a hundred had come in since she'd last logged on, before leaving Chicago.

"Best get cracking," she told Avalon, who opened her eyes, yawned and then went back to sleep.

Reaching for the pen and notepad on the bedside table, Echo scrawled a shopping list. Velvet bags. Cording. Certain herbs and stones. Some of the supplies she needed had arrived with her furniture and other belongings, but she would have to contact her wholesalers, just the same.

Biting her lower lip, she scanned the list of orders again. Something niggled at the periphery of her awareness.

And then the name jumped out at her.

Cora Tellington.

"Cora?" she said aloud. A smile broke over her face as she checked the address. Sure enough, it was *the* Cora Tellington, of Indian Rock, Arizona.

Well, she thought happily, *I'll be darned.*

Of course, she could fill the order from supplies on hand and deliver it in person, but Cora might be embarrassed and, besides, Echo wasn't sure she was ready to reveal her sideline to anyone just yet. Her name didn't appear on the Web site, and there was no toll-free number or post office box listed, either. Any receipts went directly into an online-payment service account, and she'd always shipped the merchandise from a franchise in the neighborhood.

Something else caught her attention as she studied Cora's order on the screen of her laptop.

Cora wasn't buying for herself.

"Hmm," Echo murmured, confused.

Then, because she felt a peculiar sense of urgency, she set the computer aside, got off the bed and started rummaging through boxes, gathering the necessary materials.

A feather.

A pink agate.

A prayer, printed on a tiny strip of paper.

She put all these things into a small blue velvet bag, tied the gold drawstring and placed the works inside a little padded envelope, to be mailed on Monday morning.

What on earth, she wondered, had prompted Cora Tellington to order a love-spell, not for herself, but for a man?

THE PACKAGE ARRIVED IN Monday afternoon's mail. Cora smiled when she saw it, felt a shiver of excitement and secreted it away in her purse before Maggie or any of her other employees caught a glimpse.

It was silly, she knew, to place her hopes in this kind of magic, but desperate times called for desperate measures. She'd tried just about everything else, and she was fresh out of ideas.

Of course, she could have gone to Sedona and talked to a psychic, but people knew her there. She didn't want anybody spilling the beans—if word of what she was up to ever got back to Rance, he'd have a fit and fall in it.

I did it for you, Julie, she said silently. *And for your girls.*

Julie would have laughed, Cora knew that. Her daughter had been the practical, pragmatic type, just like Rance. Indeed, the two of them had been very much alike, believing only in what they could see, hear and touch.

It was sad.

Cora came back from her mental sojourn. Hammering sounded from next door, at Echo's shop, and Eddie Walters's old truck was still parked out front.

Needing a break, after giving three perms and a weave, Cora decided to go over and see how the new shelves were coming along.

Echo was up on a ladder, painting the ceiling. Barefoot, wearing a fitted T-shirt, her long, firm legs revealed by a pair of denim shorts, she looked like a wood nymph. The dog was nowhere in sight.

"Wow," Cora said, admiring Eddie's work as well as Echo's. "The place looks great."

Echo smiled and descended the ladder, laying her paint roller in the tray and resting her hands on her hips. "The first shipment of books is due to arrive on Thursday," she said. "I might be open for business by Saturday morning."

It pleased Cora to see the old shop coming alive again. She'd bought it years ago, along with the space next door, planning to expand her own business one day. As it turned out, though, she'd had her hands full with the Curl and Twirl, and now she was thinking more and more often of retiring, maybe doing a little traveling.

Of course, she couldn't do that with Rance still running hither and yon like some crazy man, trying to work himself into an early grave, or outrun memories of a past he tended to idealize.

Cora had loved her daughter, but Julie had been a flesh-and-blood woman, with all the accompanying faults and foibles, not a paragon of virtue. In some ways, it was unfair, Rance's remembering her the way he did. He'd forgotten the way the two of them butted heads, because they were too much alike. Stiff-necked, both of them. Used to getting their own way.

A curious expression came over Echo's face; she seemed to be *pondering* Cora, like the blank spaces in a crossword puzzle.

"I haven't seen the girls in a few days," Echo said, brightening.

"Rance took them camping up on Jesse's ridge," Cora explained, relieved. "Where's Avalon?"

"Hiding under my bed, I think," Echo replied. "All this hammering and sawing is probably giving her a headache."

Eddie grinned sheepishly and waded into the conversation. "Almost done," he said.

Cora had known Eddie all his life. Known his mother, and his grandmother, too, God rest their souls. He wasn't a bright boy, but he was good with his hands. When somebody in Indian Rock needed shelves put up, or walls painted, or pipes and wiring fixed, Eddie was the person they called. That was why Cora had recommended him to Echo.

"Looks like you did a good job," Cora told him. "Just like always."

Eddie beamed, already putting away his tools. The floor was covered with sawdust, and Cora, being Cora, found a broom in the corner and started sweeping.

"You don't have to do that," Echo protested, a slight frown puckering her brow.

Cora remembered that she'd come from Chicago. Like as not, folks in a big city like that didn't sweep one another's floors, but this was Indian Rock, not Chicago. Cora went right on with her sweeping.

Echo watched solemnly, and she looked like a person with something to say. When Eddie finished up, Echo wrote him a check, and he left with his toolbox.

Avalon came downstairs the moment the door closed behind him.

"How ya doin' today, little mama?" Cora asked the dog. She'd always liked critters, but she had a special place in her heart for this one. Echo had told her about finding Avalon outside a truck stop down by Tucson, lost and soaked to the skin.

"I was walking her on Saturday night, after I got back from the party," Echo said suddenly, patting the dog's head. "We came to a park, so I let her off the leash for a run. She headed straight for an RV parked on the opposite side and about clawed the door down trying to get in."

Cora considered that. The implications were obvious.

"I want to find her family," Echo said, very softly, and very sadly. "I truly do. But I swear it's going to kill me to give her up."

If ever anybody looked like they needed a hug, it was Echo Wells, in that moment. "You'll do what's right," Cora said, dumping a dustbinful of sawdust and wood chips into the trash. "That's the kind of person you are."

Echo's eyes glistened. She blinked and looked away.

"I might be out of line asking this," Cora ventured carefully, "but do you have any folks?"

Echo met her gaze, though Cora could tell she didn't want to. "An aunt and uncle, a few cousins," she said. "We're not close."

"I see." Cora told herself she was an old busybody and she ought to keep her mouth shut. She didn't, though. "No husband or boyfriend?"

Echo shook her head. Looked away. Looked back. "I almost got married once," she said. "Justin and I booked a slot in one of those gaudy little chapels in Vegas. I flew in on schedule, put on my dress and took a cab to the McWeddings place. Justin was—detained."

Cora set the broom aside. "You mean he stood you up?"

"He said he had a meeting at the last minute," Echo said, trying to smile and failing miserably.

Uh-oh, Cora thought, as she registered the word *meeting.* She'd been toying with the idea that Rance and Echo might get together ever since the party—the girls liked Echo, and she and Rance surely looked good together—despite their bristly beginning. But Rance was a workaholic, and evidently this Justin yahoo had been, too.

"So you were all alone in Vegas? He didn't show up at all?"

"I told him not to bother," Echo said. Her voice sounded small and faraway.

"But when you got back home…?"

"Justin lives in New York," Echo replied, when Cora's sentence fell apart in the middle, like a suspension bridge bearing too much weight. "I lived in Chicago. Neither of us wanted to move at the time, so it wouldn't have worked out, anyway."

"Still," Cora said, wanting to cry.

"Justin was all business," Echo went on, evidently trying to make Cora feel better. The effort, just like the smile she'd attempted earlier, fell flat. "He cared more about his company than anything else. I wanted—"

"What did you want, Echo?" Cora asked, after a few moments of gentle silence.

"A dog," Echo said. "A husband and kids."

Cora's hopes sparked again. "You're young—twenty-nine? Thirty? You oughtn't to give up."

Echo leaned down, stroked Avalon thoughtfully. "Twenty-nine," she said. Then she gave Cora another of those pensive looks. "What about you, Cora? You haven't mentioned a husband. Are you planning to fall in love one day soon?"

It was an odd question. Made Cora think of the little package snugged away in her handbag. "Julie's dad died years ago. Best husband a woman could ever ask for, my Mike. Nope, I'm not in the market for a man. After all, I'm sixty-three years old. I've saved up some money, and I'd like to take me one of those cruises."

"What stops you?" Echo asked. She put the question carefully, as though expecting it to blow up in her face.

"Rance," Cora admitted, after weighing the matter in her mind first. "I'm afraid he'd hire another airheaded nanny and fly off someplace. Leave Rianna and Maeve at her mercy."

Echo's gaze drifted to the display window, and suddenly she looked flushed and flustered. "Speak of the devil," she said.

Cora turned, watched as Rance got out of his SUV, fresh from the camping trip. His hair was rumpled and he needed a shave. His jeans and white T-shirt looked as though he'd slept in them. He started toward the Curl and Twirl, noticed Cora and Echo watching him through the window, and changed direction.

"Where are the girls?" Cora asked the minute he stepped over the threshold.

He sighed, and a muscle bunched in his jaw. Then he grinned, that tilted McKettrick grin. "I knew I was forgetting something when I broke camp this afternoon," he joked.

"Very funny," Cora said, but she had to chuckle a little.

"They're at Keegan's, with Devon," Rance explained, and even though he was speaking to Cora, he was looking at Echo. Taking in the paint splotches, the long bare legs, the form-fitting T-shirt.

"I just remembered something I need to do before the Curl and Twirl closes for the day," Cora announced, and made a beeline for the door.

Outside, on the sidewalk, she paused and allowed herself the smallest of smiles. If Rance kept his back turned long enough, she might just be able to slip the contents of that little package under the seat of his truck.

She thought about the Web site, and all the testimonials, and the thirty-day money-back guarantee.

Time to take a chance on magic.

"ABOUT THE OTHER NIGHT," Rance began awkwardly, giving the dog a sidelong glance. At least it hadn't gone for his throat, so maybe he'd be able to work his way into its good graces after all.

Echo, looking like a strawberry ice cream cone in her tight pink shirt and little bitty jeans shorts, stayed on the other side of the room. She said nothing, just waited. Maybe she wanted to watch him squirm for a while.

Rance shoved a hand through his hair, wishing he'd taken the time to shower and change clothes before driving into town. He'd come to let Cora know he and the girls were back from the camping trip, or at least that was what he'd told himself when he'd dropped the girls off at Keegan's. Now, facing Echo Wells, he knew it for the lie it was.

"I was a little short-tempered at the party," he said awkwardly. "I'd like to apologize."

Her eyes widened. Whatever she'd expected him to say, it hadn't been that. "No need," she said, still cautious, just when he was beginning to think she wasn't going to speak to him at all.

"I caught a mess of fish while we were camping," he heard himself say. "I thought I'd fry them up for supper tonight." He paused, cleared his throat, trying to remember the last time he'd felt like a sixteen-year-old asking out the most popular girl in school. "Maybe you'd like to join us?"

She flushed. Fidgeted a little. "I'm not sure that would be a good idea—"

"The girls will be there," he put in quickly when she faltered. He grinned, more out of nervousness than amusement. "You can bring the dog."

Echo moistened her lips. "Look, you don't have to—"

"Do you ever speak in complete sentences?" Rance asked, relieved when she relaxed and even laughed a little.

She looked down at her clothes, which Rance would have liked to peel away so he could taste everything underneath in slow, wet nibbles.

"I'm a mess," she said.

Some mess, he thought, shifting uncomfortably

when a vision of those legs, draped over his shoulders while he knelt between them, flashed into his mind. "You look fine to me," he answered, silently crediting himself with the understatement of the century.

He saw the decision, tentative and hopeful, take shape in her face.

"Okay," she said.

"Okay," he agreed.

"I'll just grab a shower and meet you at your place later."

Another vision exploded in Rance's mind. Echo, naked and slick with water, coming apart in his arms as he slammed into her in a single thrust of his hips.

He had to swallow again. If he didn't get out of there quick, he'd have to step behind the counter to hide his rising interest.

"Six o'clock?" he asked.

"Six o'clock," she confirmed.

He turned, started for the door, then looked back over one shoulder. "You need directions?"

Her smile melted something inside him. "That would help," she said.

He told her how to find the house and made his escape.

Outside, feeling distracted and three kinds of grubby, he noticed that the door of his rig was a little ajar.

Weird, he thought. He'd slammed it shut after getting out.

With a shrug, he climbed into the SUV and started the engine.

All the way back to the ranch, he thought about Echo.

He wasn't a psychic.

He didn't call hotlines, hang crystals or consult tarot cards.

And he didn't need any of those things to tell him what the future held.

He was going to make love to Echo Wells—and soon.

"It doesn't mean a thing," Echo told Avalon as she shinnied into a pair of jeans, after her shower, and then pulled a white eyelet top on over her bra, a lacey number she wore whenever she wanted cleavage. "He's just trying to make up for being rude at the party."

Avalon tipped her head to one side and panted.

"We shouldn't read anything into this," Echo went on, fluffing her hair. Should she braid it, pin it up or wear it down?

She decided on the braid. Pinning it up implied too much getting ready, and wearing it down was too sexy. Not to mention that, being damp from the shower, it was bound to frizz out around her head and make her look as though she'd just stuck her finger into a light socket.

Makeup?

Echo sighed. Too much getting ready again.

She settled for lip gloss and a touch of mascara. Perfume?

Not a chance.

"Come on," she said to Avalon, hooking a leash to the dog's collar and grabbing for her purse. "We'll drive slowly, so we don't seem too eager."

Avalon sighed.

They descended the stairs, into the shop, and Echo paused a moment to enjoy the new shelves and the smell of sawdust.

Outside, she locked the shop door and approached the Volkswagen. She'd bought it with a windfall, last year. Now, looking at it, she wondered if she shouldn't have chosen a more circumspect color.

She opened the passenger-side door, and Avalon leaped obediently into the seat, waited while Echo unhooked the leash again and fastened the seat belt.

"Can't be too careful," she said. "After all, you're probably preggo."

A minute later, they were zooming out of town.

They'd traveled several miles before Echo remembered that she didn't want to seem eager, and slowed to approximately the speed of a lawn mower.

Avalon panted, watching the scenery drag by.

Echo turned the radio on, then off again.

Flipped on the CD player.

Mozart. That was what she needed. Nice, soothing Mozart.

So why did everything inside her vibrate to "Boot-Scootin' Boogie?"

The ranch house was built of logs and mortar, and stood facing a shimmering creek, dancing in the fading sunlight of a summer evening.

She pulled the Volkswagen up alongside Rance's SUV, and smiled when Rianna and Maeve burst out onto a side patio and raced toward her.

"I've got a pink car, too!" Rianna shouted when Echo rolled down her window to greet them.

Avalon gave a joyous yelp and strained at her seat belt.

After determining that it was safe to turn the animal loose, Echo got out and went around to the other side of the car to do so.

Avalon sprang out with a happy *woof* and ran in ecstatic circles around Rianna and Maeve, who seemed equally delighted.

Soon, the three of them were off at a high lope, apparently too exuberant to stand still for another moment.

Echo stood and watched them, one hand shading her eyes, a little smile playing on her mouth.

Rance was beside her before she had a chance to prepare.

"Welcome to the Triple M," he said quietly.

The low rumble of his voice found a fault line inside Echo and caused a tectonic shift. Off balance, she looked up at him, braced herself against another quake when the sunlight caught in his dark hair. He wore clean jeans and a blue sports shirt that intensified the fierce sapphire of his eyes.

The trademark grin flashed white, a pleasing contrast to his sun-browned skin, as he reached out and pushed her car door shut.

Unconsciously, Echo took a step back, and immediately felt foolish.

"I should have brought something," she said. "Wine or—or—something."

"You brought yourself," he replied easily. "That's enough."

There was a brief, electric stare-down, and Rance won.

Echo dodged first, sought out the girls again, and Avalon. They were down by the creek, and as she watched, Maeve threw a stick along the bank and Avalon raced after it.

Rance took her hand, just briefly, long enough to start her toward the house. Long enough to send a jolt through her system.

She walked alongside him, coming to a stop on the long flagstone patio, where a bottle of white wine cooled atop a black wrought-iron table.

Rance pulled back one of the chairs and gestured for her to sit down.

She sat gratefully, not trusting her knees.

Below, the creek bubbled and sent up dazzling flashes of sunshine, while the dog and the little girls played. Beyond was another house, even bigger than Rance's and Sierra's were. It had a covered porch running the length of the structure and gabled windows on the second floor.

Climbing roses and lilacs flourished in the yard, along with a venerable peony bush, weighted with fat white blossoms.

"Keegan's place," Rance said, opening the wine and pouring a glass for Echo. "Of course, there have been additions over the years, but it started as a frontier cabin."

The wine was white, dry, crisp and so cold that it frosted the glass. "Angus McKettrick built it," Echo said, and then wished she hadn't been quite so forthcoming. Now Rance would think she'd been researching his family history.

He pulled back a chair, sat down and poured himself some wine. "Yes," he said, with just the faintest trace of amusement in his voice. "All us McKettricks come from that old man and one or another of his three wives."

"Sierra's house belonged to Holt and Lorelei," Echo piped up, and almost put a hand over her mouth in the next moment.

"Yes," Rance answered.

Echo was interested, in spite of herself. "So which McKettrick son are you descended from?"

"Rafe and his wife, Emmeline," Rance answered, watching his daughters with a slight smile as they frolicked with the dog. "They had two daughters— just like I do."

Echo pondered. "No sons?"

"No sons," Rance confirmed.

"Then how did you end up with the family name?"

Rance grinned, brought his attention back to Echo. "The McKettrick women stay McKettricks, no matter who they marry. The tradition started with Katie, old Angus's only daughter, and it's never been broken, as far as I know."

Echo sighed. "I envy you," she said. "My family moved around a lot, and nobody seemed to care much about genealogy."

Rance took another sip of wine. Sighed. "There have been times," he confided, obviously teasing, "when I wished I was an orphan. Jesse and Keegan and Meg and I all grew up together, along with a flock of other cousins who spent summers here."

"You're lucky," Echo told him.

"I know," he said.

"I don't think I met Meg at Rianna's party," Echo reflected, sifting through names and faces.

"She's Sierra's sister," Rance said, after shaking his head to confirm what Echo had said. "Blows in like a tumbleweed every once in a while. Once Sierra and Travis finish the house they're building in town, Meg will probably come home. She's been making noises about it for a long time, but she has strong ties in San Antonio."

"It's a lot to keep track of," Echo said. "Your family, I mean."

"Tell me about it," Rance replied with a chuckle. "You ready to eat?"

The delicious scent of fried fish wafted from the built-in grill on the patio. Echo's stomach rumbled audibly, and they both laughed.

"Guess so," she said.

Rance called the girls, sent them into the house to wash up and laid the table with different colored plates and mismatched silverware.

"This is the outdoor stuff," he told Echo.

She grinned. "I like it. It's…festive."

Avalon approached, sat at a polite distance from the table, in a patch of shade. Echo's throat tightened when Maeve and Rianna came out of the house, each carrying a bowl. Maeve's sloshed with water, and Rianna's contained some kind of chopped meat.

Apparently, Avalon was to have a feast, too.

The girls took their places at the table, and Rance poured juice into their wineglasses. He served the fish on a huge, chipped platter, along with a green salad and a basket of rolls.

"We caught these fish ourselves," Maeve said importantly. She lisped a little when she spoke, and Echo realized she was wearing braces, the see-through kind. "Dad took us camping on Jesse's ridge."

"It's Cheyenne's ridge, too," Rianna said. "She's going to marry Jesse. They kiss *all the time.*"

Rance chuckled.

Avalon, having lapped up half the water and

tasted the chopped meat, settled contentedly on the warm patio stones for a nap.

Echo found herself wishing things would stay just this way—the four of them dining outside, like a real family, complete with dog. Such moments were rare in her life, and all too fleeting. The children, the houses and the dogs always belonged to other people, but tonight she could almost pretend that she fit right in.

"Do you think Avalon would like to ride in my birthday car?" Rianna asked earnestly, breaking Echo's train of thought.

"I told you," Maeve said, "she won't *fit*."

Rance and Echo exchanged glances, and there was something so intimate about the exchange that Echo's breath caught.

She imagined herself staying—clearing the table with Rance after supper, chatting while they washed the dishes, tucking the girls into bed once they'd had their baths…

Stop, she thought, but it was no use.

She and Rance would return to the patio, once Rianna and Maeve were settled in for the night, watch the stars pop out, glittering like rhinestones in the clear country sky. Maybe they would dance to soft music, right here in the open air, and then they would go upstairs together, and make slow, sweet love with the windows open to the breeze….

She blushed.

Rance was staring at her, as if he could see what she was thinking.

"Wine always makes me too warm," she explained hastily, fanning her face with one hand.

A slow grin spread across Rance's face. "Whatever you say," he replied.

CHAPTER 5

AFTER SUPPER, RIANNA EXCUSED herself, left the patio and soon came speeding around the corner of the ranch house in her miniature pink Volkswagen. With a delighted smile, she tooted the horn.

Echo was oddly moved by the sight, as well as amused. She laughed, peripherally aware of Rance's glance, lighting briefly on her, then shifting back to Rianna.

"It's just like *your* car!" Rianna cried.

"So it is," Echo said softly.

"Except that Echo can actually *drive* hers," Maeve put in, with an air of implacable practicality.

"I can drive," Rianna argued. "I betcha I could go all the way to Indian Rock, if Daddy would let me!"

"We've been over that," Rance interjected.

"I can't *even* take it across the bridge to Uncle Keegan's house," Rianna said, pouting now.

"Go and play," Rance told his daughters. "Both of you."

Rianna shot off down the driveway, horn blasting, with Maeve running beside her. Avalon raised herself off the patio stones, yawned and ambled off in halfhearted pursuit.

"I don't know what I was thinking, buying that thing," Rance admitted. "The kid will be sixteen soon enough, and driving a real car."

Impulsively, Echo reached out to pat Rance's hand. Her skin seared where she'd touched him, and he flinched as though he'd felt it, too. Both of them drew in an audible breath.

Color pulsed in Echo's cheeks. "She loves it," she said, somewhat lamely. "And she loves you, obviously."

"I'm not sure I deserve it," Rance said. Then he took Echo's hand, chafing her knuckles lightly with the pad of his thumb. "What about you, Echo Wells?" he asked. "Who loves you?"

She tensed, recovered and tried for a smile. The obvious answer was *Nobody,* but she couldn't bring herself to say it out loud. For one thing, it would sound pathetic, and for another, it would hurt too much.

"I'm kind of a loner," she said.

Rance did not release her hand, but his grip wasn't tight. Once the series of visceral charges subsided, it was nice. "You don't strike me as the loner type," he replied. "You said your family moved around a lot. Does that mean you're not close to any of them?"

"Yes," she answered, and looked away, because suddenly there were tears in her eyes, and she'd die if he saw them. "That's what it means."

Rance didn't answer. Nor did he let go of her hand.

Dusk was gathering, and a paper-thin moon was visible directly above the main chimney of Keegan McKettrick's house.

"It's so beautiful here," Echo said quietly. She wanted to pull away, knew she should, but the message was short-circuited somewhere between her brain and the muscles in her hand.

"More beautiful tonight than usual," Rance agreed.

She glanced at him, her gaze colliding with his and skittering away. It was a line, of course, but it beat "Haven't I seen you somewhere before?"

Gently, she pulled her hand from his. It would be easy to tumble into bed with him, on this or some other night—only too easy. Maybe other encounters would follow, but then Rance would move on, and she would be left with the landscape of her soul scorched bare.

It had happened before—with Justin—and Echo knew she couldn't afford a repeat performance.

She stood, began clearing the table.

"Echo," Rance said, without rising from his chair. "Stop."

She paused, watched as Maeve, Rianna and Avalon came back up the driveway, a plume of dust trailing behind the little pink car.

"I should get back to town," she said.

Rance stood. "All right," he answered, but he sounded reluctant, as though he'd like to suggest something else.

She forced herself to meet his eyes. "I—it was a lovely evening—"

He smiled, though a certain sadness lingered in his eyes. "Something spooked you, Echo," he said gently. "What was it?"

She bit her lower lip. How could she explain that *he* spooked her? He and all he caused her to feel? In one evening, he'd reawakened dreams she'd long since put to rest, dreams that could never come true because the two of them were so different.

He was rich, she merely got by.

He had a vast extended family, she was alone in the world.

He was practical, while she had a tendency toward magical thinking.

It would never work.

"I don't know," she lied.

He cupped her chin in one hand, brushed the side of his thumb across her mouth in a caress so gentle that it sent hot shivers through her. "I think you do," he countered. "But if you're not ready to tell me, that's fine."

Rianna zipped up in her minibug and sent one of the chairs crashing loudly onto the flagstones.

"Park it," Rance ordered. "Time for a pit stop."

Rianna sighed, sounding resigned to the unreasonable demands of grown-ups, and climbed out of the little car.

Echo reached for her shoulder bag.

"You're leaving?" Rianna asked.

"Big day tomorrow," Echo said. She intended to drive to Flagstaff and buy a cash register and credit-card processor. When the stock for her shop started to arrive, she wanted to be ready.

Rianna's small shoulders sagged. "Oh," she murmured.

"Say good night to Miss Wells and get ready for bed," Rance told his daughter. "Maeve, you too."

"But it isn't even *dark* yet!" Maeve protested.

"Do it," Rance said.

"Good night, Miss Wells," Maeve and Rianna chorused glumly. After giving Avalon a few farewell pats, the children disappeared into the house.

Rance walked Echo to her car, Avalon keeping pace at her other side.

Echo was busy for a few moments, getting Avalon settled on the car seat, and when she turned around, she smashed directly into Rance. He felt like a stone wall, and the impact dizzied her a little.

He slipped his arms loosely around her waist,

bent his head and touched his lips to hers. It was a brief kiss, over in a heartbeat, but it left Echo shaken and confused—and absolutely certain that her earlier premonition was correct.

Sooner or later, Rance McKettrick was going to seduce her and, against all sense and reason, she was going to let him.

RANCE BARELY SLEPT THAT night, and the next morning he took the girls to town for breakfast at the Roadhouse before dropping them off at Cora's shop. He was disappointed to notice that Echo's ridiculous pink car was gone, though he figured it was just as well if they didn't run into each other right away. He'd enjoyed the previous evening a bit too much for comfortable reflection.

His mother-in-law, alone in the Curl and Twirl except for an old lady swathed in a plastic cape and sitting under one of the hair dryers, took in his slacks, white shirt and tie.

"Are you planning to board that jet again?" Cora asked warily, once Rianna and Maeve had gone into the adjoining studio to practice their baton-twirling. The value of such a skill mystified Rance, there being no market for it in the real world, and he put it down to the fathomless peculiarity of the female mind.

Rance shook his head, both at Cora's question and the feminine gender. "I'll be in my office at McKettrickCo," he said. "More meetings. If the girls get to be too much for you, I can pick them up, take them back to work with me."

"They're never too much for me," Cora said. Then her mouth softened into a smile, and her eyes twinkled with mischief. "How was supper last night?" she asked.

"It was delicious," Rance hedged. "Trout. I fried them up myself."

"You know that isn't what I meant," Cora persisted. He'd called when he got back to the ranch and invited her to join the party, but she'd demurred, as soon as he'd mentioned that Echo would be there.

Rance grinned and leaned in, in case the old lady could hear over the roar of that hair dryer, which covered the top of her head like a space helmet. "Well," he said, "first I sent the girls to bed. Then, when I was sure they were asleep, I stripped Echo naked, threw her down in the tall grass and ravished her."

Cora's eyes widened. Then she punched him. "You scoundrel," she said. "You had me going for a moment there!"

Rance laughed, wishing he *had* ravished Echo. He might have gotten a decent night's sleep then, instead of tossing and turning until the wee small hours. He was about to leave for work when Cora stopped him.

"Why don't you have supper at my place tonight? You and the girls."

He raised an eyebrow. "Do I smell a trap?"

"I might invite Echo, if that's what you mean,"

Cora said. "She's lonely, Rance, and I don't think she eats right. She's too thin."

Personally, Rance thought Echo's figure was perfect, but he wasn't going to argue the point with Cora. He frowned. "She seemed to have a good appetite last night," he said. More than that, she'd wanted him as much as he'd wanted her—another insight he wasn't about to share.

She was scared, maybe just of him, maybe of all men.

"She's been burned," he mused aloud, without intending to voice the thought in the first place.

Cora nodded sagely, glanced back at the woman under the dryer, who was immersed in a tattered copy of *People*, and confided, "His name was Justin. She flew all the way to Vegas to marry him in one of those silly little chapels, and he didn't show up."

Rance was surprised at how this news impacted him; he felt it like a blow. He was at once grateful that Echo hadn't gone through with the marriage and sorely tempted to find this Justin character and change the shape of his face.

"She told you that?"

"Women tell other women things they'd never say to a man in a million years," Cora said wisely. "Not directly, anyhow."

The reminder nettled. Women *did* keep secrets, and they spoke a language all their own. It had been that way with Julie; she hadn't said a word to him when she wasn't happy, at least in the beginning, when they could have turned things around—she'd gone to Cora instead. He'd found his wife crying, several times, asked what was wrong, and gotten the same answer: *Nothing*. That "nothing" had grown into a pretty big "something."

He wondered if Julie had confided all of it to Cora, a question that had kept him awake many a night, but he couldn't bring himself to ask. McKettrick pride. It was one of his best qualities— allowing him to succeed on a scale well beyond the reach of McKettrickCo—and one of his worst.

"I'll think about supper," he promised Cora in parting, and he would. But it would be at the tail end of a lot of other things he wanted to ponder.

WHEN ECHO AND AVALON returned to the shop that afternoon with the cash register and the credit card machine, Echo, feeling oddly ill at ease, went to her laptop, resting on the counter, and logged on. The e-mail was waiting, along with six more orders for love spells.

"Pitcher looks like my dog," the spelling-challenged stranger had written. "She run off from my back yard in Dry Creek, Arizona, three weeks ago. She's gonna have pups and there worth some real money, so I want to get her home. Ain't paying no rewards." The man had signed his name, Bud Willand, and contact information followed.

Echo glanced at Avalon, who was resting quietly in a patch of sunlight streaming in through the display window. She'd passed by the exit for Dry Creek on her way north from Tucson.

"Did you belong to somebody named Bud Willand?" she asked.

Avalon sighed and stretched.

After hesitating to wrestle with her conscience, Echo dialed the phone number listed in the e-mail. She couldn't *not* call, but she had a very bad feeling, just the same.

"Yo" came the brusque answer.

"Is this Mr. Willand?" Echo asked.

"Bud," Mr. Willand confirmed.

"I believe you sent me an e-mail about a lost pet? Can you tell me what you call her?" It would be an easy enough test; if Avalon *was* Bud Willand's dog, she would respond to her name.

Willand gave a gruff, faintly contemptuous chuckle. "Kids named her Whitey, not that it matters. Damn critter never comes when you call her, anyhow."

"Whitey," Echo repeated, watching Avalon for any sign of recognition.

The dog didn't so much as twitch.

"I don't think this is Whitey," she said.

"I'd like to take a look at her just the same," Willand replied. "Kids miss her somethin' awful. And, like I said, she don't answer to nothing but a bowl of table scraps."

"I really don't—"

"She's a good huntin' dog, though. Take her out every fall in my camper."

Echo closed her eyes, remembering the way Avalon had clawed so desperately at the door of that RV, the night of Rianna's birthday party, and been virtually inconsolable when the woman inside wasn't her owner.

She couldn't imagine gentle Avalon as a hunter, though. Couldn't bear to think of her tied up in someone's backyard, subsisting on table scraps.

Still, there was the camper reference—she hadn't mentioned anything like that on the missing-pet Web sites, although she had updated the information once since that night—and it wouldn't be right or fair to ignore that.

Echo gave Bud Willand directions to Indian Rock and her shop, hoping all the while that he wouldn't show up.

Within half an hour, she'd forgotten all about Mr. Willand and any claims he might have on Avalon. The first shipment of books arrived, and she got busy sorting them and entering them into an inventory database on her computer.

It was just after five when Cora dropped in.

"Place is starting to look like a bookstore," she commented happily.

Echo grinned, pleased and exhausted. "It's coming together," she said. It would take a lot of work to open the shop by Saturday morning, but she was determined to do so.

"I'd be glad to help," Cora said. "First, though, I think you ought to come over to my place for a good supper." She glanced fondly down at Avalon, who was still sunning herself. "You can bring the pooch, too, of course."

"That's so kind of you," Echo answered, pushing back sweat-dampened bangs and giving a tired sigh, "but I was planning to grab some yogurt and keep working."

"Yogurt," Cora scoffed good-naturedly, "can't compete with my three-bean-bacon casserole."

Echo's stomach grumbled. "Probably not."

"You come on home with me," Cora insisted. "After supper, we'll head back here and finish up."

Avalon stood and stretched, went to Cora's side and licked her hand.

Echo laughed. "I guess it's decided," she said. "Just let me clean up a little."

"You look fine," Cora said. "I've got to stop by McKettrickCo to pick up the girls. Rance came and got them—took them out to lunch, then back to his office. I'm beginning to think there might be hope for that man yet."

Echo smiled, though any reference to Rance made her nervous. "He'll be joining us?" she asked tentatively.

"That depends," Cora answered. "Big things happening in the company right now. There's a possibility they might go public, and since the McKettrick clan is divided on the issue, Rance may be up to his backside in alligators right about now."

"Oh," Echo said, at a loss. She knew nothing

about McKettrickCo except that it was an international corporation and, as such, probably chopping down rain forests and exploiting unskilled laborers.

"Come on, now," Cora prodded. "We'll have us a good time, whether Rance shows up or not."

Five minutes later, Echo was in the Volks, with Avalon buckled in on the passenger side, following Cora to McKettrickCo's local offices. The building was impressive, fitting in well with the landscape, and there were a number of cars parked in the lot, although it was surely past closing time.

Echo waited in her car, hoping Rance would join them at Cora's for supper and, with equal intensity, hoping he *wouldn't*. She felt like a giant rubber band, stretched to its limits.

When Cora came outside again, Rianna and Maeve were with her, but there was no sign of Rance.

Rianna and Maeve waved to Echo, grinning, and Cora shepherded them into her truck. When she started the engine and backed out of her parking space, Echo pulled in behind her.

Cora's house was a two-story Victorian, painted white and trimmed in forest green, with a picket fence and lilac bushes blooming in the front yard. A flag waved from a metal holder fixed to a pillar of the wraparound porch, which was partly screened in. A big maple tree provided shade, and a wooden swing hung from one of its sturdy branches. The driveway was gravel, leading to an old-fashioned detached garage.

Cora parked the truck inside, while Maeve and Rianna bounded back through the open door to meet Echo and Avalon on the sidewalk.

The girls greeted Avalon with a lot of exuberant ear-rumpling and some back-stroking, and Echo would have sworn the dog was smiling as she basked in their attention.

Echo thought briefly of Bud Willand and his children. *Was* Avalon the missing Whitey? Would the Willand kids welcome her the way Rianna and Maeve had, with happy, rollicking love?

The pit of Echo's stomach quavered a little. If Avalon *was* Whitey, she would have to give her up, and the prospect filled her with dread.

"How come you look so sad?" Rianna asked, pausing to study Echo's face with solemn interest.

"I'm just a little tired," Echo hastened to explain.

Cora, evidently having entered the house from a side or back door, appeared on the front porch, beckoning.

"There's lemonade in the fridge," she called.

Maeve opened the creaking gate, and they all trooped through. Looking at that wonderfully simple house, with its gleaming windows and neatly kept lawn, flower beds and shrubbery, Echo felt another pang.

What would it have been like to grow up in such a place?

She imagined snow at Christmas, a festive wreath on the door and colorful tree lights glowing in the living room window. In the autumn, there would be jack-o'-lanterns on the step, while crimson and gold leaves pooled around the trunk of the maple. In the spring, pansies, nasturtiums and geraniums would billow brightly over the edges of terra-cotta pots.

Echo's throat tightened with an impossible longing.

Rianna, young as she was, seemed to understand. She took Echo's hand and squeezed it lightly. "I miss my mom," she whispered.

Tears burned behind Echo's eyes.

Maeve's small back stiffened, and she turned to face her sister. "You don't *remember* Mom," she accused.

"I still miss her," Rianna insisted.

"Let's get some of that lemonade," Echo said.

"We all need to wet our whistles," Cora added. She was smiling, but her eyes were sad and serious as she gathered her granddaughters close against her sides. Over their heads, Echo's and Cora's gazes connected.

They had cold lemonade in the backyard, at a wicker table, and then the children played with Avalon while Cora and Echo sat quietly in the leaf-dappled sunshine.

"Their mother grew up right here under this roof," Cora said softly. "She played in the grass, with her dog, Farky, just like Rianna and Maeve are doing now. I never thought I'd still be here, and my Julie gone. "

Echo didn't know how to respond.

Cora managed a resolute smile. "I'm an old fool, running on about somebody you didn't even know," she said. "Forgive me."

"I don't mind listening, Cora," Echo answered. "And you're anything but an 'old fool.'"

"Would you like to look at some pictures?" Cora asked, with touching shyness. "Of Julie, I mean?"

"I'd like that very much," Echo said.

Cora hurried into the house and soon returned with an album, well worn. She pulled a chair closer to Echo's and laid the large book reverently on the tabletop, opening to the first page.

There was a much younger Cora, smiling, posed in front of a Christmas tree and holding a beautiful baby clad in pink. "My husband, Mike, took that picture," she said.

Maeve and Rianna appeared, as if magnetized, standing on either side of their grandmother to peer, rapt, over her shoulders. Undoubtedly, they'd seen the photographs in that album often enough to memorize every detail of every image, but from their expressions, they might have been seeing them for the first time.

"Show Echo the one of Mommy in the cowgirl outfit," Rianna prompted breathlessly. Looking up at Echo, she added proudly, "Mommy was Little Miss Rodeo when she was five."

"Wow," Echo said, honestly impressed. Julie Tellington was Shirley Temple–cute in her fringed skirt, vest and boots, beaming into the camera lens with the confidence of a thoroughly cherished child.

"She wasn't the least bit spoiled, either," Cora related fondly, devouring the photo with her eyes. "We tried to have more children, Mike and I did, but we felt blessed to raise our Julie."

Echo couldn't speak. She yearned for a child of her own, one she would love as fiercely as Cora had loved hers. "She was beautiful."

Cora nodded. Sniffled slightly. Her hand curved around the edge of the aging picture with a tenderness that bruised Echo's very soul. To love the way Cora had was a terrible risk, laying the heart bare, with all its most delicate nerves exposed.

How had Cora borne such a loss?

Rianna reached out with grubby, grass-stained fingers and touched the photograph briefly. Echo was glad when Cora didn't reprimand the little girl, but waited until Rianna slowly withdrew her hand.

A series of sequential photos followed—Julie on the first day of school, competing in various baton-twirling contests, always in an outfit as elaborate as the cowgirl costume, and probably hand-made, opening presents on her birthdays, and at Christmas. Dressed for trick-or-treating, in a variety of imaginative getups—a bumblebee one year, a giant hot dog the next, then a sunflower with floppy yellow petals and green felt leaves.

Cora admitted modestly that she'd sewn constantly when Julie was little, and still made costumes for Rianna and Maeve when they were called for.

Midway through the album, Rance began to appear—a teenager clowning as he and Julie washed an old car, the spray of the hose frozen forever in a bright geyser, a handsome young man standing proudly beside Julie on prom night, their wedding. Later, he posed with Julie and the kids, and their smiles seemed to light up the picture.

There were more photos—taken at picnics, on holidays. Echo wondered sadly if anyone else had noticed Julie's smile growing almost imperceptibly dimmer, from one occasion to the next.

Finally, they reached the album's end.

Avalon gave an uncertain little yelp, and everyone looked up to see Rance standing in the yard, watching them. His face was in shadow, but he came out of the shade smiling.

Echo's heart caught painfully.

"I hope I didn't miss supper," he said.

Avalon approached him, and Echo watched, oddly stricken, as he leaned down to pet the dog in greeting.

"We didn't eat yet," Rianna informed her father.

"Good," he said, looking at Echo as he came nearer. His gaze dropped, momentarily, to the album.

"I'll get you some lemonade," Cora said, getting up and clutching the album against her chest, almost as though she feared he might snatch it from her.

"Thanks," he said mildly, still watching Echo.

Cora went inside the house, taking the photo album with her.

Rianna and Maeve followed, leaving Rance and Echo alone in the backyard, except for Avalon, who waited for Rance to sit down at the table, then settled companionably at his feet.

"Long day?" Echo asked, noting the signs of fatigue around Rance's eyes, barely suppressing an urge to smooth his slightly rumpled hair.

"The usual," he said. "I take it Cora showed you one of her albums."

She nodded. "Julie was lovely," she said.

Rance acknowledged that with a brief motion of his head. Relaxed a little.

Rianna returned with a glass of lemonade. "Are we going public?" she asked, handing the drink to her father.

The moment quivered.

Then Rance laughed, both at his daughter's words and Echo's obvious confusion. "That hasn't been decided yet," he told Rianna. "As of right now, McKettrickCo is still a family business."

Echo, having finally caught up with the conversation, wanted to ask which side Rance was on, and promptly decided it was none of her business.

"Are we for or against?" Rianna inquired.

"We're undecided," Rance replied.

"Uncle Jesse?"

"Undecided," Rance said.

"Uncle Keegan is definitely *against*," Rianna declared.

"Is he ever," Rance confirmed. "Far be it from him to live out the rest of his days as a man of leisure."

"What would you do, Daddy? If you didn't have to work at McKettrickCo anymore, I mean?" Rianna looked so hopeful as she asked that question that Echo had to avert her eyes.

"I'd spend more time with you and your sister," Rance said quietly.

Echo's gaze flew to his face.

"That would be good," Rianna said, beaming. In that moment, despite her Rance-dark hair, the child looked to Echo so much like Julie that it was as though she'd come back to life.

Rance took a sip of his lemonade. "That would be good," he agreed.

Maeve came out of the back door then, carrying a stack of plates topped with silverware. Cora was right behind her, bearing a blue-and-white casserole dish in both hands.

Avalon sat up on her haunches and sniffed appreciatively.

Cora took one of the plates, once Maeve had set them on the table, dished up a portion of the savory-smelling concoction, and put it on the ground for Avalon.

"I hope you don't mind," Cora said, after the fact, glancing at Echo.

"I don't mind," Echo whispered, wishing, just as

she had the night before, on Rance's patio, that time would stand still, instead of flowing on and on, like the creek in front of the ranch house. Knowing it wouldn't, she folded the homey backyard tableau carefully and tucked it away in the mental scrapbook where she kept only the most precious things.

CHAPTER 6

TWILIGHT THICKENED INTO dusky darkness, there in Cora's backyard, the girls playing with Avalon, Cora watering her flower beds with a trickle from the hose, Echo and Rance sitting quietly at the table, now cleared of supper dishes.

Echo's feelings—a sense of calm renewal, contrasted with the uneasy conviction that she was on dangerous ground—showed clearly in her face.

Rance watched, both wary and fascinated, while her expressions changed—now a soft, reflective smile as she watched the kids and the dog romp in the fresh-cut grass, then a slight worried frown, creasing the smooth skin between her eyebrows.

Periodically, she settled back in her chair, relaxed. In the next moment, though, she would be on its edge again, stealing surreptitious glances at her watch.

Finally, with a sigh of resolution, she got to her feet.

Rance's gaze focused first on her bare legs, below the ragged fringe of her denim shorts, then rose with purposeful deliberation to connect with her eyes.

She flushed, probably caught somewhere between flustered irritation at his audacity and a tacit acknowledgment of their mutual attraction. It was primordial, this thing happening between them, as elemental as a volcanic eruption, and as unstoppable.

They were going to collide, like two powerfully opposing weather systems, high in an uneasy sky. It was irrational, it was bound to be cataclysmic, and it was inevitable.

Category five, Rance thought.

He stood because Echo had. An old-fashioned gesture, yes. And one imprinted on the DNA of every McKettrick male. No matter what kind of scoundrel you were, in business or any other area of life, you rose when a lady did. You opened doors and you carried heavy things.

"You're not leaving already, are you?" Cora asked, turning from the flower beds to look at Echo.

Echo wrenched her attention from Rance—he literally felt the shock, like old paint being stripped from a wall—and smiled at Cora. "It's almost eight o'clock," she said reasonably.

She was a princess, with invisible wings. Perhaps, at some unknown hour, she would turn into a frog.

Rance frowned inwardly. Or was frogdom solely the province of princes? He was a little sketchy when it came to fairy tales.

Cora made a face, then shut off the hose and wound it into a green, shiny coil. "I promised I'd help you unpack books tonight, and I always keep my word."

"You're tired," Echo protested. She seemed to have forgotten Rance existed, but he wasn't fooled. She was aware of him in every cell of her body, just as he was of her. She was deliberately ignoring him. Pretending he wasn't there.

Good luck, he thought. Women sometimes disliked or even hated him. They threw things and they yelled and cried. More often, they crooned and wheedled and flirted, and scored his bare back with their fingernails when he made love to them.

But they never ignored him.

"Nonsense," Cora argued. "I'm full of energy."

"We can help," Rianna said hopefully. "Can't we?" But even as she spoke, she was yawning.

"Tell you what," Rance interjected, knowing what he was about to suggest would throw the proverbial wrench into Echo's works and loving the prospect because it electrified the atmosphere. "It sounds like there's some heavy lifting to do. You girls stay here with Granny, and *I'll* help out with the books."

"It really isn't necessary," Echo said, with delicious uncertainty. "The job can wait until tomorrow."

"Not if you want to be open for business on Saturday morning, it can't," Cora put in. Even in the gathering darkness, Rance saw the spark in his mother-in-law's eyes. She didn't miss a whole hell of a lot. She yawned copiously, just as Rianna had done, and Maeve did the same. "Now that you mention it," Cora added, "I *could* stand to put up my feet for a while. Maybe watch a little TV."

Echo bit her lower lip, glanced uncomfortably in Rance's direction. He could tell she was torn and, rounder that he was, he was enjoying the crackle, and the quicksilver thoughts flickering in her wondrous eyes, like a slide show on fast-forward.

Get lost, a part of her said.

Make love to me until neither of us has anything left to give, said another.

Decisions, decisions.

Rance smiled to himself. *Always glad to oblige a lady,* he thought.

"It seems we keep getting thrown together," she said fitfully.

"Go figure," Rance answered.

"You two run along now," Cora added, with a shooing motion of both hands. "The girls and I will have some ice cream and see what's on the tube."

Echo flushed again, rousing something primitive in Rance—not a desire to conquer, as he might have expected, but to protect.

Resigned, Echo thanked Cora for supper, said good-night to the girls, and called Avalon to her side.

Rance promised to pick the girls up in an hour or two, and walked Echo and the dog to her car, parked out front, wheels touching the sidewalk. The SUV loomed behind it, and Rance couldn't help drawing a parallel between the vehicles and Echo and himself.

He backed off a little, both physically and mentally.

Waiting until she'd settled the dog and then herself in the pink bug, he then climbed into the SUV, started the engine and followed her through quiet residential streets lined with simple, well-kept houses onto the main road, back to her bookshop.

An old truck was parked out front, and a man got out of it as soon as Echo pulled up.

Rance felt uneasy, though he couldn't have given a solid reason for it. He'd never met a man he was physically afraid of, which probably meant he was feeling territorial. Unless Rance missed his guess, and that didn't happen often, the stranger wasn't Echo's type—he was too scruffy for that. Needed a shower, a haircut and a shave, for starters. Probably a job, too, from the looks of his clothing and his rig.

Echo hesitated after she got out of the bug, then made a visible decision to round the car and step up onto the sidewalk, where the man waited. Rance shut off his own rig and was standing beside her before she'd come to a full stop.

"I'm Bud Willand," the stranger said.

Rance noticed that Echo had left the dog in the car.

"Echo Wells," she replied. Her voice was small and a little tremulous—she hadn't wanted to give up her name. Or to have this conversation at all, most likely.

Willand sized Rance up, the way men do when matters of primitive instinct might arise, and wisely kept his distance. Turning his attention to Avalon, who was watching them all through the passenger-side window, tongue lolling, he said, "That looks like Whitey, all right."

Echo tensed.

Rance wanted to put an arm around her shoulder, but refrained.

Willand turned slightly, toward Echo's car. "Hello there, girl," he said to the dog. "Looks like you been livin' in style since you jumped the fence down home."

Avalon shrank back a little in the seat, trying to see around Willand's bulky frame and find Echo.

She stepped into view. "It's okay, Avalon," she said very softly.

Willand moved toward the car.

"Wait," Echo said, but it was too late.

He opened the door and Avalon snarled, then lunged. She became a blur of white, struggling so wildly against the seat belt that she got tangled in it. If she hadn't, she'd have bitten a chunk out of Willand's hide for sure.

Willand cursed and jumped back, stumbling

against the curb and nearly landing on his ass on the sidewalk.

Echo moved between him and White Fang. Her eyes glittered as she looked back at Willand, and her chin stuck out a little. Meanwhile, Avalon settled down.

"This isn't your dog," Echo said clearly.

"The hell it isn't!" Willand snapped. "She's just as damn mean as ever, too!"

"Avalon," Echo said evenly, glancing briefly at Rance before facing Willand again, "is *not* mean." She stepped closer to the dog, soothed it with a few gentle pats on the head and some shushes.

"Avalon!" Willand spat. "What kind of stupid New Age name is that for a dog?" He glared at the animal. So much for the jovial approach.

Slowly, Echo unfastened the seat belt. The dog sat quietly, leaning against her mistress, but Avalon's gaze, a strange mixture of predator and prey, was fixed on Willand. "Call her," Echo said. "If she's yours, she'll come to you."

Willand swore again, this time more viciously than before.

Rance waited, every muscle poised.

Willand went around the back of his pickup and lowered the tailgate with a bang. "Whitey," he called. "You *git* in this truck!"

Avalon growled, low, and then looked piteously up into Echo's face.

"You're not taking this dog anywhere," Echo said.

"The hell I'm not," Willand argued, lumbering back to the sidewalk. "That's a purebred, right there, and she's worth a lot of money."

Rance stepped in front of Willand when the stranger would have advanced on Echo. Maybe he planned on beating the dog into submission, and maybe he was just stupid. "Seems to me the matter has been decided," Rance said. "The dog stays."

Willand gave him a look of pure hatred. "If you know what's good for you, mister," he said, "you'll stay the hell out of this."

"The dog stays," Rance repeated, giving the words no inflection at all. "Echo, take Avalon and go inside."

"No," she said.

"You leave that dog right here," Willand ordered, without looking away from Rance's face. "She's going with me."

Rance didn't look away, either. In point of fact, he was spoiling for a fight, and if Echo and the dog hadn't been there, he would have indulged the impulse and worried about the consequences later.

"Echo," Rance said, one more time, "*go inside.*"

She thrust out a sigh, took the dog by the collar and led her to the door of the shop. After a few moments of purse rummaging, both woman and canine were off the sidewalk and out of harm's way.

"That is *my* dog," Willand said, running the back of one hand across his mouth. Rance caught a whiff of stale beer, sweat and bad dental hygiene. "My wife is waitin' at home, watchin' the road for me and Whitey. I ain't goin' back without her."

Out of the corner of his eye, Rance saw Echo peering through the glass door of the bookshop, cell phone in hand.

God bless her, she was ready to call the police.

He almost smiled at that.

The stare-down went on.

Finally, Willand folded. Slammed the tailgate closed, then went around to the front of his truck. "I'll be back for my dog," he warned.

Rance followed. Now, with Willand's truck blocking her view, Echo was probably on her tiptoes, trying to see what was going on.

"How much?" Rance asked. With guys like Bud Willand, it always came down to cold, hard cash.

Willand, having wrenched open the driver's-side door, narrowed his eyes. "Say what?"

"How much?"

"You admittin' that dog is mine?"

"I'm not admitting anything," Rance replied. "For the last time—*how much?*"

Willand shoved a hand through his greasy hair. Checked out Rance's SUV, then his clothes. "I could get five hundred bucks for a dog like that, easy," he said speculatively. "More, if there's pups, like I figure there is."

Rance pulled his money clip from the pocket of his white shirt. Without taking his eyes off Willand, he counted out twice the price the other man had mentioned.

Willand grasped at it.

Rance drew back his hand, the bills folded between his thumb and index finger. "You're a country boy," he said, "so I figure you'll understand what I'm about to tell you. If you ever set foot in this town again, for any reason, you'd better bring an army, because you're going to need one to keep me from turning you inside out. Is that clear?"

Willand's attention was on the money. "Sure," he muttered.

Rance was almost disappointed. He tucked the bills behind the cigarette pack rolled up in the sleeve of Willand's stained T-shirt. "Get out."

Willand nodded. "Piece-of-shit dog, anyhow," he said. Then he got behind the wheel of his truck, slammed the door and laid rubber.

Rance watched until the taillights of the old rig disappeared into the darkness. The lights went on inside the bookstore, and Echo stuck her head out.

"He's gone?"

Under any other circumstances, Rance would have laughed at the inanity of that question, but he knew what Echo was really asking, beyond the rhetorical. She wanted to know if Willand would be back.

"He's gone," Rance confirmed, moving toward her.

She stepped back to let him into the shop. "For good?"

"Probably," he answered, entering.

"She really isn't his dog," Echo said, closing the door behind him. "Or, if she is, he mistreated her. She obviously hates him and—"

She paused and her eyes filled with tears.

Rance laid his hands on her shoulders, but lightly. "It's okay, Echo," he said. He wanted to kiss her again, a lot more thoroughly than he had the night before, out at his place, but the moment called for something else. He drew her against him instead and held her.

"How did you make him go away?" she asked, her voice muffled by the fabric of his shirt.

He stroked the back of her head, closing his fingers around that fetching braid, found it thick as a calf rope, but a lot softer. "Never mind that," he said. "If you see or hear from Willand again, you just let me know. I'll take it from there."

She tilted her head back, looked up at him and sniffled. "I'm sorry, Rance," she said.

"What for?" he asked, honestly puzzled.

"For getting you involved. He could have had a gun, or a knife—"

"I can take care of myself," Rance assured her. He wanted to add, *And I can take care of you,* but he didn't, because it was too soon. Because the time for it might never come at all.

She let out a shuddery sigh and pulled back out of Rance's arms. Sniffled again. "Thank you," she said.

"Any time," he replied, oddly bereft now that he

wasn't holding her anymore. Now that she'd with-drawn.

He shook off a sudden case of the dismals and looked around at the boxes taking up most of the floor space. "Guess we'd better get started," he said, "if you want to open Saturday morning."

Echo smiled at him, but it was a cautious draw-bridge of a smile. *Keep your distance,* it said. "You've been at your office all day, working hard," she argued. "I can handle this, Rance. Really."

"I'm sure you can," Rance said. "Where's the coffeepot?"

"The coffeepot?"

He grinned. "I could use a little caffeine," he told her. Maybe the stuff would mix with the adrenaline coursing through his system—like meeting like in some weird chemical reaction—and the two would cancel each other out. "Since it's probably politically incorrect to ask you to make coffee, I'll do it myself."

She blinked. "You're not leaving?"

"Not unless you call the cops and have me thrown out," he said.

To his surprise, she laughed. "You *are* stubborn. And I seriously doubt that political correctness is at the top of your priority list."

"Guilty on both counts," he replied. "I can't help it. I'm a McKettrick."

She started for the stairs at the back of the shop.

He followed, even though he hadn't been invited. Near the top, she turned, looked down at him with her heart in her wide eyes. "It's too soon," she said, very quietly.

"I know," he answered.

She looked relieved and disconcerted, both at the same time.

At least they were on the same page.

ECHO LOVED HER APARTMENT, small as it was. Loved the featherbed and the big windows and the shelves jammed with cherished, oft-read books.

Now, though, she wondered how it looked to Rance. The man traveled by private jet. He chartered helicopters and lived in a house that was probably worth more money than she'd be likely to earn in three lifetimes.

She tried not to stare as he glanced around, taking it in.

Avalon, stretched out luxuriously on her airbed, gave a loud, snorting snore.

Echo fumbled with the coffeemaker. Ran the water so hard that it splashed up and soaked the front of her shirt. She was cranking down the ancient faucet when Rance's hand closed over hers.

She shut her eyes briefly. Withdrew her fingers.

He turned off the water.

"Echo," he said.

She forced herself to look at him.

"Relax," he told her. "Nothing is going to happen until you're ready."

She bit her lower lip, trying to hold back her

response. It popped right out of her mouth, anyway. "But it *is* going to happen."

He smiled. Took the coffeepot out of her hand, filled it with water. "I think so," he said easily. "Tell me about the man who made you so skittish."

She held the front of her T-shirt away from her skin, wiggled the fabric a little, in a futile attempt to dry it. It was an ordinary thing to do, and she hoped she looked calm, though her heart was racing. "Who says I'm skittish?"

Rance poured the water into the back of the machine, took filters and the coffee canister down off the shelf above the counter. "I do," he answered. "Every time I get close to you, you practically jump out of your skin."

"I do not," she protested.

He gave her a look.

"Okay, you do make me a little nervous."

"Sorry about that," he said, but he didn't sound sorry at all. He sounded pleased. He finished with the coffee, turned and stood leaning against the counter with his arms folded, watching her. Waiting.

"We were supposed to get married," she told him, without meaning to. "Justin and I, I mean."

"Justin," he repeated, as though testing the name. "What went wrong?"

"He changed his mind at the last minute." She looked away, made herself look back. It was a point of pride, being able to stand toe to toe with Rance McKettrick, though God only knew why she should feel that way. After all, the man was a virtual stranger. "It was probably for the best."

"Probably," Rance agreed.

He seemed to fill the room, with his broad shoulders and his big personality. He sucked out all the air—made her want to throw open the windows. Made her want to do other things, too. Things she blushed to think about, because they all involved getting naked.

"Maybe we should go downstairs," she said.

Rance's gaze drifted to the bed, then back to her. "Maybe we should," he agreed, albeit reluctantly.

For the next hour, they unpacked boxes, drank coffee and talked about everything but the way the earth seemed to tilt whenever they accidentally touched shoulders or made eye contact.

They'd made considerable progress when they decided, by tacit agreement, to call it a night.

Rance inspected the locks on his way out, frowning thoughtfully.

Echo's throat tightened at his concern. When was the last time anyone had worried about her safety?

"I have Avalon to protect me," she told him, and then she was embarrassed, because maybe he hadn't been thinking along those lines at all.

He was a man. They thought about hardware—nuts and bolts, locks and screws.

"Have them changed," he said. "You need a dead bolt, and a chain."

She nodded, ridiculously touched.

He went out and waited on the sidewalk until she worked the lock.

Grinned at her through the glass.

It was all she could do not to jerk the door open again and ask him to stay. Not because she was afraid—that would have been a much more acceptable reason, to Echo's way of thinking, than the real one.

She wanted Rance McKettrick.

It was that simple—and that complicated.

He hesitated, then turned away and headed for his SUV.

A moment later, he was back, rapping lightly on the glass with his knuckles.

Barely able to breathe, Echo wrestled with the lock and pulled open the door.

"I was wondering," Rance said, "if you've ever ridden a horse."

She swallowed, totally confused. "A horse?"

He grinned. "You know. Big critters. Four legs. A mane and tail."

She giggled, more from nerves than amusement. "No," she said. "I have never ridden a horse."

"Sunday?"

"I beg your pardon?"

"Would you like to go riding? On Sunday?"

Indian Rock was a small town, with five different churches. Echo had already noticed that the other stores, with the exception of the supermarket, were all closed that day, and she'd adjusted her plans accordingly. "I was going to work," she said, sounding lame. "Try to get the inventory organized. Log titles into the computer."

"Are you scared of horses?"

The challenge made her stiffen her spine, even though she knew she was being played. "No."

"Then I'll pick you up around one." He took in her shorts and T-shirt. "Wear jeans," he added. "It's rough country."

Before Echo could protest, he was gone again.

She relocked the door, shut off the lights and went upstairs.

Because of all the coffee, she was wide awake.

At least she *told* herself it was the coffee.

BY THE TIME RANCE GOT TO Cora's, Rianna and Maeve were in their pajamas, sound asleep at either end of their grandmother's couch, sharing a faded quilt he knew had been Julie's.

Cora put a finger to her lips, then beckoned for Rance to follow her to the kitchen. The album she and the girls had been looking at earlier, with Echo, rested on the table.

"I could make some decaf," Cora said.

Rance shook his head.

She smiled. "You can leave the girls overnight. They're fine where they are."

Rance nodded, drew back a chair at the table and sat down. The ranch house was big, and without his daughters it would be empty, as well. He was in no hurry to get back there.

Cora's smile dimmed a little. "You all right, Rance?"

He sighed, then laid a hand on the cover of the album. An old and fathomless sorrow washed through him. "I'm fine," he said.

Cora's gaze followed his hand. "Let her go," she said very softly. "Julie, I mean."

They needed to talk, about so many things. But every time Rance got too close to the subject of his late wife, he felt so raw inside that it took his breath away. He was afraid he'd break down, and he couldn't do that—not in front of Cora.

Despite his privileged upbringing, he'd known a lot of loss in his life—his parents had divorced while he was in college, after his only sibling, his younger sister, Cassidy, had died of leukemia, within mere weeks of the diagnosis. She'd been seventeen.

Seventeen.

Where was the justice in that?

And what if it happened again—to Maeve or Rianna? What if one of them had inherited the same renegade gene that had brought Cassidy down?

"I have," he said belatedly, realizing he'd let Cora's words go unanswered. "I have let Julie go."

"Have you?" Cora asked, pulling back a chair and joining him at the table.

Rance rubbed his chin. His beard was coming in, and he was tired to the bone. Tired of McKettrickCo, tired of the rat race that had been his refuge for so long.

Suddenly, he wanted to be a rancher, like generations of McKettricks before him. He wanted to run
cattle on the land, ride horses, plant hayfields.

Chuck out the three-piece suits jamming his
closet at home and wear jeans and western shirts
and boots again, the way Jesse did. Sell the SUV
and get himself a truck.

He chuckled at the pictures going through his
mind. Tried, without success, to shake them off.

"What is it?" Cora asked, very gently.

He couldn't look at her. "Did you ever wish
you'd done something different with your life?"

"Not for a single, solitary minute," she replied
with certainty. "I'd marry Mike Tellington all over
again. Raise my daughter just the way I did. Run the
Curl and Twirl, too."

Rance forced himself to meet Cora's gaze. "It
hasn't been easy for you," he said, and then felt like
an idiot for stating the obvious.

"It hasn't been so bad, Rance. Sure, it was hard
losing Mike, and then Julie, too, but I have Rianna
and Maeve. I try to think about what I have, not
what I'm missing."

"You're a wise woman, Cora."

She gave a little snort at that. "I don't know how
wise I am, but I can count my blessings well enough."

Rance absorbed that in silence. He had blessings
aplenty, Rianna and Maeve being the most important ones, his pioneer heritage being another, but
sometimes he felt empty, just the same. As if a cold

and bitter wind could blow right through him and not even slow down.

"What about you, Rance?" Cora prompted. "What would you do differently, if you could go back in time?"

"I'd have been there when Julie took that spill at the horse show, for one thing," he said. She'd broken her neck, going over a jump. Rance had been in Hong Kong at the time, making deals, driving the hard bargains he was famous for. It had all seemed so damn important back then.

Cora touched his hand. "Don't, Rance," she said. "Don't go back over that ground. Julie died instantly—there was nothing you could have done."

His eyes burned. "You had to handle it all. The arrangements. The girls. All while you were grieving yourself."

"Situation like that," Cora said, sounding choked, "a person does what they have to do. I wish you'd been here, too, Rance, but I don't hold it against you that you weren't."

A long, difficult silence fell.

"It wasn't perfect," he said. That was as close as he could get to the truth both of them were avoiding, to what lay behind the oh-so-respectable facade of his memories. "But I loved Julie."

"Of course you did," Cora replied. "And she loved you. You were a good provider, Rance. You were a faithful husband and a fine father. Nobody could have asked any more of you."

Julie had asked more of him. A lot more. And he'd put her off, thinking there was plenty of time.

Julie might still be alive if he'd swallowed his damnable pride. If he'd given even an inch of ground.

"Life moves on, Rance," Cora said, squeezing his hand. "Takes us with it, kicking and screaming sometimes, but we don't get much say. When they lowered my Julie's casket into the ground, I wanted to die, too. Right then and there. But I had Maeve and Rianna to think about. I had to go on."

Rance nodded. Looked away and blinked hard.

"You've been stuck in neutral for a long time," Cora said. "But you're a young man. You have two daughters. Rance, you've got to go on."

It wasn't as if he had a choice, any more than Cora had. Time he accepted that, and stopped running from a past he couldn't change.

"Mind if I crash in the spare room tonight?" he asked.

Cora rose out of her chair, patted his shoulder as she passed.

"Make yourself at home," she told him.

CHAPTER 7

"YOU WANT TO DO *WHAT?*" Keegan asked the next morning, leaning halfway across his shiny desk at McKettrickCo and bracing himself against the wood with both hands, like a man about to do a standing push-up.

"You heard him," Jesse said from his place by the window. "Our cousin Rance has come to his senses."

"Come to his senses?" Keegan echoed, furious. He looked as though he might blow an artery at any moment. "He's lost his freaking *mind!*"

Rance sighed. "Take a breath, Keeg," he said.

Keegan thrust himself back, threw his hands out from his sides. "God*damn* it, Rance!" he yelled.

"You can't just throw over everything this family has worked for for the last fifty years!"

"Sure he can," Jesse said.

"You stay out of this!" Keegan roared.

Jesse didn't so much as flinch, nor did his piss-off grin falter.

The office door popped open, and Myrna Terp stuck her head in. "Is everything all right in here?" she asked. Having raised three sons herself— Morgan, Virgil and, alas, Wyatt—and worked in the Flagstaff operation until the new branch of McKettrickCo was opened in Indian Rock a few months back, Myrna was no stranger to conflict, verbal or otherwise.

"Yes!" Keegan answered.

"Everything's fine," Jesse told Myrna in calm tones. "Rance is going to retire from the company and concentrate on ranching, that's all."

Myrna opened her mouth, closed it again and re-treated, shutting the door softly behind her.

Keegan sank into his cushy leather chair, braced his elbows on the edge of the desk and covered his face with both hands.

"You are taking this way too hard," Rance said. "It's not as if I'm selling my shares to an outsider and moving to China."

Keegan lowered his hands. Stared at Rance as though he'd never seen him before. "It's the woman, isn't it?" he asked, his voice dangerously quiet. "The one with the pink car."

"Echo," Rance said, suddenly defensive, "has nothing to do with this. I've got two daughters to raise, Keeg. I have more money than *their* grandchildren could ever spend. What do I want with a job?"

Jesse began to clap, slowly and quietly.

Keegan threw him a murderous glance.

Jesse grinned, unfazed as always.

"Maybe *you* want to work yourself to death," Rance told Keegan, "but *I* don't."

"It's the woman," Keegan insisted grimly. A vein jumped under his right temple, and his jawline looked hard enough to bite through a brick.

"It's *not* the woman."

Jesse rolled his eyes. "Of *course* it's the woman, Rance. Until she came to town, you wanted to set up branch offices on other planets."

"Whose side are you on?" Rance demanded.

Jesse ignored the question.

"You'll regret this," Keegan said, glaring at Rance again. "Buying cattle. *Planting hay,* for God's sake. You're a businessman, Rance—not a rancher."

"I'm a McKettrick," Rance said. "The Triple M is in my blood."

"Oh, go ahead, then," Keegan railed. "Ride the range. Sit around campfires and sing with the coyotes, for all I care. You'll be bored out of your skull within six months. You'll want to come back. Trouble is, McKettrickCo will be *gone.*"

"You need a vacation," Jesse told Keegan. "Go somewhere and get laid."

"Shut up," Keegan bit out. "Unlike you, I do not subscribe to the theory that getting laid is the solution to everything from global warming to fallen arches, all right?"

Jesse laughed. "There's your problem," he said. He left his post at the window, strolled to where Rance stood and laid a hand on his shoulder. "If you're serious about heading up to Flag for that cattle auction," he added, "I'll go with you. Just give me a call at Lucky's."

Lucky's was a bar and grill, with a card room in the back. Jesse spent a lot of his spare time there, playing poker.

"At least *Cheyenne* works," Keegan said, once Jesse was gone.

Cheyenne, who would be Jesse's bride in a matter of weeks, was McKettrickCo's newest executive. Working in conjunction with the local high school and a junior college in Flagstaff, she'd set up a work-study program for kids and displaced homemakers and even a few senior citizens. So far, though still in the early stages of development, the idea was a success.

Rance didn't need the fat paycheck he drew from the company, but he'd hate to see a new board of directors put all those people out of work.

"I'll vote with you, Keeg," he said.

Keegan sighed. "I'm not sure that's going to be enough," he admitted. "Even if you stay on."

"You know I'll help any way I can."

Keegan studied him for a long time, then nodded. "Yeah," he said. "I know. But who's going to do your job, Rance?"

"I was in charge of expansion," Rance answered. "As far as I'm concerned, this company is big enough. Maybe too big."

"Maybe you're right," Keegan said. "Hell, maybe Jesse's right, too. Maybe I need to get laid."

Rance laughed. "It couldn't hurt."

Keegan grinned. For a moment, he looked like the old Keegan, the one who'd fished in the creek on the Triple M and ridden the hills on horseback with him and Jesse. The one who'd seen ranching as a fine, free life.

But then Keegan turned sober again. "Is it serious, Rance? With Echo, I mean?"

Rance shoved a hand through his hair. Looked away, then met his cousin's gaze squarely. "Damned if I know," he said. "*Something's* going on. We haven't slept together yet, but it's bound to happen."

Keegan leaned back in his chair, cupping his hands behind his head. "Be careful," he counseled. "I barely met the lovely Ms. Wells, but there's something fragile about her. She's breakable, Rance."

Rance recalled the way Echo had stood up to Bud Willand the night before, when the ne'er-do-well wanted to take her dog. She *was* delicate—small-boned and slender enough to blow away in a high wind. But she was strong, too. She'd come to a new town, where she didn't know a soul, and she was about to open a business.

It took guts to do that.

"I don't *want* to break her," Rance said.

"No," Keegan agreed, watching him pensively. "I know that. But she's the first woman you've really been drawn to since Julie. Don't use her, Rance. That's all I'm saying. Somebody's done Echo Wells a real number, somewhere along the way. Maybe more than once."

Rance narrowed his eyes. "You got all that just by meeting her at Rianna's birthday party?"

"Yeah," Keegan said. "She's been hurt, Rance."

Haven't we all? Rance wondered. Keegan surely had—he'd lost his folks in a plane crash when he was still in high school, and later his marriage had gone sour. He rarely saw his daughter since the divorce.

Even Jesse, for all his easy ways, had been lonely as hell until he'd met Cheyenne. He'd been the wildest of the three of them, dancing on a razor-sharp ledge above an abyss, tempting death. Daring it to come and get him.

And then there was Rance himself—he'd never stopped grieving over the death of his sister, Cassidy, and toward the end, he and Julie had done each other the worst kind of injury. They'd given up, gone their separate ways, even though they'd still lived under the same roof.

"I'll tie up all the loose ends by the end of next

week," Rance told Keegan, resting a hand on the doorknob.

Keegan nodded and looked away.

ON SATURDAY MORNING, ECHO rose even earlier than usual. She put coffee on to brew, pulled on a pair of old jeans and a baggy T-shirt, and took Avalon out for a predawn walk.

When they returned, Echo paused on the sidewalk.

The shop window sparkled, and the latest best-sellers were prominently displayed behind the glass. Echo had climbed a ladder, the night before, to hang a butcher-paper banner above the door—Grand Opening Saturday at 9:00 a.m. it proclaimed. The till waited on the newly varnished counter, along-side the credit-card machine. Now all she needed were customers.

Would they come?

Echo bit her lip. Yes, she thought, her spirits rising on a swell of optimism. People would come—probably out of curiosity at first. But if they were welcomed, and if she listened to them, they would return again and again.

Remembering what Rance had said, early on, about competition from the chains, she was a little deflated, but the sensation lasted only a moment.

She was too excited to be discouraged.

She unlocked the door, led Avalon inside and locked up again. No dead bolt and chain yet, but she had a call in to Eddie Walters, the local handyman.

Upstairs, she took a quick shower, wolfed down scrambled eggs and toast in her bathrobe, and reconsidered the clothes she'd laid out for her first day in business. The lightweight navy pin-striped pantsuit had seemed sensible when she'd chosen it the night before, but now the general effect seemed a little stiff.

More like something a banker would wear to refuse a loan or foreclose on something.

Not good, Echo thought. Half her wardrobe was still in boxes; her small closet contained mostly sundresses, summery tops and jeans.

Jeans wouldn't do—she wanted to present a friendly image, but not too casual.

The sundresses were all pretty, made of light cotton or floaty stuff.

Floaty stuff: out. Sure, she had a few decks of tarot cards and some crystals among her stock, but she didn't want to come off as Glenda the Good Witch. Indian Rock, as Rance had once pointed out, was not Sedona.

Finally, she selected a sleeveless navy dress with tiny white polka dots. Back in Chicago, she'd worn it to casual luncheons and backyard fund-raisers, with the single strand of pearls Justin had given her as a preengagement present.

She'd given the pearls to a casino employee in Vegas, a weary, resigned-looking woman wiping out ashtrays along a line of slot machines, along with her plastic bridal bouquet.

Looking back on that humiliating day, when she'd been all dressed up with nobody to marry, she smiled. *Thank you, Justin,* she thought for the first time. *Thank you.*

Once she was dressed, with her hair braided and her usual lip gloss and touch of mascara applied, Echo twirled.

Only Avalon was there to see, but Avalon was enough.

"Show time," she told the dog.

Avalon panted and smiled her dog smile.

Together, they went downstairs.

Cora, Rianna, Maeve and a number of other people were waiting on the sidewalk, smiling through the glass. Cora juggled a tote bag and a huge bakery box.

Echo grinned as she opened the door to let them all in, and it didn't bother her a bit that Rance hadn't come.

"Daddy bought a whole *bunch* of cattle!" Rianna announced the moment she crossed the threshold. "Trucks and trucks and trucks full of them!"

"He's going to be a rancher," Maeve added solemnly. "And he's wearing shit-kickers, just like Uncle Jesse's."

"Maeve McKettrick," Cora scolded, her tone as good-natured as her manner, as she bustled to set the bakery box down on the counter. "Watch your language."

"Granny bought you a cake," Rianna told Echo. "That's what's in the box."

"Picked up some paper plates and napkins and plastic forks, too," Cora said. "I'll just get them out of the truck."

Cheyenne Bridges, whom Echo had met briefly at Rianna's birthday party, introduced her mother, Ayanna, and said her brother, Mitch, would be along later, with Jesse.

Sierra materialized out of the crowd, too, accompanied by a slender blond woman with enormous blue eyes and a great haircut. She wore jeans, boots and a black cashmere turtleneck. "Echo Wells," Sierra said, "this is my sister, Meg. Echo, Meg McKettrick."

Meg smiled and put out a hand. "Hi," she said. "It's about time this place had a bookstore."

Sierra was already scanning the shop. "Amen," she agreed.

Cora returned with a bulging grocery bag, beckoned to Echo and proudly unveiled the sheet cake, iced in white butter cream, with the words "Welcome to Indian Rock, Echo Wells" written in blue frosting across the top.

It was an ordinary-enough sentiment, but Echo had never seen her name on a cake before. Her eyes burned, and for a moment she was too choked up to speak.

Ever perceptive, Cora patted her arm. "You get behind the counter, there, and I'll take your picture," she said, immediately hauling a small digital camera out of her tote bag.

Echo swallowed hard and went to stand behind the cake. Avalon followed, and just as Cora snapped the photograph, the dog stood on her hind legs, forepaws resting on the counter's edge, as though posing.

Everyone laughed, and the tightness in Echo's chest eased.

She cut the cake, setting a smidgeon of it on the floor for Avalon, and began working the cash register. Cheyenne, who had already set aside a stack of cookbooks for herself, stepped in to help bag people's purchases.

Customers came and went, most buying, all sampling Cora's welcome-to-town cake. There were only crumbs of it left when Rance appeared in the open doorway of the shop.

He wore jeans, a black cowboy hat, boots and a blue chambray work shirt—ordinary clothes, in the same way the greeting on the cake was ordinary. And yet the sight of him seemed to stop time itself, for Echo. Everyone else in the store receded, as though behind a silent, murky waterfall—visible, but indistinctly so.

Rance smiled, took off the hat. Set it aside on a bestseller table, now stripped nearly bare, and approached the counter.

"Howdy, ma'am," he said, very seriously.

Echo stared at him for a moment, then laughed. The waterfall vanished, the people were back, and every clock in the world started ticking again. "Howdy yourself," she replied.

He peered into the cake box, now almost empty, and looked comically forlorn.

"That's what you get for showing up late," Cheyenne told him, edging Echo aside to work the register herself. "Take a break," she added, when Echo hesitated.

Echo made her way to the stairs at the back of the shop, knowing Rance would follow, and sat on the third step up. He took the second, smiling up at her.

"Looks like the place is a hit," he said.

Echo shrugged, but she felt ridiculously proud. "You should have seen the cake," she told him. "It had writing on it. 'Welcome to Indian Rock, Echo Wells.'"

"I wish I *had* seen the cake," Rance teased. "I might have gotten some of it then."

Suddenly, Echo was ambushed again. Tears sprang to her eyes, and she turned her head to hide them, but Rance was too quick.

He took her hand. "What's the matter?" he asked.

She blinked, hoping her mascara wouldn't run. "Nothing," she answered. "Everything is wonderful. It's just that—"

"What?" Rance prompted.

"It's silly."

He squeezed her hand but said nothing.

"Nobody ever gave me a cake before," she told him.

"Not even on your birthday?"

She swallowed, thinking of all the childhood birthdays that had come and gone. She hadn't made the connection at Rianna's party. And all those celebrations that never happened were ancient history, anyway, along with the little-girl disappointment that accompanied them. What was the big deal now?

"I told you it was silly," she sniffled.

Rance raised her hand to his mouth, kissed it lightly. "Are we still on for that ride tomorrow afternoon?"

For a moment, Echo misunderstood. Her body heated, and warm, secret places expanded, deep inside her. Then she remembered the invitation he'd extended, after the Bud Willand incident and the unpacking of all those boxes of books.

She was just starting to hope Rance hadn't noticed her first and entirely spontaneous reaction when the grin spread across his face.

He *knew* what she'd been thinking, damn it.

And his next words confirmed that.

"I was planning to saddle a couple of horses," he said, "but I'm open to any kind of ride you might have in mind, Echo Wells."

Another rush of heat swamped Echo, because she couldn't help imagining what it would feel like to straddle Rance McKettrick's hips and take him deep, deep inside her.

He chuckled, and it was a low, *naked* sound, as though they were alone in his bedroom, alone in his house, alone in the *universe*. He leaned toward her, spoke in a tone only she could hear.

"When the time comes," he told her, "I'm going

to peel off your clothes, real slow. And I'm going to taste everything I uncover. Take my time. You're wound up tight inside right now, but when you turn loose, it'll raise the rafters."

Echo went damp all over.

Rance grinned again, well aware that he'd gotten the response he was after, and got to his feet. "I just came to say hello," he told her, as though he hadn't just carried out a virtual seduction on the stairway between her shop and her apartment. "There's another truckload of cattle due at the ranch anytime now, so I'd better go sign for them."

He was talking about *cattle?*

After nearly bringing her to a climax with just the *promise* of his lovemaking?

Echo was mortified.

She was also so aroused that she wondered how she'd get through twenty-four hours without the satisfaction only this one impossible man could possibly give her.

Rance bent, touched his mouth to hers, nibbled slightly at her lower lip. "One o'clock," he told her. "Wear jeans if you want to ride…a horse."

Echo watched, dumbstruck, as he turned and walked away, weaving through the crowd of shoppers, pausing to speak to Cora, and then to his daughters.

Mercifully, the rest of the day went by quickly, because the shop stayed busy. Echo didn't have much time to ponder the mysteries of Rance McKettrick, at least not consciously, but her very cells seemed to hum with naughty subliminal expectations.

At five o'clock, she closed the shop, went upstairs to change her clothes and took Avalon out for a second walk.

Back home, they shared a grilled cheese sandwich, and Avalon plodded to the airbed, exhausted.

Echo was tired, too, but she knew if she tried to sleep, she'd start thinking about Rance, so she spent the next three hours filling orders for her mail-order clients. When she took that pile of padded envelopes to the post office on her lunch hour Monday, she'd have to take care that Cora didn't see her.

One look at those packets and Cora, being as perceptive as Rance, might just recognize the size and shape, and put two and two together.

Echo huffed out a sigh. "Get real," she muttered. "Nobody is *that* perceptive."

But she wondered.

She finished her work, checked the locks downstairs, took a cool shower and crawled into bed.

She tallied the day's receipts in her head.

She made out a mental grocery list.

She turned onto her left side, then onto her right.

The apartment was too hot.

She tossed back the covers.

Sweltering.

She got up and opened one of the back windows to let in a breeze.

That didn't help, either, because Echo Wells

had her own heat wave going, and it had nothing whatsoever to do with summer weather in northern Arizona.

KEEGAN WAS PROBABLY RIGHT, Rance reflected, leaning on the top rail of the fence overlooking the long-empty pasture behind his house. He'd lost his mind, buying all these damn cows.

Who did he think he was? Angus McKettrick, the legendary old man who had founded the Triple M, way back in the 1800s?

Still, the night air felt good, and there were a million stars shining overhead, and it was a fine thing to listen to the cattle setting down in the deep grass.

He turned, looked back at the house. It was dark, except for a few of the downstairs windows. Rianna and Maeve had long since fallen asleep, reading the books Cora had helped them pick out at Echo's grand opening.

Echo.

It was a good name for her, he decided. Just when he thought he'd put her out of his mind, she'd come back to him and set all his senses to vibrating.

According to Maeve and Rianna, the name was made up. She had another, and evidently it was a secret, and a person had to know her well before she'd say what it was.

Rance intended to get to know Echo Wells's *real* well.

He sighed, took off his hat, shoved a hand

through his hair. He'd done hard physical labor that day, for the first time in more years than he cared to think about, and he needed a shower, bad. Like as not, every bone and muscle in his body would be aching like a son of a bitch by morning.

Hell of a thing if he couldn't mount a horse tomorrow, he thought, because he was all stove up like some broken-down old bronc-buster with too many rodeos behind him.

He grinned.

Maybe he wouldn't be able to mount a horse, but he wouldn't have much trouble mounting Echo. Lay her down in the sweet grass, and cowboy-up.

Somebody did her a real number, he heard Keegan say. *She's breakable.*

With a cousin like Keeg, a man didn't need a conscience.

"Shit," Rance muttered, and resettled his hat.

"Something on your mind?"

He started a little. "Think of the devil," he said, "and he'll appear."

Keegan chuckled and stepped up beside him, out of the darkness, then leaned against the fence. "You'd better hire some ranch hands," he told Rance, "if you're serious about playing the old-time McKettrick."

Rance sighed. "It's going to sound strange," he said quietly, "but sometimes it feels as if they're still here—Angus and the boys. Once or twice, just at twilight, I'd swear I saw a horse and rider where they couldn't be." He braced himself, expecting Keegan to call him a sentimental fool, or worse, but it didn't happen.

"I know what you mean," Keegan said. "I've had one or two experiences like that myself. Maybe Sierra's right. Could be, time isn't what we think it is. Past, present, future—maybe it's all *now*."

"You been listening to that spook-talk again?" Rance asked. Sierra was convinced that she and Travis were sharing Holt and Lorelei's old place with some of her ancestors. Said Doss and Hannah McKettrick were as alive as anybody—and they'd been married in 1919.

Sierra wasn't the first person in the family to make a claim like that, either. Eve, Sierra and Meg's mother, had always sworn strange things went on in that house, and Meg believed it, too.

One summer, when they were kids, Meg had hauled off and sucker-punched Rance, right in the nose, for saying she was crazy, believing in ghosts.

He hadn't minded the pain or the blood, he reflected, with a slight smile, but he'd sure as hell hated being slugged by a girl, especially since he couldn't hit her back.

Keegan let the question pass and put one of his own. "Do you think I ought to try to get custody of Devon?"

Rance didn't look at Keegan. His cousin had just said a hard thing, and he needed to stand with it for a little while.

"Is that what you want, Keeg?" he asked when the time seemed right.

Keegan sighed. "I know I miss that kid something awful," he answered. "That old house over there on the other side of the creek is big, and it's empty. I guess that's why I work the way I do. Because then I don't have to think about how lonesome I get whenever I stand still for too long."

Rance hesitated, then slapped a hand to his cousin's shoulder. "I know all about empty houses," he said.

"You've got Rianna and Maeve," Keegan pointed out.

"Yeah," Rance said. "They're my own kids, but I couldn't tell you much beyond that. I hardly know them, Keeg."

They were silent for a long while, just listening to the sounds the cattle made and the babble of the creek behind them.

"They're female," Rance said.

"Most girls are," Keegan replied.

"Cora has to translate practically everything they say. Who's this Barbie broad, anyway?"

Keegan laughed aloud. "Barbie's a doll, Rance."

Rance frowned, confused. "You dating her or something?"

Keegan gave another guffaw. "The toy kind," he explained when he caught his breath. "Devon has about fourteen of them."

"Oh," Rance said, bemused.

"Thanks," Keegan told him, after another lengthy silence.

"For what?"

"Making me feel like less of an idiot. Compared to you, I'm an expert on kids." Keegan's grin flashed. "So, thanks again."

Rance chuckled. "Don't hold your breath waiting for me to say 'you're welcome.'"

CHAPTER 8

CORA CAME TO GET THE GIRLS first thing the next morning, meaning to take them to Sunday school, like she always did. Having breakfasted on Rance's cooking—burned toast and runny eggs—they were more than ready to go. He wasn't too sure about Rianna's outfit—she had on flowered pants and a striped shirt—but Maeve looked presentable, if uncertain, in a yellow dress.

"Lord have mercy," Cora said, taking in Rianna's getup.

Rance gave his mother-in-law a sidelong glance. He had to clean up the kitchen, and then ride the pasture fences to make sure they were still sound;

it had been two decades, at least, since there were cattle on the place.

Cora smiled. "I could stay and attend to these dishes," she volunteered.

Rance shook his head. "You go on to church," he said. "And be sure to remind the Lord about that mercy you mentioned. I could use a little."

She laughed.

"I am not going to be seen in public with you," Maeve told her sister. "You look like a clown."

Rianna put out her tongue.

Maeve advanced on her.

"Girls," Cora said firmly.

They both subsided.

"How do you do that?" Rance asked Cora, genuinely baffled. "They've been about to tear each other's hair out by the roots all morning. I had to threaten them with boarding school to get them to behave."

"You'll learn," Cora told him. She sounded confident, which was way more than Rance could claim.

She shooed the girls out, and paused on the threshold to study Rance. The door of Cora's truck slammed in the near distance, silencing the birds. Maybe they were waiting, like Rance was, for a blood-curdling, smashed-finger scream from either Rianna or Maeve.

"You're doing fine, Rance," Cora said gently. A slight grin tilted up one corner of her mouth. "But I wouldn't mention boarding school again."

He sighed. "It seemed like a better option than, say, *prison.*"

Cora laughed. "There's a picnic after church today," she said. "It'll probably run into the evening, so maybe Rianna and Maeve ought to spend the night with me."

"Good idea," he answered, trying to sound casual. "You have a good time with Echo and don't worry about a thing."

He'd been scraping plates at the sink. Now he stopped and stared at Cora in irritated amazement. "Do you have the whole town of Indian Rock bugged or something?" he asked.

She indulged in a little smirk. "I know all, I see all," she said. "Plus, Echo told me the two of you were going riding this afternoon."

With that, Cora closed the door, leaving Rance alone with his thoughts, his shortcomings as a father, and a stack of pans he'd have to sandblast to get clean.

WEAR JEANS IF YOU WANT to ride a horse.

Rance's sultry implication had been running through Echo's mind most of the night.

She put on a sundress, without any underwear.

Then she changed into jeans and a T-shirt, *with* underwear.

Avalon watched the whole process from the airbed, looking bored. They'd taken a good long walk together, that morning, and the dog had eaten well. Now she seemed to want a nap more than anything else.

Echo was torn. She didn't like leaving Avalon home alone, but the animal *was* pregnant—her belly was beginning to bulge with the proof, now that she'd filled out a little. It didn't seem right to drag her along to the Triple M, especially since Rianna and Maeve weren't going to be there.

The obvious solution was to call Rance and beg off, make some excuse, and spend the day restocking the shelves downstairs and filling more orders from the web site. There was, of course, the added benefit of avoiding all risk of ending up in Rance McKettrick's bed.

If that could be considered a benefit.

"I haven't had sex in two years," Echo confessed to Avalon.

Avalon yawned luxuriously.

"Of course you wouldn't sympathize," Echo said. "*You're* going to have puppies."

Avalon rested her muzzle on her forepaws and eyed Echo sleepily.

"Not to mention that I've gotten so desperate for companionship that I carry on conversations with dogs."

Avalon yawned again and closed her eyes.

Echo sighed and went back to her closet.

RANCE HAD FORGOTTEN THE challenge he'd issued when he'd told Echo to wear jeans if she wanted to ride a horse. When he got to the bookstore, at ten minutes to one, and saw what she had on, it all came back to him.

Silky pants with wide legs—pink, of course—and a lacy top that managed to look demure while hugging her upper body like a second skin. Over one arm, she carried a pair of freshly pressed blue jeans.

How the hell was he supposed to interpret that?

"I don't like leaving Avalon by herself," she said, instead of hello.

"Bring her, then," Rance replied, still stupefied by all that blatantly feminine fabric—and the smooth skin he imagined beneath it.

"She's in no condition to go trailing all over the countryside behind a couple of horses."

"Are we going to need horses?" Rance asked. It wasn't a jibe; he honestly didn't know.

The pink of Echo's blouse leaped into her face and pulsed there. "I have no idea," she said. "Do we have to decide right now?"

Rance shook his head, managed a smile. *We have all night,* he wanted to say, but he wasn't about to push his luck. One wrong move on his part, and she'd decide to stay home and baby-sit the dog.

Avalon settled the question by coming downstairs, with one end of her leash in her teeth.

"I guess she wants to go along," Echo said.

"Fine by me," Rance replied.

Five minutes later, the three of them were in the

SUV, Avalon riding in the back seat with the leash coiled beside her.

Echo put the window part way down, and the wind played with the tendrils of hair that were always escaping from her braid.

They went through the drive-in for burgers and fries, ate in the parking lot and headed for the ranch. Avalon, having consumed a quarter-pounder, belched copiously and then lay down for a snooze.

Rance, feeling unaccountably anxious, decided to take Echo on a tour of the Triple M before heading home. She'd seen Travis and Sierra's place, of course, so he took her by Jesse's, high on its hill, with the old schoolhouse Jeb McKettrick had built for his bride still standing.

If Jesse and Cheyenne were around, Rance saw no sign of them, and he wasn't in the mood to visit, anyhow. He told Echo what he knew about Jeb and Chloe, and she listened with a wistful smile.

"What a wonderful story," she said when he'd finished.

He showed her the swimming hole where he and Jesse and Keegan had passed so many carefree days, and every other site he could think of, besides the graveyard.

Finally, there was nothing to do but head for his place.

There, in the driveway, he brought the SUV to a stop and shut off the motor. Then he just sat there, wondering what to do next.

If Jesse and Keegan could have seen him right then, they'd have ribbed him until he was laid to rest in Rafe and Emmeline's section of the cemetery.

They might have stayed right where they were, he and Echo, if Avalon hadn't whimpered to get out of the rig.

Even then, they both stood in the driveway, looking everywhere but at each other, while the dog squatted.

Echo broke the impasse, gazing into the pasture beyond the house, where some forty head of cattle were munching grass. Rance planned to purchase at least a hundred more, and hire a couple of ranch hands to help him ride herd on them.

She walked toward the fence, and Rance followed, as did the dog.

"No chasing," Echo told Avalon.

The dog sat down, panting.

Watching Echo out of the corner of his eye, Rance tried to imagine her living there, on the Triple M. Feeding cows from the back of a truck, mucking out stalls. He couldn't picture her doing those things—she was a city girl, even if she *had* moved to Indian Rock. She'd be unhappy on the ranch, just like Julie was.

She surprised him. "It's so beautiful out here," she said. "Makes me wonder how you can stand to leave."

He watched her, until she caught him. Then he looked away, pretended an interest in the cattle. "There've been times," he confessed, "when I couldn't stand to *stay.*"

"Why?"

He was a long time answering, because he'd so often asked himself the same question. "This land is a part of me," he said, feeling his way. "Like another body, beyond flesh and blood and bone. So I guess maybe it was *myself* I wanted to escape."

She took it in slowly, the mountains, the trees, the wide expanses of grass, then she turned those mystical eyes of hers on him. He felt exposed, opened up, as though his soul had been laid bare to her. He'd never experienced anything like it before, even with Julie, and it scared him. At the same time, beneath the fear, exhilaration stirred.

"Do you know how lucky you are?" she asked. "You live on sacred ground, Rance. You *belong* in this place, with these people. You're part of a story that reaches back for generations."

He'd always known he was lucky, but hearing it put that way gave him an emotional jolt. "Why do they call you Echo?" he said, because he figured it was his turn to ask a question, and because he needed to catch his balance.

She hesitated, but she didn't hedge. "When I went to live with my aunt and uncle, after my parents were killed, so I've been told, I repeated everything anybody said to me. My uncle nicknamed me Echo, and it stuck."

Rance wanted to touch her, take her into his arms, shield her from anything and anybody who might do her harm. But he knew he couldn't protect her—he'd learned that lesson with Julie. "What's your real name?"

She smiled, and turned her head, not just looking at the land now, but breathing it in. Storing it up, as though to take some part of it away with her. "I might tell you one day," she said. "Not now, though."

He had to accept that. He took her hand. "Let's go saddle up a couple of horses," he told her. "Of course, you're going to have to get out of those fluffy pants." He hadn't intended the statement as an innuendo, and he felt the heat of embarrassment creep up his neck.

Echo laughed, touched his arm. "It's okay, Rance," she said. "I know what you meant."

They went back to the SUV, where she'd left her jeans, the dog trotting behind, happily sniffing the ground. Inside the house, he filled a mixing bowl with water and set it on the floor while Echo changed clothes in a nearby bathroom.

Avalon seemed content to stay behind and snooze in a patch of sunlight on the kitchen floor when they headed for the barn.

He saddled Snowball, Cassidy's old mare, for Echo, and Comanche, his own pinto gelding, for himself. He knew Echo had never ridden before, but she was game to try, and that impressed him.

He helped her mount up, out in front of the barn, and she sat grinning in the saddle, obviously nervous, but excited, too.

Echo.

It was a pretty enough name, but now that he really thought about it, it didn't suit her. It belied her substance, sounded hollow. And this woman was anything but hollow.

He drew Comanche up alongside Snowball, showed Echo how to hold the reins, one resting loosely in each palm.

"Never wrap them around your hands," he said. "Snowball's probably the gentlest horse in Arizona, but any horse can be spooked. You could be dragged if she threw you and you were tangled up in the reins."

Echo swallowed, nodded. Again, Rance was struck by her courage. It was a quality he valued above everything but integrity.

"What if she runs?" Echo asked.

"She won't," Rance promised. "We're going to take it slow."

Clearly relieved, Echo let out an audible breath. "Okay," she agreed.

They rode down the driveway, over the bank, along the side of the creek, headed upstream, moving at an easy pace. Practically raised on the back of a horse, as most McKettricks were, Rance would have let Comanche have his head if he'd been alone. Snowball, docile as she was, would have kept pace—he sensed the mare's desire to run, saw it quivering under her hide. Muscle memory, he thought. Cassidy had ridden bareback, fearless as an Apache warrior.

Cass, Rance mourned silently. *I miss you, little sister.*

Snowball missed her, too. He knew that now, and it broke something loose, deep inside him.

They spent the next couple of hours riding the land, he and Echo, and it was more like making love than anything they could have done in bed.

"SUSAN?" RANCE ASKED, grinning, when they stopped, miles down the stream, to let the horses rest. They'd been playing the Rumpelstiltskin game between long intervals of companionable silence, for some time by then.

"No," Echo said, relieved to be standing on solid ground, waiting for the circulation to return to her legs.

"Allison?"

"Nope."

"Laurie?"

"Wrong again."

Rance laughed, bent, picked up a flat stone from the bank. Sent it skipping across the sun-sparkled water. "Sandy?"

"Give it up, Rance. You'll never guess my name in a million years."

"They why don't you just tell me what it is?"

"Because I like being a woman of mystery," she said.

He moved a step closer. Cupped his hands on either side of her face. "Oh, you're that, all right," he told her.

Then he kissed her.

There were kisses, and then there were near-death experiences.

For Echo, this bold and fiery contact fell just short of the latter.

Dazed, breathless as a near-drowned swimmer clawing her way up onto a bank, Echo pressed her hands against Rance's chest and turned away.

"What the hell…?" he muttered, and somehow she knew he wasn't referring to her sudden retreat, but to the kiss itself.

She turned back to study his face. Had he felt it, too?

He met her gaze squarely, and she *knew,* somehow, that he had, even though he might not have defined it in the same way.

For Echo, a jagged tear had opened in the fabric of the universe itself, and something wholly new and terrifyingly beautiful waited on the other side.

"Are we going to run away from this?" Rance asked, very quietly. "Or shall we find out where it leads?"

Echo put a hand to her throat, too stricken to answer right away. Once she stepped through that rip in time and space, she would never be the same. And she instinctively understood that, while the other side was a fiercely beautiful place, it was not a safe one. There would be new dangers there, things she'd never encountered before and had no idea how to deal with.

Joy was a certainty, but so was sorrow.

Did she dare take the risk?

Her life was mundane. It was also familiar. She knew the paths, because she'd traveled them so many times. Of course there were surprises, some good and some bad, but not many.

Not many.

"Echo?" Rance prompted, when she didn't, *couldn't* speak.

Her mouth was parched; she wanted to drop to her knees amid the moist, shiny pebbles littering the creek side like confetti and drink as thirstily as the horses did. "I…am…so…scared," she managed.

"Me, too," Rance admitted. His voice was a rasp. "Right about now, I'd like to get back on that horse and ride full out until he drops someplace far from here." The stark honesty of his statement rocked Echo almost as profoundly as the kiss had. "I suspect you want the same thing. But the truth is, if we run in opposite directions, we'll never know what might have happened. I don't mind telling you, that prospect scares me even more, because the landscape out there looks pretty bleak."

Echo nodded. Everything had changed. Maybe it wasn't even *possible* to go back to being the person she'd been just a few minutes before.

Then it struck her. Her world hadn't shifted on the fulcrum of a single kiss, or even on her first en-counter with Rance McKettrick a few days before, on the sidewalk in front of the shop. Her destiny had been permanently altered the moment she decided to leave Chicago. She'd left her false self, her *safe* self, behind for good. And while she certainly found Rance attractive—indeed, she felt magnetized— the truest change had nothing to do with him.

"What do we do now?" she asked.

He grinned, though a look of grave wonder showed in his eyes. "I have a few ideas," he said. "But this one's up to you, Echo. I'm not going to push you in one direction or the other."

She summoned up a shaky smile. "Could you help me back up on that horse, please? I don't think my legs are working right."

He smiled, set her foot in the appropriate stirrup, and hoisted her into the saddle, with one strong hand splayed across her backside. His fingers might have been electrified, and so many needs spiraled through Echo's body that if he'd taken her down off Snowball's back, peeled away her clothes and taken her right there on the rocky ground of the creek bank, she would have welcomed him.

They rode slowly back toward the ranch house, and instead of subsiding, as she thought it might, her visceral desire for this man only grew stronger.

The sun was sliding westward when they reached the barn, though there were still hours of daylight ahead.

In silence, Rance attended to the horses, re-moving their saddles, checking their hooves for stones, putting them away in their stalls, filling their feeders with hay.

Echo watched the whole process, knowing she could fetch Avalon from the house, get into her car and leave, and save herself by doing so.

Instead, she perched on an overturned bucket in the wide, sawdust-strewn place between the rows of stalls, and watched Rance do a rancher's work. Only when all the horses had been fed did he turn to look at her.

Again, he surprised her. "A swim might loosen your muscles a little," he said. "That was a long ride for a first timer, and one way or another, you're going to be mighty sore by morning."

He'd shown her the swimming hole earlier; it was a tree-sheltered, Garden of Eden kind of place. Fitting, she supposed. Given the way she felt, they might have been the only two people on a whole new earth.

"I didn't bring a suit," she said, brought up short by her practical side.

He helped her to her feet when she tried to rise and found out that the predicted soreness had arrived ahead of schedule. "You won't need one," he said.

More hot shivers spiked through her.

He held tightly to her hand and led her not toward his SUV, but in the direction of the house.

"I thought we were going swimming," she said. She didn't even recognize her own voice; it seemed she'd given it over to some inner stranger. Some reckless woman with a powerful craving for forbidden fruit.

"We are," he answered. "There's a pool on the far side of the house."

"Oh," she said, letting him tug her along.

They passed through the massive kitchen, where Avalon still slumbered, dreaming dog dreams that made her legs twitch. The room was all Echo had seen of Rance's home, besides the spacious powder room where she'd changed into her jeans earlier.

Now they came to a dining room, furnished in rustic elegance, and then a living room beyond, where the biggest natural rock fireplace she'd ever seen seemed dwarfed by the space around it. Books on the walls, colorful rugs lying like splotches of paint on a slate-tile floor.

They passed through a bedroom next, a suite, rather, with floors of inlaid hardwood and a fabulous fresco of wild horses, running free, taking up one entire wall. The bed, a huge four-poster, faced an expanse of windows, a living tapestry of trees and mountains and sky. Lying in that bed, Echo imagined fitfully, would be like sleeping outside, in the midst of nature.

Suddenly, it came to her that she was trespassing, and she balked a little.

Rance stopped, looked down into her eyes and shook his head. Clearly, he'd read her thoughts again—an unnerving prospect in and of itself. All her life, or at least since she was very small, Echo had felt semitransparent, like a ghost wandering unnoticed among the living, and while she'd chafed at that sometimes, she'd grown used to it, too. But this man *saw* her, left her no place to hide.

"This was my parents' room," Rance said. "Mine's upstairs."

Did that mean he'd never slept here, with Julie?

He brought her through a wide doorway, and there before them was a secret grotto of a pool, enclosed by semiopaque walls of glass brick. She soon saw, when Rance flipped a switch on the wall, that the roof was retractable, opening the space to the broad high country sky.

Echo was so enchanted that she forgot, for a few moments, to be afraid.

"Shower's over there," Rance said, pointing to a wooden door flanked by flourishing plants that would normally grow only in tropical places.

She bit her lower lip.

He grinned, awaiting her decision. She could shower alone, or with him.

The choice was hers to make.

She was still carrying on the internal debate when he caught her off guard again.

"Help yourself," he said. "You'll find towels and a robe and anything else you could need inside. I'll go rustle us up something to eat."

With that, he was gone.

Echo stood very still for a long time. She knew what would happen when Rance came back, they both did. Although she wasn't a virgin—she'd given herself freely to Justin, and not so freely to a couple of other men, too—she wasn't into casual sex.

As if there could be anything *casual* about sex with Rance McKettrick.

If that kiss back by the creek had been any indication, the experience would be downright apocalyptic.

Did she want that?

Other men had pleased her, in a sedate, clothes-on sort of way.

But Rance wasn't just going to please her. His lovemaking would be the naked kind, fevered, sweaty, skin to skin.

With Justin, she'd had pleasant little climaxes that left her sighing.

With Rance, it would be different. She had already felt the first tremors on the steps in the bookshop, when he'd seduced her with words. Again, when he kissed her. Now, the very air itself seemed to tremble with the prospect of all he could make her feel.

With Justin, she had purred and snuggled.

With Rance, it would be an elemental, frenzied exchange, a slamming collision, a desperate struggle for satisfaction.

Echo went into the bathroom, moving like a woman in a trance. She took off her clothes, opened the glass door of the enormous shower and adjusted the taps. The hot spray at once soothed her and washed away the last shreds of her resistance.

When she stepped out into the pool area again,

wrapped in a bath sheet, Rance was there. She knew by his damp, towel-ruffled hair that he'd showered elsewhere. And now he was in the water, watching as she approached.

A plate with a couple of sandwiches rested on a low table between two patio chairs, and Echo was suddenly ravenous. Paradoxically, her throat might have been cinched tight and tied, for all the food she could have gotten past it.

She pretended confidence, since she had none of her own, and walked to the side of the pool, where tiled steps led down into the water.

"This is some swimmin' hole," she said.

Rance laughed, but his eyes were intent, missing not the lightest nuance. He wore nary a stitch, of course, and the water was clear.

Echo was careful not to look beneath the surface, but, in fact, his ruggedly handsome face, his wide shoulders, muscular chest and strong arms gave her plenty to consider.

In a rush of boldness, she dropped the towel, and Rance's startled expression was so delicious that the embarrassment she expected to feel never came.

Let him look, said her inner Amazon, emerging for the first time, ever, from some subconscious jungle.

Echo took a few moments to exalt in the beauty of her own body and the power it gave her. Rance gazed upon her, rapt, as though she were some shining and golden creature, appearing suddenly out of nowhere, and moved back slightly, giving her space to step into the pool.

The water was delicious—just the right temperature, neither too cool nor too warm.

Echo closed her eyes, held her breath and bobbed, allowing the water to close around her, and then broke the surface abruptly, joyously, as though baptized into a freedom undreamed of by ordinary men and women.

Rance laughed and splashed her, sending a sparkling sheet of water cascading over her.

She responded in kind.

But when the battle ended, they were standing almost toe to toe, and Rance's dark lashes were beaded with gleaming droplets of pool water. He reached out, set his strong hands on either side of her waist and pulled her to him.

She put her arms around his neck and stood on tiptoe to kiss him, before he could kiss her.

Their tongues touched, a spark was ignited, and a flame burst from it that no amount of water could have extinguished.

Instinctively, Echo wrapped her legs around Rance's hips, while the kiss went on, deepening from exploration to passion, and then beyond. She felt his erection between her thighs, and would have taken him in then, if he had cooperated.

Of course, being Rance McKettrick, he didn't cooperate.

He kissed her senseless and caressed her breasts

until she broke free of his mouth and leaned back to offer herself. He feasted then, laving her nipples with his tongue, suckling at them until her clamped legs went limp.

He lifted her into his arms, carried her out of the water, up the steps, into the bedroom with the horses racing along the wall. He laid her sideways on the bedcovers, wet as she was, with her legs dangling. And then he knelt, easing her thighs farther apart.

She arched her back, gasping, when she felt his breath warm on the nest of curls, gave a strangled cry when he parted them and touched his lips to her. Gripping her ankles, he set her feet on the edge of the mattress, now nibbling, now suckling, now teasing her with butterfly-light flicks of his tongue.

He brought her to the verge of climax, left her quivering there.

She whimpered in soft dismay.

Rance rose and stretched out on the bed, shifting her in the process, until she was kneeling on the pillows, astride his head. She gripped the headboard, and grasping her hips, he lowered her onto his mouth for the real ride.

Echo's vulnerability was complete, and so was her surrender. The first climax made her groan aloud and sag limply in the heat of quick release. Now, she thought, he would take her.

But he didn't.

He made her come again, more intensely this time, staying with her as she rocked and bucked, a low howl of primitive abandon tearing hoarsely from her throat. Her palms sweated where she gripped the headboard; indeed, her whole body was slick with perspiration. He suckled until her body convulsed from its molten core, like some little-earth, spewing fire.

"Make…love…to…me…now!" It was both an Amazon's demand and a supplicant's plea. She wanted Rance within her, part of her, hard and powerful, at once conquering her and paying homage to the holy underlying power that gave her life.

He answered by giving her still another orgasm, one so ferocious that it seared through flesh and bone and imprinted itself on her very soul, like a brand.

Even as he laid her down for the taking, reeling and spent, caught in the charged space between the last shattering climax and the inevitable next, Echo knew that whatever happened between her and Rance after this, she would bear his mark forever.

CHAPTER 9

THRUST UPWARD ON THE VIOLENT swell of some already-forgotten nightmare, the remnants of it trailing behind him like rags, Rance opened his eyes to a room silvered by the light of a full moon.

Echo had gone; he knew that even before he looked for her.

For a few fanciful moments, he imagined her receding, like a sound, like her name, growing fainter and fainter with distance.

He supposed it was for the best—they'd mated, like a wild stallion and a mare, with plenty of carrying on. Facing each other, in the bright light of day, might be a tall order.

Yes, sir. He was relieved, that's what he was. Relieved.

So why did he feel like an old bucket with a leak?

He glanced at the clock next to the bed—a little after two in the morning. How long had she been gone?

No telling. He'd slept like a dead man, after the last bout of lovemaking; a circus parade could have come past the foot of the bed, brass band and all, and he'd never have known it. One slight woman, slipping back into her clothes and sneaking out wouldn't so much as stir a breeze.

He got up, because he knew he wouldn't get back to sleep again. Prowled naked into the master bathroom, where he'd undressed and showered earlier, after the horseback ride, before getting into the pool. Echo, standing under the spray just on the other side of the wall, had clearly been surprised to find him already in the water.

He smiled at the recollection of her, standing there, wrapped in a towel but otherwise just as God made her. She'd looked wary and, at one and the same time, fiercely female.

Now he showered again, pulled on a terry-cloth robe and headed for the kitchen.

He didn't realize how much he'd been hoping to find Echo there until he arrived and found that she was really and truly gone. She'd left the lights burning, taken the dog and hit the trail for town.

Rance sighed and fired up the coffeemaker.

While the java was brewing, he went upstairs to his bedroom and pulled on his last pair of clean jeans, a shirt he'd already worn twice, socks and boots. In the bathroom, he brushed his teeth and combed his hair.

He wasn't much of a housekeeper, he had to admit. That was part of the reason he hadn't brought Echo up here—there was laundry scattered everywhere, and nobody had scrubbed the fixtures since the last time Cora put on a Hazmat suit, as a charitable act, and waded in with hot soapy water and a hard-bristled brush.

Part of the reason.

Gathering up an armload of dirty clothes and musty towels, Rance advanced on the bedroom.

The sheets hadn't been changed in a while.

Everything was covered in dust.

And he had shared this room with his wife.

They'd conceived Rianna here—Maeve, he suspected, as Julie had often joked, had gotten her start in the back seat of an extended-cab pickup, after a Fourth of July rodeo in Flagstaff.

There was so much history in that room.

He and Julie hadn't just made love there, they'd fought there, too.

They'd said things they couldn't take back.

And one morning, Julie had climbed out of that bed, having slept in it alone for too many nights, put on her fancy English riding gear and headed for a horse show down in Scottsdale. She'd left

Maeve and Rianna with Cora on her way out of town, with no way of knowing that she'd never see them again.

Rance squeezed his eyes shut for a few moments, remembering.

He'd been asleep in a hotel room in Hong Kong, exhausted after the fourth day-long meeting in a row, when the phone jangled him awake.

Keegan had been on the other end of the line, Jesse on an extension.

"I've got some bad news," Keegan had said. Then he'd choked up, and Rance's heart had seized so hard he'd thought it would never start beating again.

Rianna and Maeve, he'd thought. One or both of them had been hurt, or killed.

It was his worst fear.

Jesse had stepped in then. "Julie's dead, Rance," he'd said. "She took a spill off a horse at a show this afternoon and broke her neck."

Rance had been stone silent for a breath or two. Then he'd let out a bellow of grief that had brought hotel security to pound at his door. Just recalling that night, he felt that agonized cry rising inside him again, hammering at the back of his throat.

They'd come for him the next day, in a chartered jet—Keegan, Jesse and his dad. Gathered him up and brought him home, like the shards of a relic, almost irretrievably broken, but worth gluing back together.

One by one, he'd put the pieces in place again.

But he hadn't realized, until just now, that the cracks still showed.

He took the laundry to the chute in the corner of the closet, opened the small door, and stuffed the wash down it. After that, he gathered more dirty clothes from the floor, tore the sheets and blankets off the bed, sent it all after the first batch.

Julie's face, framed in gold-trimmed ebony, smiled at him from a photograph on the bedroom mantel. In the old days, when the house was new and much smaller, the room had been Rafe and Emmeline's, and he and Julie had both felt a connection with them, sleeping there.

Rance crossed to the fireplace, took the picture in both hands.

He couldn't remember the nightmare he'd had earlier, in that bed downstairs, but he knew it had been about Julie. Maybe the afternoon horseback ride had spawned the dream—more likely, though, it had sprung from the lovemaking.

He'd been with a number of women since Julie's death, all of them carefully selected for their inability to touch him in any deep place. Echo was the first one he'd bedded under his own roof, and, like it or not, she'd gotten past all his defenses.

As he looked into Julie's eyes, his own burned.

He'd loved her since he was twelve years old.

All through high school and college, he'd loved her with everything he had. Loved her so recklessly, so completely, that he hadn't known how to respond when she'd told him she wanted a separation, that she meant to move back to town with the girls, stay at Cora's for a while, until she could get some perspective.

He'd sweet-talked her out of it—promised not to travel so much, bought her jewelry, told her sure, she could start her career as a graphic designer, as soon as the girls were older. And it wasn't as if they needed the money, he'd said, damnably certain that he was right.

A month later, she was dead.

And now there was no way to tell her that he'd been a proud, stupid fool, and he was sorry.

He polished the glass on the front of his shirt, put the picture back on the mantel, in its usual place.

Whatever he had with Echo Wells, it wasn't love. He'd had that with Julie, and this didn't feel anything like it.

Guilt assailed him, roiled up out of his midsection and soured at the back of his tongue. He knew it was irrational, but the plain fact was, he'd never felt this way before, as if he'd betrayed his wife.

He turned, left the room and went downstairs.

The coffee was ready, and he poured a cup, then proceeded into the laundry room. While the washing machine chugged away, a few minutes later, Rance stood at the kitchen window and stared out, wishing to God the sun would come up.

When it did, he would put a bridle on Snowball

and ride her bareback over the hills. He'd take it easy, because the horse was out of shape, and no one but Maeve had taken her far from the barn since Cassidy died—until yesterday.

Maybe together he and that old horse could out-distance all they'd lost.

CORA WALTZED INTO THE SHOP first thing the next morning, Maeve and Rianna tagging after her, and plopped a newspaper down on the counter, right under Echo's nose.

"You made the front page of the Indian Rock *Gazette*," Cora said proudly.

Echo, who hadn't slept since leaving Rance's bed a little after midnight, had to concentrate to focus her eyes. There she was, on opening day, with the big cake in front of her and Avalon's big dog head jutting up at her side.

Town Welcomes Newcomer Echo Wells, the headline read.

Echo blinked.

Was it possible that she'd opened the bookstore only the day before yesterday?

"I took my camera right down to the newspaper office and had them download the picture into their computer," Cora rambled on. "There's no weekend edition—most everybody gets the *Republic* on Sunday—but here you are on Monday, big as life!"

Echo smiled and scanned the brief article, which

included her name, the store's telephone number and address, her business hours and a rather cute remark about dogs who read books.

"Thank you, Cora," she said.

"A little publicity never hurts," Cora answered.

"What's all this?" Rianna asked. She'd come around the end of the counter, and found the box full of little mailing packets Echo intended to take to the post office at lunchtime.

Echo glanced at Cora, who was peering curiously over the counter, then turned her attention back to Rianna. "Just some stuff I'm sending out," she said. "Samples."

"Samples?" Rianna asked, puzzled.

"Rianna McKettrick," Cora said, "you stop that snooping."

"We get samples sometimes," Rianna went on, staring solemnly up at Echo. "Laundry detergent and things like that. I never heard of sample *books,* though."

"Well," Cora announced, apparently making no connection between the packets in the box and the one she'd received her mail order love spell in, "I guess we'd better get out to the ranch and see how Rance is faring with the cowboy life."

Echo's face felt warm, and she looked away.

How in the world was she going to face Rance, after the things they'd done together?

"Are you all right?" Cora asked, pausing on the periphery of Echo's vision as she turned to go. "You look a little peaky. I hope you're not coming down with something."

"I'm fine," Echo insisted, making herself look at Cora. Her smile felt wobbly, and a little on the brittle side. Cora liked to play the matchmaker, it was true, but Echo's having several hours of headboard-slamming sex with her late daughter's husband probably wasn't what she'd had in mind.

A little hand-holding, maybe. A few backyard suppers, with the girls in attendance. Innocent things like that.

Fortunately, Cora accepted Echo's answer at face value. She looked at the box of mailers once more before she left, though, and a small frown creased her forehead.

The sideline, while something she wasn't in the habit of talking about it, was no deep, dark secret, but Cora hadn't actually asked for an explanation, so Echo hadn't offered one. She wouldn't have, anyway, while Rianna and Maeve were there to overhear.

The bookstore did a brisk business all morning and, at noon, Echo closed the shop, loaded Avalon and the packages into her car and drove to the post office.

The postal clerk, a good-natured woman who had come to the grand opening and bought a sizable stack of romance novels, remarked on the volume and suggested the purchase of a bulk-mail permit.

Echo smiled, thanked her and left.

When she and Avalon returned to the store, there were four people waiting on the sidewalk out front.

Things got quiet again around one o'clock; Echo used the lull to dash upstairs, build a tuna sandwich and fill her grumbling stomach. When she heard the bell over the shop door, she hurried back down to the first floor, chewing hastily.

Rance stood examining the spine of a military thriller.

Echo nearly choked on her food.

She glanced around the shop, and was relieved and, paradoxically, alarmed to find that they were alone.

She couldn't tell anything by his face, or the way he stood. He was dressed for ranching, as he had been the day before, and simply seeing him again awakened memories that speeded up her heartbeat and made her breath run shallow.

He laid the thriller on the counter, produced a money clip from his shirt pocket.

Was he going to act as if nothing had happened between them?

Was that good—or bad?

She drummed up a smile, slipped behind the counter to ring up the purchase. "Do you read that author a lot?" she asked. Rance might have been a tourist passing through town, someone she'd never seen before and would never see again, rather than a man she had made love to, not even twenty-four hours before.

"No," Rance answered.

So much for small talk, Echo thought, somewhat desperately.

She blushed miserably as she made change and bagged the book.

"Echo," Rance said. "Look at me."

She did, but it wasn't easy. She knew, even before the words came out of his mouth, what he was going to say next, and braced herself.

"Things are moving too fast between us," Rance told her.

He was right, of course. Echo completely agreed. At the same time, she felt as though the floor beneath her feet had just dissolved, leaving her dangling over the mouth of a black hole, with nothing to grip except the edge of the counter.

Her knuckles hurt, she was holding on so tightly. "Yes," she said.

Rance looked pained, as well as solemn. "I need you to understand that this isn't about you, Echo."

This isn't about you. The classic.

Justin had used that line, after standing her up at the altar. She'd been alone in a city of strangers, wearing a wedding dress and clutching a cheap silk bouquet. How could that—or this—not be about her? She wasn't just a bystander, untouched by these events. She was a *casualty* of them.

"Right," she said, with quiet bitterness. "It's all about *you,* isn't it, Rance?"

He paled beneath that tan of his. "Echo—" he began.

She shoved the book at him, tucked into its anonymous plastic bag. She couldn't afford the printed kind, with a logo—hell, she didn't even *have* a logo. "Get out," she said.

"Echo, I—will you listen to—"

"Just get out. Please."

Avalon rose onto her haunches, growled.

At least I have one friend, Echo thought. But then Cora's image leaped into her mind. *Okay, two,* she allowed silently. *And probably temporary on both counts.*

Rance took the book, turned and walked out of the shop.

Cora appeared within five minutes. The woman must have radar.

"What happened?" she asked without preamble, glancing back over one shoulder as Rance drove away.

Echo wanted to sigh, but she refrained, busying herself behind the counter, straightening things that were already straight. "Exactly what I should have expected," she said, because keeping secrets from Cora was obviously impossible and, anyway, she was tired of trying. "Things are happening too fast, according to Rance. And, of course, none of it is 'about me.'"

Cora frowned thoughtfully. "I should ask those love-potion people for my money back," she muttered.

Echo opened the cash register, took out a twenty dollar bill and handed it over.

Under any other circumstances, the look on Cora's face would have made Echo laugh out loud. As it was, she was barely holding herself together.

Cora stared at the money. "What…?"

"Take it."

"But—"

"I'm the one who sold it to you, Cora. I own the Web site."

Cora blinked. "You're…?"

"I am," Echo confirmed. "All those little mailers you saw? The ones Rianna asked about? Every one represents a hopeful customer."

Suddenly, a smile spread across Cora's face. "Well, I'll be switched," she said. "Is that a coincidence, or what?"

"Or what," Echo answered grimly. "I'm a fraud. I ought to return every single one of those people's money. I can't do that, because I've put almost everything I have into opening the store—but I can refuse all future orders. I can shut down the Web site."

"Wait a second," Cora said. "It says right on the site, 'Order at your own risk.' How is that fraud?"

"I've set myself up as some kind of expert on love." She gave a soggy little snort of laughter. "What a joke."

"Did you make up all those testimonials? The ones on the Web site, I mean? I was especially struck by the one from E. Simmons of Trenton, New Jersey."

"Of course not," Echo answered, trying to

remember what E. Simmons had said, and failing completely. "That would be dishonest!"

Cora chuckled. Then she turned toward the front window again, staring at the empty place where Rance's big, obnoxious SUV had been. After a few moments, she smiled mysteriously and slid the twenty dollar bill back in Echo's direction. "Well, here's one from C. Tellington of Indian Rock, Arizona—It ain't over till it's over."

"What are you talking about?" Echo asked, though she was afraid she knew. It should have been obvious all along, but she'd been so preoccupied with Avalon, getting her bearings in a new place and opening the shop, that she simply hadn't followed that one little thread of logic back to the spool.

Cora turned back, but she seemed to be looking through Echo to someone or something standing beyond. "Everybody's heart is like a cup," she mused softly, as though feeling her way toward some private conclusion. "They stumble from place to place and person to person, trying to get them filled. They get cracked, those cups, and even broken. Some people throw them away, thinking that will stop the pain. Poor fools. Nobody can fill a cup but Almighty God Himself. Nobody."

Echo knew Cora was a church-going woman, but she herself had only a nodding acquaintance with God. He minded his business, and she minded hers. "You're not going to start preaching, are you?" Echo asked weakly.

Cora chuckled again. Shook her head. "No," she said. "I'm just having a little revelation here, that's all. But you've got a cup, Echo, and so does Rance. Just like everybody else. I don't know what kind of shape yours is in, but Rance's needs some mending, and that's for sure."

"I don't see what all this has to do with—"

"I know you don't," Cora said fondly, reaching across the counter to pat Echo's hand. "But you think about it."

As if she had a choice.

"Okay," Echo said.

Cora left.

Echo watched her go, more confused than before.

Presently, she put the twenty-dollar bill back in the till.

Ten minutes later, Cheyenne Bridges's mother, Ayanna, walked in.

"You need help," she announced.

"True," Echo said, but she wasn't referring to the bookshop. She thought for a moment. "I *could* use someone, part-time. I'm afraid it's minimum wage, though, and as for job security—well, that's something I can't promise."

Ayanna beamed. "Then I'm the perfect candidate. Thanks to my daughter and future son-in-law, I don't have to worry about money. I used to stock shelves and bag groceries over at the market, but it was a lot of lifting, and when my back wasn't out, my feet were killing me. The truth is, though, I miss having somewhere to go, and something to do. I'm not cut out to be a lady of leisure."

Echo laughed, despite everything. "Me, neither," she confessed. "Have you had any experience working in a bookstore?"

Ayanna shook her head, causing her dangly silver earrings to make delicate music. "No," she said forthrightly. Her hair was salt-and-pepper, pulled back from her face, and her clothes were colorful. She would probably make very good company, and she seemed both intelligent and competent. "Have you?"

Again, Echo laughed. "No," she answered. "I'm faking it, mostly." Even as she spoke, a UPS truck pulled up out front, bringing more books to replace the ones sold on opening day. Each one would have to be cataloged into inventory, and she still needed to set up a business account at the bank. Then there were the figures to be posted to the bookkeeping program on her computer.

"I can work a cash register," Ayanna said, patting Avalon's head when the dog rounded the end of the counter to lean against her in silent adoration. "I was a waitress for years, and I've rung up a lot of sales. Just show me what you want me to do. We can figure out all the details later, and if the setup doesn't work for either one of us, we'll shake hands and call it good. What do you say?"

Echo smiled, already feeling better. Life went on.

"You're hired," she said.

The UPS man came and went, leaving piles of boxes higher than Echo and Ayanna's heads. Customers entered, bought books and left again. Several commented on the newspaper article.

During a lull in the middle of the afternoon, Echo ducked out to the bank, taking Saturday's profits with her in a zippered plastic pouch. When she returned, Ayanna was bagging up a sizable sale for a heavy-set woman dressed for ranch work.

She gave Echo a friendly smile and left.

Avalon followed her to the door and stood whimpering when it closed in her face, nose pressed to the glass.

Echo and Ayanna exchanged glances. Ayanna probably didn't know Avalon's story, but given the size of the community, she might.

"What do you suppose that's about?" Echo asked.

"Most likely she's lonesome," Ayanna said, presumably referring to Avalon. "That was Nell Jenson. She and her husband, Roy, have a spread outside of town, and at least half a dozen dogs."

Fresh sadness touched Echo's heart in that moment. Maybe it was wrong to keep Avalon in town, cooped up in the shop or the tiny apartment upstairs so much of the time. Maybe she'd be happier on a ranch, running with a pack.

So many "maybes" and nothing, it seemed, for certain.

"I found her, you know," Echo confided. "The dog, I mean. Outside a truck stop, down by Tucson.

She'd obviously been on her own for a while. I'm not sure if she'd been dropped off, or just gotten lost."

Ayanna, who had been sorting the cash in the register drawer, paused to look at Avalon, then Echo. "It was good of you to pick her up," Ayanna said. "A lot of people wouldn't have."

"I couldn't just leave her," Echo replied softly, watching with a heavy spirit as Avalon turned sadly from the door, crossed to the foot of the stairs and lay down with a deep sigh. "She was so bedraggled and hungry, and it was raining."

Bud Willand came to mind, and Echo shivered. Rance had gotten rid of the man somehow, but she wasn't convinced she'd seen the last of him.

Or of Rance.

Do not think about Rance McKettrick.

"I've put notices on all the lost-pet Web sites," Echo went on. "I've had one response, but I don't think the man was on the level. If Avalon *did* belong to him, he must have abused her. As gentle as she is, she'd have bitten him if she could."

"Animals," Ayanna said, "are good judges of character."

"You wouldn't want a puppy, would you?" Echo asked.

Ayanna managed to frown and smile at the same time. "So there's going to be a birth, is there? No, I certainly wouldn't want a puppy, but Jesse and Cheyenne might. I'll mention it to them. How soon is she due?"

"No idea," Echo admitted. "I've been thinking of taking her to a vet, just to make sure she's okay. Is there a good one in town?"

"Doc Swann," Ayanna answered. She approached Avalon, crouched in a soft billow of turquoise, pink and green skirt, and lifted one of the dog's ears, then the other, rubbing the flesh gently between a thumb and forefinger. "Could be she has a microchip. You know, one of those things they implant, with all the pertinent information recorded on it?"

Echo tapped a palm to the middle of her forehead. "I didn't think of that." She brought the Flagstaff telephone book out from beneath the counter, Indian Rock and other nearby communities being listed in their own sections, and flipped through the business directory.

Finding Dr. Swann's number, she placed a call and explained what she needed, while Ayanna went on stroking Avalon's glossy coat. For a woman who didn't want a puppy, she certainly looked smitten.

"Bring her right over," the receptionist said. "We're not busy at the moment."

Echo cupped a hand over the receiver. Closing time was more than an hour away, and although there was no one in the store at the moment, she hesitated to lock up early. "They can see Avalon now, if you can stay here for a while," she told Ayanna.

Ayanna nodded.

Avalon's leash was behind the counter, and she stood eagerly when Echo got it out. She was always up for a walk, and since Dr. Swann's office was just two blocks down Main Street, there would be no need to take the car. Besides, a little fresh air would do them both good.

As they strolled down the sidewalk, Echo congratulated herself.

She'd gone at least ten minutes without once thinking about Rance McKettrick.

CHAPTER 10

RANCE WATCHED, WITH HIS damnable McKettrick pride jammed up tight in his throat, as Jesse got out of his mud-spattered truck at the top of the driveway and ambled toward him. It hadn't rained for weeks. Did the man drive that rig through the creek, just to make it look like that?

As he approached, Jesse resettled his hat and grinned that got-it-dicked grin of his. As far as Rance could tell, his cousin saw life as one big casino, and he was always on a winning streak. "You wanted to talk," Jesse said, spreading his hands in an affably unspoken "I'm here. So talk."

Rance had called Jesse after the disastrous inter-

lude with Echo at the bookstore, out of pure desperation. Dragged him out of a poker game in the back
room at Lucky's, where he was, as usual, winning.

Now he wished he hadn't done it. Better if he'd
just suffered in silence—after all, he'd had a lot of
practice at that.

He scowled, lifted his own hat and shoved a hand
through his hair. "What if I said I changed my mind?"

Jesse laughed. "Then I'd have to knock you on
your ass. I had pocket aces, with a third in the flop
and a good chance of one more on the river."

Most Americans spoke English.

Jesse spoke Texas Hold 'Em. Fluently.

"You think you're man enough to do that?"
Rance asked, stalling.

"Knock you on your ass? You better believe it."
Jesse paused, and his grin was super-charged.
"'Course, there might be a problem when you got
back up again."

Rance was grudgingly mollified. The truth was,
he and Keegan and Jesse used to get into it, and
plenty, when they were kids. Usually behind one of
the barns on the Triple M. They'd fought like young
bulls back then, and then laughed about it afterward.

He kind of missed those times.

Jesse took in the house and yard in a quick,
sweeping glance. He was probably looking for
Rianna and Maeve, who always greeted him with
shouts of joy and shinnied up him as if he were a

pole at the county fair. They were in town with
Cora. "What's going on, Rance?" he asked quietly,
but the glint in his eyes indicated that he'd already
guessed the answer.

"Something happened," Rance said. He turned
and led the way to the patio, the place where he'd
served Echo and the kids a fish supper just the other
night. Why did it seem like somebody else's experience, and not his own?

"No shit," Jesse replied, hauling back a chair,
sinking into it and setting his battered hat on the
tabletop. "You wouldn't have called me if it hadn't."

"Maybe I would," Rance said, still on his feet,
and still uncertain, "if you'd carry a damned cell
phone like everybody else."

"I hate them," Jesse answered. "They always ring
at the wrong time." He settled back, touched the tips
of his fingers together and regarded Rance thoughtfully. "You good for a cold beer?"

Rance chuckled and relaxed a little. "Sure," he
said, grateful for the request because, one, he could
use a beer himself, and two, it would give him a
minute or so to nail up the framework of what he
wanted to say. He'd already had three-quarters of an
hour, though, since making the call to Lucky's and
asking Nurleen to put Jesse on the horn, and he'd
made no significant progress.

All too quickly, the task was completed. Rance
handed Jesse a bottle, watching as he twisted off the
lid and took a long drink.

"Sit down," Jesse said after swallowing. "You make me nervous, standing there like you expect your clothes to burst into flame and you're figuring out how fast you can get to the creek."

Rance thrust out a sigh. Sat down. Took a draught of his own beer.

"Something happened," Jesse prompted when Rance didn't say anything right away.

"You know damn well what it was," Rance accused. "You just enjoy watching me sizzle on a grill."

Jesse grinned. "That, too," he admitted. "My guess is, you're in over your head with Echo Wells. You took her to bed, didn't you? And worse yet, you enjoyed it. Now you're hammering yourself into the ground for committing the unforgivable sin."

"I used her, Jesse."

"Did you?" He picked at the label on his beer bottle with one thumbnail. "I assume the lady was amenable to the idea. You didn't knock her over the head and drag her into your evil lair, or anything like that?"

Rance felt a rush of heat climb his neck and pulse painfully along his jawbones. "Of *course* I didn't," he bit out. "What do you think I am?"

"I think you're scared shitless, for one thing."

"Thank you, Dr. Phil," Rance said, seething.

Jesse laughed, swigged more beer and turned his hat in a slow circle on the tabletop, watching the process with quiet interest. When his eyes met

Rance's again, they were solemn. "Rance, Julie is dead. You didn't betray her, okay?"

"I took something from Echo," Rance said glumly. "I didn't mean to, but I did."

"She was a virgin?"

"No," Rance replied. "Thank God."

"Then what's bugging you so much?"

"There's nowhere to go from here, Jesse. I can't marry her. I'm not ready for that."

Jesse's eyes twinkled. "Did she propose?"

Rance, in the act of raising his beer to his mouth, set it down again. "No."

"Did the subject of marriage come up at all?"

"No." Something else sure had, though. And that part of Rance's anatomy was still a little tender.

"So what's the problem? Shit, Rance—give the woman some credit. Maybe she just wanted a good roll in the hay, the same as you did. Maybe she doesn't expect anything from you. Just because *you're* old-fashioned, doesn't mean she is."

Rance thrust out a ragged sigh. What Jesse said made sense, in a Jesse kind of way. So why didn't he feel one damn bit better?

"Rance?" Jesse urged, when the silence went on too long to suit him.

"Is it old-fashioned to think that sex that good ought to mean something?" Rance asked, of himself more than Jesse.

"Yeah," Jesse said. "It is. But it's honorable as hell. Old Angus would be mighty proud of you."

"I told her I wasn't ready for a relationship. Like some damn fool. I even said it wasn't about her, it was about me."

Jesse rolled his eyes. "Oh, my God," he marveled. "You *didn't*."

"I did."

"Well, do you?"

"Do I what?"

"Do you want a relationship with Echo Wells?" Jesse asked, measuring the words out one by one, like scoops of grain for a blind mule with a short attention span.

"I don't know."

"Do you want more hot sex?"

Rance grinned. "Hell, yes." The grin died and fell right off his face. "But she told me to get out of her shop."

"Well," Jesse said, "you probably weren't going to have sex in the shop, anyhow. Not that it's such a bad idea, now that I think about it. Ask her out again. Tell her the truth—that you can't make any promises and you don't expect any in return."

"She'll hand me my head."

"Maybe," Jesse agreed. "But maybe she'll understand. Could be, she feels the same way. You'll never know if you turn coward, Rance."

"I'm *not* a coward."

"Come on. Where this woman is concerned, you've got a yellow streak a mile wide. I've never seen you so bent out of shape. Even Julie didn't rattle your cage like this."

Rance took a moment to recover. Sometimes the truth burned like a brand fresh from a hot fire, and though none had been used on the Triple M for a long time, he caught the scent of scorched hide, all right.

And it was his own.

"What would you do?" he asked, and even though he'd made an effort to sound as if he didn't give a damn, his voice came out rusty as the hub of an old tractor wheel, left out in the weather for too many seasons.

Jesse didn't actually look smug. Just easy in his skin, like always. Content, too, because he had Cheyenne now—the two of them were living together, and different as they were, it seemed they'd found a balance, reached some kind of accord. Jesse still played a lot of poker, and Cheyenne thrived on her job at McKettrickCo.

"Probably the same as you," Jess said, after considering Rance's question for an uncomfortably long time. "I don't mind telling you, when I met up with Cheyenne again, I wanted to split myself right down the middle and run in two different directions. I'd gotten pretty comfortable. I had everything I wanted—the game, the money, the horses, that ridge up there, on the ground floor of heaven—or I *thought* I had everything. Cheyenne turned the whole works upside down, and me with it."

"This isn't like you and Cheyenne," Rance interjected. "You're in love. This is just sex. There's a big difference."

"I think you're scared you might find out it's more than 'just sex.' You fool a lot of people, Rance, but I know you too well. It was bad, losing Julie the way you did. You'll always care about her. But there's more to this than not letting go, isn't there?"

Rance sighed. "Julie was going to leave," he said. "Move in with Cora for a while."

"I figured it was something like that," Jesse replied.

"It wasn't the first time," Rance heard himself say. As close as he was to his cousins, he hadn't leveled with either one of them. He still wasn't ready to lay all his cards on the table. "I was gone too much, and she didn't like living so far out of town. She wanted to start a career, and she'd have had to go to Phoenix or Flag to do that."

Jesse waited calmly.

But Rance couldn't get the rest of it out. Much as he wanted to tell Jesse, to tell *somebody,* he just couldn't bring himself to say more.

Jesse studied him. "Now what?" he asked.

"What do you mean, 'now what'?"

"You gonna stay solid, Rance, or split yourself and run?"

"I don't know."

"Then what do you *want* to do?"

"Stay in one piece, I guess. Stand toe to toe with this thing and see what happens."

Jesse grinned, pushed back his chair and stood.

"My work here is done," he said. "Cheyenne's working late, and I promised to bring her a burger from Lucky's."

Rance didn't rise, nor did he reach for the bottle and down the dregs of his beer. He just looked up at his cousin. "Was it worth it, Jess?" he asked, very quietly. "Taking a chance, I mean."

Jesse put on his hat. He looked like a saloon gambler with a fast horse waiting outside, but he was in no rush. Life unfolded for Jesse. The cards came. Sure as hell, when the time was ripe, the right woman turned up, too.

"Best wager I ever made," he said. "I always thought I was a winner before. Wasn't till I hooked up with Cheyenne that I knew what it really means to win."

Rance watched, in pensive silence as his cousin turned and walked away, adjusting his hat as he went, and not once looking back.

DR. SWANN, A HANDSOME white-haired man with kind eyes, gave Avalon a quick examination, paying special attention to her belly.

"She's got a few weeks to go, I'd say," he told Echo kindly, "but there's definitely a litter in there."

"What about the microchip?" Echo forced herself to ask. She'd related the story about finding Avalon alone in the rain, and explained that she'd posted notices on every reliable missing-pet Web site she could find.

If there was a chip, she didn't want to know.

At the same time, she *had* to know.

The veterinarian deftly felt Avalon's ears. "Yep," he said presently. "It's right here."

Echo gripped the edges of the plastic chair she was sitting in, though she tried to be subtle about it. The room seemed to sway a little, and she closed her eyes.

If the Doc, as Ayanna referred to him, had noticed her reaction, he didn't let on. "We can take it out, of course, but we'll have to send it up to a lab in Flagstaff to retrieve the information. We're not equipped for it here."

Echo gave a wooden nod and swallowed. The name, address and telephone number of Avalon's real owners would be on that chip. She'd have to get in touch with them. But what if they weren't nice people? What if they'd dropped her off on purpose?

She squeezed her eyes shut again, tight, and when she opened them again, Doc Swann was standing directly in front of her, holding out a little paper cup filled with water.

"Those folks must care a lot about this dog, if they had a chip implanted," he said gently.

Echo accepted the water with another nod, this time of thanks, and gulped it down. For a moment or two, she was afraid it would come right back up. Then she got another mental picture of Avalon jumping against the door of that RV, on the street running alongside the park, and she knew the doctor was right.

Somebody out there loved Avalon.

They'd probably looked high and low for her, and waited for the phone to ring or a letter to come. Maybe they'd given up hope, though—thought the dog was dead, or gone forever.

"Let's find out who they are," Echo said. Her eyes were so glazed with tears that Avalon was just a white haze with a patch of pink—her panting tongue—in the middle.

Doc reached down and patted Echo's shoulder. "I'll take care of it, if you'll just step out for a few moments," he said. "And call you as soon as I hear back from the lab." He paused as Echo got awkwardly to her feet, and Avalon rose off her haunches, ready to follow. "Sometimes," he went on, "the chips are faulty, or they get damaged. It's possible we won't be able to recover anything."

She waited in the hall, and when Doc Swann opened the door and handed her the leash, Avalon sported a small bandage on her right ear.

As much as Echo hated the idea of losing this dog, the prospect of never finding her rightful owners made her feel even worse.

This was about doing the right thing for an innocent, trusting animal, she reminded herself. Not about her.

Now, where had she heard *that* before?

"I KNEW YOU'D BE BACK," Keegan said on Tuesday morning, when Rance showed up at McKettrickCo in shoes that looked spit-shined and the least uncomfortable of his three-piece suits. "I just thought it would take longer."

"I've got meetings in Taiwan," Rance said. "I called San Antonio, and the company jet is on its way here as we speak."

Keegan opened his eyes wide, then narrowed them. He looked frazzled, as usual, sitting behind his too-tidy desk. "Meetings in Taiwan," he repeated thoughtfully. "Rance, what the hell is going on with you? What happened to the gentleman-rancher plan? Did you mean that speech about spending more time with Rianna and Maeve, or were you just blowing smoke?"

Rance's back molars ground together, and he made a conscious and none-too-successful effort to relax his jaw. At this rate, he'd be gumming his food before he was forty. "You know something?" he challenged, leaning over the top of Keegan's desk, his hands braced on the smooth wood. "This isn't the reaction I expected from you. You did your damnedest to talk me *out* of resigning, remember?"

"I remember," Keegan replied, undaunted by the overbearing approach, which, because of his size, Rance had used effectively ever since he reached his full height.

Realizing that, he backed off a little.

"What are you running away from?" Keegan pressed, pushing back in his chair and tenting his fingers under his chin. "Or should I say, *whom?* As if I didn't know."

"It isn't Echo," Rance said, a mite too quickly.

Who was he kidding? This had everything to do with the lady in pink.

"Right," Keegan agreed with wry skepticism. "Spare me the bullshit, all right?" His frown deepened. "Taiwan. I'll say this for you, cousin— when you run away, you don't fool around."

"This trip could make a big difference in the company's bottom line," Rance argued, straightening his tie. God, he hated ties, and herding this conversation in another direction was like funneling a pack of feral cats into a gunny sack, but something made him try, hopeless as it was.

"Save it," Keegan said. "You're not worried about the bottom line. That's *another* thing you told me when you resigned."

Rance's steam finally ran out. He looked around for a chair, dragged one up and fell into it. "Why is talking to you harder than driving nails into a rock with no hammer?"

Keegan laughed. "Because you're lying through your teeth, mainly."

"I'll be away for a *week,* Keeg. Not six months. I can make this up to the girls when I get back."

"You used to say that about Julie," Keegan recalled. Like Jesse, he could be a hard-ass when he thought the situation called for it—more of the McKettrick DNA. "Every time she had to change plans because you were making a last-minute business trip. The day came, obviously, when there were no more chances to make things up."

Rance let out a whoosh of breath, as though he'd caught a ramrod square in the center of his solar plexus. "Man, Keeg. That was harsh."

"The truth usually is. You want to go to Taiwan and make this company bigger, you go right ahead. Just keep this in mind—you never know when the bill's going to come due. Julie's death ought to have taught you that."

Rance closed his eyes momentarily, and when he opened them again, he couldn't quite look Keegan in the face. "Are you through yet?"

"I'm through," Keegan confirmed. "Can you turn that jet back?"

"Probably not," Rance answered. "The folks over in Taiwan won't be too happy if I cancel, either. They did a lot of scrambling to make this work—I was on the phone with them half the night."

"Then I guess I'll see you in a week."

"I guess so," Rance said. He walked out of Keegan's office on his own two feet then, but it didn't feel that way on the inside. In the figurative sense, he crawled on his hands and knees.

"MY DADDY'S GONE TO TAIWAN," Rianna told Echo glumly, on Wednesday afternoon, when she came to story time at the bookstore. The weekly event had been Ayanna's idea, and on this, the first day, it had drawn a good crowd of bored kids. She was also starting a readers' group for the parents.

Echo had felt Rance's absence like a dry socket

after a tooth was pulled, even though no one had said anything about his leaving, until just now. She realized with deep chagrin that a part of her had been waiting for some news of Rance, or to catch a glimpse of him, however distant or brief.

But it wasn't as if she'd been pining. The shop kept her busy, even with Ayanna's help, and she'd been listening for the telephone ever since she'd taken Avalon to see Dr. Swann on Monday afternoon.

"Where's Maeve?" Echo asked, wanting to take Rianna in her arms and give her a reassuring hug, but not quite daring. She could identify with the child's dejection; despite the obvious differences, such as wealth and the fact that Rianna *had* a father, however preoccupied he was with his own concerns, as well as a sister and a devoted grandmother, loneliness was loneliness. Adults had choices, but kids had to accept whatever was offered, whether it was enough or not.

"She says she's too old for story time," Rianna said. She glanced over one small shoulder at the other children, gathering around Ayanna in an eager circle. Avalon, lying in her usual patch of sunlight, got up to walk stiffly to Rianna and give her an affectionate nose-nuzzle.

Rianna giggled and patted Avalon's head. Nothing like a little dog therapy when life got you down, Echo thought. Her heart ached. When would Avalon's owners be found? When would the call come?

As if the universe had heard the questions, and

decided to give the rare, immediate answer, the telephone rang exactly then.

"Echo's Books and Gifts," Echo said, talking a little too loud, hoping it was another kind of call and knowing it wasn't.

"This is Cindy at Dr. Swann's office" came the cheerful reply. "We've heard back from the lab in Flagstaff. Do you have a pencil handy?"

Do you have a pencil handy?

Such an ordinary and entirely reasonable question.

Tears glazed Echo's eyes. "Yes," she said, with a slight sniffle.

Rianna, still watching, gazed at her curiously.

Avalon's expression was one of purest trust.

"Let's see," Cindy said, the words accompanied by the brisk tapping of a keyboard. "The animal's name is Snowball. Her owners are Herb and Marge Ademoye, of Santa Fe, New Mexico." She followed up with a telephone number in the 505 area code.

Snowball, Echo thought, oddly detached. Snowball, like the mare she'd ridden with Rance on the Triple M.

She thanked Cindy, hung up and rounded the end of the counter to sit on her haunches, looking into Avalon's saintly brown eyes. "Hello, Snowball," she said.

Snowball made a soft, whimperlike sound and licked her face.

"I thought her name was Avalon," Rianna said, looking concerned.

"Nope," Echo answered, bravely sucking a torrent of tears back up into her sinuses. "Snowball."

"We have a horse named Snowball," Rianna replied. "She belonged to my Aunt Cassidy."

Echo blinked. Rance hadn't mentioned a sibling, but, then, there was a lot she didn't know about him. Even with her heart splitting down the middle, she noticed that Rianna had spoken of her aunt in the past tense.

Of course, that didn't mean Cassidy was dead or anything. People outgrew horses, and sold them or left them behind for others to look after.

"She was only seventeen when she died," Rianna said. "I wasn't born yet, so I didn't know her."

Suddenly, it was almost too much to bear, the way the world was. If she hadn't had to call the Ademoyes and finish the workday, Echo would have fled upstairs, thrown herself down on her bed and cried herself into a stupor.

She touched Rianna's cheek. "You'd better hurry," she said gently, "or you'll miss the beginning of the story."

Rianna nodded, gave Echo and Avalon/Snowball another long, pensive look, and went to join the other kids.

Echo straightened, went behind the counter again and picked up the telephone. She made three tries, each time transposing the digits of the Ademoyes' number, before the call went through.

"Hello," answered a woman's recorded voice. "You've reached Herb and Marge Ademoye. We're not available to take your call, but we check our messages regularly. Please leave your name and number, and we'll get back to you at the first opportunity. Thank you."

Echo, always self-conscious talking to a machine, said awkwardly, "This is Echo Wells, and I live in Indian Rock, Arizona. I have your dog, Av—Snowball—"

Snowball's ears perked at the sound of her name.

Echo's throat tightened so that she could barely give her contact numbers.

She hung up, but she was already waiting for the Ademoyes to call.

Waiting for Rance McKettrick to return from Taiwan.

Waiting.

She had a long history of that.

As a little girl, she'd waited for her parents to come and take her home.

Then, finally realizing that they never would, she'd waited for her aunt and uncle to love her.

Giving up on that, too, eventually, she'd waited to meet the right man.

She'd met Justin and *thought* he was the right man. Unfortunately, he hadn't agreed.

Swallowing the lump in her throat, Echo straightened her spine and lifted her chin. She would not indulge in self-pity. *Everybody* had sorrows, secret and otherwise. Everybody, at one time or another, felt lonely.

The day went on.

Ayanna finished the story hour.

Grateful mothers returned to collect their children and bought stacks of books in the process. Ayanna, full of quiet triumph, helped Echo ring up the purchases, tally the day's receipts and close the store.

After Ayanna went home, Echo loaded Snowball into the car and drove to the supermarket, where she bought fried chicken and potato salad in the deli section. Back at the shop again, the two of them shared the meal.

Although she liked her apartment, Echo was reluctant to go upstairs. She might as well have been in a lighted aquarium, she thought, as the shop at night, with all the lights burning, but in a strange way it made her feel less lonely, knowing pedestrians and people driving by in cars could see her.

"That's pretty pathetic, isn't it?" she asked Snowball, who was munching on a big piece of chicken skin. She didn't seem as fond of the potato salad.

The telephone rang.

That was what telephones did, on a fairly regular basis, but Echo was still so startled, she nearly dropped her fork.

"Echo's Books and Gifts," she said.

Silence.

"Hello?"

"Oh, I'm sorry," said a familiar feminine voice. "I'm trying to drive and talk on the phone at the same time. I've got to get one of those earpiece things before I end up committing vehicular homicide."

Echo blinked.

The woman laughed warmly. "This is Marge Ademoye," she said. "I'm calling about Snowball. H-how is she?"

Echo didn't miss the catch in Mrs. Ademoye's voice when she asked about her dog.

"Snowball," Echo said, "is just fine."

"Thank God," Marge said. "Herb and I have been just frantic."

"She's good," Echo reiterated.

"She got away from us, almost three months ago now, at a rest area along Highway 10," Marge explained, and Echo knew the other woman was crying. "We looked and looked, and called until our throats were raw, but she was just—gone." There was a pause, then Marge said, in a muffled, over-the-shoulder tone, meant for someone else, "I'm talking to the woman who found Snowball," she said, probably addressing her husband. "Herb's been in the back of the RV, taking a nap," she explained, speaking to Echo again. "You said you live in Indian Rock, Arizona?"

"Yes," Echo answered, while Snowball watched her with her head tilted to one side, her brow furrowed and her ears cocked slightly forward.

"We're in—where are we, Herb?—South Dakota. We travel a lot, with Herb retired, and all. Herb was a dentist for thirty-two years."

Echo smiled, even though her eyes were burning again and the glands under her ears and in her neck felt swollen to the bursting point. "Snowball will be right here waiting for you," she managed. "I'll take good care of her until you arrive."

Marge's words were heartfelt. "Thank you so much."

"You're welcome," Echo answered.

Goodbyes were said, and she hung up the phone.

"Your people are coming to get you," she told Snowball.

Then, blinking away more tears, she looked up and was surprised to see her own reflection in the darkened glass of the display window.

Darned if she wasn't visible, which meant she was not transparent, she was solid.

Go figure.

CHAPTER 11

ECHO KNEW SHE WAS DREAMING.

Knew she was *really* lying in her own grown-up bed, in the apartment above the bookshop in Indian Rock, Arizona, with Snowball-aka-Avalon snoring snug and furry and warm against her side.

Somebody else's dog.

The knowledge bubbled up from the bedrock of her sleeping mind, and she *might* have made a soft, despairing sound of protest and clung a little more tightly to the lost dog that had, paradoxically, *found* her.

She was seven years old in the dream she knew she was dreaming, and couldn't seem to escape. If she'd looked into a mirror, she would certainly have seen Rianna's face, not her own, but she was, in that peculiar and conflicting way of dreams, still herself.

She stood in a discount superstore with her aunt, uncle and cousins, and it was almost Christmas. *Almost* Christmas, because, for Echo, Christmas never really arrived. It was always a promise, shining out there ahead somewhere, the special preserve of children who were loved and wanted.

Even at seven, she understood that she didn't fall into that category.

But there was the doll.

The magnificent doll, nearly as tall as she was. It wore a sparkly blue dress, the skirt a cascade of starched ruffles. Margaret, that was her name, and she smiled down at Echo from her splendid box, through the cellophane window protecting her from eager little fingers and reflecting the colored lights from the big, glittering tree at the end of the aisle. She had long, curly auburn hair, a tiny tiara and a wand in one hand, with a jeweled star at the top. Her shoes looked as though they were made of glass, like the ones Cinderella wore to the ball, though even as small as she was, Echo was sure they must have been plastic.

I had forgotten that doll, said the wakeful part of Echo's mind.

Had you? asked the Universe, gently skeptical.

In the dream, the child-Echo swallowed, gazing up at the doll in forlorn wonder. She touched her uncle's hand—tugged at it. It was an act of unprecedented bravery; her mother's brother and his harried wife never abused her. They just never seemed to actually *see* her. Like the stray cat that sometimes slunk up onto the back porch, looking for a handout, Echo was expected to eat and go away.

"That's what I want for Christmas," Echo told her uncle, very quietly, although no one had asked. "That doll."

Her cousins, two girls and a boy, clamored for skates and soccer balls and boom boxes.

Her uncle looked down at her, in a rare noticing moment, and frowned, as though surprised to find her there, standing beside him, zipped up in her hand-me-down coat. But Echo felt a stirring of hope, just the same. She whispered a prayer—back then, she still called the Universe "God"—*please*.

It was all she knew to say.

When Christmas morning came, the skates and the boom-boxes and the soccer balls were there, but no doll.

She got a coloring book and crayons, and a jewelry box with a little ballerina inside. It danced on a tiny circle of glass when the key was turned. She sat, among gifts she would otherwise have cherished, and wondered what Christmas tree Margaret, that magical doll, stood under, in what living room.

Somebody else's doll.

Echo awakened with tears on her face and Snowball trying to lick them away.

Somebody else's doll.

Somebody else's dog.

And Rance, whether she liked it or not, was somebody else's *man*. Rianna and Maeve were somebody else's daughters. It didn't matter that Julie McKettrick was dead and gone. She'd been there first, Julie had—first with Rance, first with the children.

Julie's life, however brief, had been a shout.

And I am only the echo.

Echo clung to Snowball, and she sobbed.

BUD WILLAND STUDIED THE picture on the front page of the Indian Rock *Gazette,* which he'd found on a table in one of the casino restaurants, way down in Phoenix, and figured it for a sign. Echo Wells and that piece-of-shit dog, with a cake between them.

The payoff, given to him by her fancy boyfriend, was gone. He'd poked the last of it into a slot machine, not fifteen minutes back. They were all rigged, those damn machines. Suckered you in, with lights and music and motion and color. Made you think you had a chance, but all the time, they were bleeding you dry.

Bud seethed.

He'd found that dog out in the alley, going through his garbage, a couple of months back. Skinny as hell, and dirty, too. He'd wanted to run it off, but his woman said it was some kind of purebred, and there might be a reward. So they'd corralled the critter, found it was wearing a collar, but the little ring where the tag should have been was sprung.

Della said they ought to check the newspapers, and then she marched right out and tied the dog up in the backyard. Gave her a pan of water and the leavings from breakfast, and named the animal Whitey, once they'd hosed her down so they could see what color she was.

Days went by, though, and there was nothing in the papers. Bud would have taken that fleabag out on the highway and left it, while Della was at work, just to be shut of it, except that one day his buddy, Clovis, came by and said they could make some money. All they had to do was breed Whitey to Clovis's dog, another white Lab. When the pups came, they'd sell them and split the takings.

Clovis had paid almost a thousand bucks for the dog he had. Practically got divorced over it, too, since he'd been out of work at the time and the rent was due, and he'd used most of an insurance check to buy Ranger. Women just didn't understand business—or the value of a good hunting dog.

Clovis brought Ranger over, and it took. All they had to do was wait, him and Clovis. Make plans for spending the proceeds.

They'd gone halves on some kibble for Whitey, to fatten her up. Wanted those pups to come out good and solid. Then, one day, while nobody was home, Whitey wriggled out of that collar some way—left it on the ground, still hooked to the rope knotted to one of the clothesline poles—and jumped the fence.

Bud and Clovis had looked all over the county for that damned dog. Then, just when they'd given up all hope, Clovis's teenage daughter, who was good with computers, found a notice on a Web site and told them about it. Showed them the picture.

Sure as death and taxes, it was Whitey.

They'd as much as called Bud a liar, that Echo woman and her boyfriend, when he went up to claim his rightful property. Of course, Bud hadn't mentioned the grand the boyfriend had given him to Clovis—he would have wanted half, and a man had a right to the occasional windfall.

Now, sitting in that casino restaurant, flat broke but with a full tank of gas in his truck, Bud was forced to reconsider the situation.

The boyfriend had warned him off, and he hadn't seemed like the kind to make an idle threat. Bud was no pansy-ass, but he wasn't a fool, either. The man from Indian Rock was younger, stronger and probably faster, and he'd had that make-my-day look in his eyes.

Still, he couldn't be everywhere at once, and judging by his clothes and that rig of his, not to mention that he could peel off a thousand dollars and hand them over to a perfect stranger without so much as a flicker of regret, he probably had some high-powered job. Which meant he couldn't be hanging around Echo Wells's bookstore twenty-four/seven, on the lookout for trouble.

Idly, Bud flipped through the pages of the thin newspaper.

And there, on the third page, was a picture of the boyfriend, part of a community service ad for McKettrickCo.

Rance McKettrick.

Bud recognized the name—just about anybody in Arizona would have—and it sent a little chill skittering down his spine. The McKettricks were definitely not people a sane man would mess with.

Pulling his pay-as-you-go cell phone from his shirt pocket, hoping he hadn't used up his minutes like he'd used up just about everything else in his life, Bud dialed the number in the ad.

"McKettrickCo," a woman said in a cheerful, singsong sort of voice.

Bud cleared his throat. "This is Ben Jackson," he said. "I'm calling from the University of Arizona, down in Tucson. I'd like to speak with Mr. Rance McKettrick, if I could. About—the educational program."

The woman hesitated, and Bud would have sworn she'd made him for a fake. If she looked at the caller ID panel on her telephone, she'd see a Tucson area code. With luck, she'd take that at face value, instead of calling back to check.

Not that Bud had had any luck to speak of lately, anyway. Della had had some big plans for his cut of the puppy-money—as much as eight thousand if they got a big litter, with half a dozen buyers already lined up—and she'd been pouting ever since that lousy dog took a powder. Always ragging on him about drawing unemployment, while she worked ten hours a day doing pedicures for a lot of snotty women. Like he ought to be flipping burgers or something.

He was a *welder,* damn it. He'd worked hard to get his ticket, and he'd been a foreman on his last job. A man had to have standards.

"Mr. McKettrick is out of the country for the rest of the week," the woman at McKettrickCo said. "However, I'd be happy to put you through to Ms. Bridges. She's in charge of our work/study program."

Bud smiled. The boyfriend was not only out of town, he was out of the United States.

Yes, indeed, it was a sign.

He thanked the lady politely, said he'd call back another time, and hung up.

Bud thought about calling Della and telling her he'd have a surprise for her when he got home that night, but the cell phone was dead. No more minutes.

He dropped it in a trash can as he left the casino.

THE STORE WAS SO BUSY that morning that Echo had to call Ayanna and ask her to put in some extra hours. Ayanna arrived within thirty minutes, but there was something a little off about her manner, as if she'd suddenly turned shy.

Echo was puzzling over that when a teenage girl

rushed into the store, bypassed all the carefully displayed books and gifts, and marched straight up to the counter.

Echo, just finishing up with another customer, smiled politely. "May I help you?"

"I want a love-spell," the girl said.

Echo went as still as if she'd just stepped over a log in the deep woods and found herself ankle deep in a nest of snakes.

"You sell them, don't you?" the visitor asked. "I don't have to order from the Web site? I'm in a hurry—I need a date for the summer dance."

"The summer—"

"Word's all over town that you're selling love-spells," Ayanna confided, stepping over Snowball, who was lying behind the counter, almost under Echo's feet. Ever since the crying jag, after the doll-dream, the dog had stuck close.

The teenage girl, who was a few pounds overweight and had a bad complexion, looked desperately hopeful. "You *will* sell me one, won't you?"

Echo had thought no one in Indian Rock knew about her sideline except Cora. Obviously, she'd been wrong. Had the woman blabbed the news all over town?

Echo finally found her voice. "Listen—er—"

"Jessica," the girl supplied.

"Jessica," Echo confirmed. "The spells are just—well, they're for fun, mostly. Just a little bag, with a stone and a feather and a prayer inside—"

"Nineteen-ninety-five, plus shipping and handling," Jessica said, laying a twenty dollar bill on the counter. "Since you don't have to handle or ship, can you give me a break on the price?"

"They're really not—"

Jessica wasn't listening. "F. Finklestein of Waycross, Georgia, got a date for the prom within twelve hours," she said. Clearly, she'd been reading the testimonials on the site, and she wasn't going to be easily dissuaded. "The dance is in a week. All my friends have dates, and I've even got a dress. You've got to help."

Jessica's eyes teared up.

Ayanna busied herself on the other side of the shop.

"My sister, Alicia, says it will *take* magic to get me a date," Jessica confided, leaning in a little.

Inwardly, Echo sighed. Then she bent down, got a red velvet bag out of the box behind the counter and handed it to Jessica, along with her twenty dollars. "My gift to you," she said softly. "Good luck, Jessica."

Jessica blushed. "Thanks," she said. She managed a faltering smile and clutched the little pouch in one hand, pressing it to her too-ample chest. "Maybe J. Borger, of Indian Rock, Arizona, will be writing in to say she got a date for the Summer Dance."

"I surely hope so," Echo answered.

As soon as Jessica had left the store, Echo rounded the end of the counter and headed for the door.

"I'll be back in a few minutes," she called to Ayanna.

Next door, she found Cora in an empty chair at one of the work stations, reading a movie magazine while she waited for somebody's color job to process.

"Did you tell anyone about the love-spells?" Echo asked.

Cora blinked, lowered the movie magazine, which was practically an antique, since it showed Jennifer Anniston and Brad Pitt cuddling onboard a yacht somewhere tropical. An indrawn breath turned Cora's mouth to an O.

"I might have mentioned it to one of the girls at the post office," she said sheepishly, laying aside the magazine and standing to face Echo. "I'm so sorry—"

Echo realized she must look angry, and consciously corrected her body language. There were very few things she was sure of these days, but one of them was the authenticity of Cora Tellington's friendship. "It's okay," she said on a sigh.

"What happened?" Cora asked.

Echo told her about Jessica's visit, and her high hopes of getting a date for the dance.

Cora smiled. "Poor Jessica. She used to be in one of my twirling classes. I've always said she'd be a beautiful girl, once her skin cleared up and she lost a pound or two."

Echo sagged a little. "I don't want her to be disappointed," she said, biting her lower lip. And then a flood of guilt washed over her, because she'd sold more than a thousand little bags with prayers and rocks and feathers in them to hopeful people all over the United States and Canada. How could she have been so irresponsible? Testimonials notwith-standing, there must be a lot of Jessicas out there, waiting for some special boy to ask them out.

And it wasn't going to happen.

She slapped a hand over her mouth and sank into one of the cheap plastic chairs in the waiting area.

Cora rushed over, looking alarmed. "My good-ness, Echo—are you all right?"

Tears glazed Echo's eyes, sudden, unexpected, and hot as acid. "What have I *done?*" she whispered miserably. "It started out as a lark—I never thought—"

Cora sat down in the chair beside Echo's. "Honey, honey—get a grip."

Echo began to hyperventilate.

Cora, adept in a crisis, put a hand on the back of Echo's neck and forced her head down between her knees. "Breathe slowly and deeply," she counseled. "Very, very slowly."

Echo tried to surface. "What have I done?" she repeated in a gasp.

Cora shoved Echo's head back to knee-level. "Breathe," she repeated.

Echo concentrated. She began to feel ever so slightly better, and Cora let her sit up. Then she thought of Jessica Borger again and burst into tears.

Cora cupped a cool, competent hand on either side of Echo's wet face. "This isn't about any love-spell, is it?" she asked.

Echo thought of the dream she'd had the night before.

Somebody else's doll.

Somebody else's dog.

Somebody else's man.

Was she falling for Rance McKettrick?

"No," she said with a quick shake of her head, answering her own question, not Cora's.

"I didn't think so," Cora replied. "It's just a theory—purely an intuition—but I think you're upset about Rance rushing off to Taiwan or Singapore or wherever he went."

Echo was stunned. "No," she protested.

Cora patted her shoulder. "If I were you," she said, lowering her voice, ostensibly so no one in the shop would overhear, "I'd be encouraged. I've never seen Rance McKettrick with such a burr under his hide. He'd fight a grizzly with his hands tied, but *you* sure put a scare into him. A big-enough one to send him flying halfway around the world just to catch his breath." She grinned, evidently relishing the idea of Rance on the run. "Good job," she finished in a confidential whisper.

Echo stared at her, completely at a loss for words.

Cora got up, went into the restroom and came out with a cold cloth.

Echo took it gratefully and swabbed her face.

"I shouldn't have come here," she said. "I should have stayed in Chicago."

"Nonsense," Cora argued. "You belong right here in Indian Rock."

"Did I tell you I found Avalon—Snowball's owners?"

"No," Cora said.

"It's going to kill me to give her up," Echo said, sniffling. "If I'd stayed in Chicago, where I had a perfectly nice life going, I wouldn't have found her and gotten attached—"

"And where would that have left that poor animal? If you hadn't come along, she might have starved or been hit by a car. No, sir, Echo. Don't you ever regret loving that dog, or anyone or any*thing* else."

"The thing about love," Echo said miserably, "is you always end up losing out."

Cora sat down again and gave her a quick hug. "Oh, but what you miss if you won't take the chance," she said.

Echo remembered, suddenly, that she owned a business, that it was the middle of the workday, and she'd left Ayanna in charge. She stood up, handed the cloth back to Cora and smoothed her pink-and-white floral sundress.

Time to start acting like a grown-up.

"Thank you, Cora," she said.

"I hope you'll forgive me for opening my big mouth over at the post office," Cora replied, standing, too, and giving Echo a motherly pat on the shoulder. "And don't worry so much. There isn't any hocus-pocus to those little bags you sell. It's the *belief* that makes them work."

Echo nodded and walked numbly out of the Curl and Twirl.

When she stepped inside her own shop, next door, she found no less than six women waiting, all wanting to buy love-spells.

She tried to give them away, as she'd done with Jessica, but the new customers, and the dozen or so after them, wouldn't hear of it. They forked over their twenty dollars, every one of them, and rushed out to cast spells over some unsuspecting man.

At five o'clock, with considerable relief, Echo closed the shop.

At six, there was a loud knock at the door. She went partway downstairs, in the jeans and lavender T-shirt she'd changed into after work, and squinted to see who was so all-fired eager to get in.

Jesse and Keegan McKettrick stood outside on the sidewalk, both of them grinning at her through the glass window in the door.

She turned the latch and opened up.

"If you want love-spells," she said, "you can't have them."

They looked at each other.

"Love…?" Jesse asked.

"Spells?" Keegan finished.

"Never mind," Echo said, blushing.

Jesse grinned. "We came to ask you out to supper," he said. "Cheyenne's at a meeting up in Flag, so I'm on my own. And then there's the chaperone factor—we wouldn't want Rance to get the idea Keeg here was trying to move in."

Keegan gave his cousin a look that would probably take the hide off anyone but another McKettrick.

The heat under Echo's skin ratcheted up a degree or ten—did Jesse and Keegan know what had happened between her and Rance? "I'm not dressed up," she pointed out, once she'd recovered from her private mortification.

"You look fine to me," Keegan said, with a note of lingering appreciation. "Anyway, it's just the Roadhouse. Burgers and beer."

Jesse checked out the shop, then studied her. "You're not a vegetarian or anything like that, are you?"

The question threw Echo. She'd been about to dash up the stairs to check on Snowball and retrieve her purse, but she paused and looked back at him over one shoulder. "Now, why would you ask that?"

Jesse grinned. "Well," he answered, "there's some New Age stuff in here, and I noticed the crystal hanging from your rearview mirror. Reminded me of Sedona, and a lot of folks there don't eat meat."

"Right," Echo said, completely confused. Having lived her whole life in and around Chicago, she wasn't familiar with the Sedona mystique, though she'd heard several references to it since she'd arrived in Indian Rock. Maybe on Sunday, she and Snowball would go check the place out.

Provided Herb and Marge Ademoye hadn't come to collect Snowball before then, anyway.

The thought sobered her. Took a little of the shine off having a dinner date with two gorgeous men. "Er—no, I'm not a vegetarian."

"Good thing," Jesse said, rocking back on the heels of his cowboy boots for a moment. "What with Rance being in the cattle business and all."

"I'll—just get my things," Echo told both men, wondering what Rance's cattle had to do with her food preferences.

Upstairs, she crouched beside the airbed and told Snowball—it was still a struggle not to think of her as Avalon—that she was going out for a while. She stroked the dog, made sure her water dish was full, grabbed her purse and went back down to the shop.

Keegan was looking at titles in the business section of the store, while Jesse checked out a deck of tarot cards.

"Ready?" Keegan asked.

"Ready," Echo confirmed.

She'd noticed a big truck and a sleek black Jaguar parked outside, with her Volks sandwiched in between. She automatically got into her own car, while Jesse climbed behind the wheel of the pickup.

The Jag was Keegan's, and he led the way to the Roadhouse, a truck stop at the edge of town.

They were seated in a corner booth with menus in hand, before it occurred to Echo that this might be more than a neighborly invitation. Jesse and Keegan were Rance's cousins, after all, and they were checking her out. Sitting across from her, they suddenly looked imposing.

How much did they know? Echo didn't think Rance was the type to kiss and tell, but men were a strange species. Maybe he'd told them all about last Sunday afternoon and evening.

The thought made Echo duck behind her menu.

"The steaks are good," Jesse commented. "You might want to avoid the seafood, though. We're a ways from the ocean, here in Arizona."

Echo relaxed a little.

When the waitress came, she ordered the fried chicken dinner. She felt a yen for comfort food, and there was nothing like a little grease to soothe a person's jangled nerves.

Jesse and Keegan both ordered T-bones.

After that, there was no excuse for using the menu as a shield, and Echo felt strangely exposed.

"You planning on sticking around Indian Rock?" Jesse asked casually, after the salads arrived and the waitress had disappeared again.

Were they going to tell her to stay away from Rance? The idea both irritated and amused her. "That's the idea," she said lightly.

"Good," Keegan said, and smiled.

They all noshed on their salads for a while.

"I guess you lived in Chicago before you came here," Jesse said.

"That's right," Echo confirmed.

"Indian Rock must be quite a change," Keegan observed.

"Quite a change," Echo said, enjoying herself. If they wanted to grill her, they were going to have to come right out and admit it. She wasn't giving up a thing.

"Pretty drastic, in fact," Keegan said.

They were McKettricks, Echo thought. They'd probably already run a background check on her. What were they hoping to find out? Did they think she was a gold digger, looking for a rich husband?

She didn't say anything at all.

"Especially since you didn't know anybody here in town," Jesse added.

Internally, Echo rolled her eyes. This, she figured, could go on all night. "Are you guys trying to give me the third degree?" she asked mildly.

Jesse's grin flashed, remarkably reminiscent of Rance's, even though the two men bore no other resemblance to each other. "Is it that obvious?"

"Painfully so," Echo said cheerfully.

"Rance has been through a lot," Keegan told her.

Echo felt a brush of sadness against a tender place in her heart. Nodded.

"Rianna and Maeve, too," Jesse added.

"Yes," Echo agreed, and the word came out sounding hoarse. "It must have been awful for everybody, when Julie died. Cora told me a little about that."

Jesse and Keegan looked slightly relieved.

The main courses arrived, and the salad plates were removed.

Keegan watched the waitress's shapely backside as she sashayed away from the table, but Jesse's gaze was fixed on Echo's face.

"I guess what we want to know," he said, "is what your intentions are toward Rance."

Echo was grateful she hadn't bitten into a piece of fried chicken yet, because she might have choked if she had. "My intentions?" she asked.

Keegan elbowed Jesse. "*That* was subtle," he said.

"Nothing about this is subtle," Echo said. "I think it's sweet that you're looking out for Rance. A little old-fashioned, maybe, but sweet."

"Are you serious about him?" Keegan asked. Now that the issue of subtlety was out of the way, he was taking the direct route.

"No," Echo answered. "We've had supper together a couple of times. That's all."

Both men looked disappointed. Echo had expected relief, so she was a little taken aback.

"You've never been married," Keegan said, frowning slightly.

"Nor do I have a criminal record," Echo answered. "But I'm sure you know that already.

I'm not in the market for a husband, wealthy or otherwise, so you can stop worrying."

Jesse grinned. "You've got great credit, too," he said.

"Rance," Keegan imparted grimly, "is going to kill us."

"No harm done," Echo told him, sawing at her chicken with a knife and fork. She thought it was kind of nice that Jesse and Keegan looked out for Rance the way they did. Wondered what it would be like, to have somebody watching your back like that.

It gave her a lonely feeling.

"Out here in the country," Jesse said, watching the culinary struggle with a twinkle of amusement in his eyes and a quirk to his mouth, "we eat fried chicken with our fingers."

Relieved, Echo reached for a drumstick. She wondered if they knew about Justin, and how he'd left her standing at the altar in a cheap wedding chapel in Las Vegas. She hadn't mentioned that to Rance, but Cora might have told them.

"So," she said, grinning, "maybe you two want to know how I voted in the last election, or something of that nature?"

CHAPTER 12

JESSE AND KEEGAN FOLLOWED Echo back to the store
in their separate vehicles, then stood on the sidewalk
at her elbows, like a pair of Secret Service agents
flanking a First Lady. The instant she opened the
front door, she knew something was wrong.

The breeze, which should have been coming
from behind her, cooled her face and raised the
small hairs on her forearms.

She took a step inside, dropped her handbag on
the floor. "Avalon?" she called, thick-throated.
Then, remembering, "Snowball?"

No answering bark.

The rear door slammed. An engine revved, then
backfired.

Her intuition, already in overdrive, kicked in big-time.

"My dog!" Echo yelled, bolting for the store-room, behind the stairs. "He's stealing my dog!"

"He," she knew instinctively, was Bud Willand.

"The alley," she heard one McKettrick man say to the other.

"Snowball!"

Tires peeled out on hard dirt, flinging gravel, though Echo, in mid-dash, couldn't be certain whether the sounds came from the front of the shop or the back. Or both.

The alley door, padlocked since she'd taken possession of the property, stood gaping. She bolted through the opening, fists clenched at her sides, ready to fight.

Sure enough, an old truck careered along the narrow passage between the back of Echo's shop and someone's detached garage, on the other side, hurling up so much dust that Echo could barely make out the figure of her dog, sitting stalwartly in the back.

Echo ran after the truck.

Meanwhile, a second truck, Jesse's, screeched to a halt at the end of the alleyway, broadside, blocking the first truck's escape. Keegan covered the only other escape route, parking his Jag and hitting the ground running.

He went by Echo, who was running at top speed, as though she were standing still, but even before he reached the scene, Jesse had wrenched open the door of Bud Willand's truck and dragged him out by the shirt.

"Chill, man," Willand blustered. "I was only taking back my own property!"

Jesse flung Willand hard against the side of the truck. "I'd shut up if I were you," he said.

Willand sank to the running board and sat with his head in his hands.

Meanwhile, Echo tugged at the tailgate, trying to free Snowball, who leaned over the top and laved her forehead with a sandpaper tongue.

Keegan eased her aside, opened the latch on the tailgate and lowered it, before lifting Snowball in both arms and setting her on the ground.

Echo dropped to her knees and put her arms around Snowball, their foreheads touching.

"Damn piece of shit dog *bit* me," Willand complained.

"Just goes to show how glad she must have been to see you," Jesse said. "And I *told* you to shut up."

Keegan, meanwhile, was on his cell phone. "Wyatt?" he said. "Keegan McKettrick. We've got a case of breaking and entering and burglary in the alley behind the Curl and Twirl."

"McKettricks," Willand muttered. "Christ, if it weren't for shit-luck, I'd have no luck at all."

"Keep talking," Jesse said. "I have a penchant for violence."

Echo got back to her feet, wobbling a little. She wasn't a runner, and besides, her shoes were all wrong. "Thank you," she said as Keegan flipped his cell phone shut.

He gave her a tilted grin and nodded. "You okay?" he asked.

"Yes," she said, though now that the adrenaline rush was subsiding, she thought she might faint.

The legendary Wyatt Terp, whom Echo had never met but had heard about from Cora, arrived at Jesse's end of the alley in record time, with siren blaring and light-bar spewing splashes of official blue and red.

"What happened here?" Wyatt asked, sprint-trotting toward them.

"This man," Echo said, pointing at Bud Willand's cowering bulk, still quivering on the running board, "broke into my shop and stole my dog."

"Give me a break," Willand said.

"Can I hurt him?" Jesse asked Wyatt.

"No," Wyatt responded with a note of unmistakable regret.

Wyatt ambled back to the rear of Echo's shop and inspected the damage. "Breaking and entering, all right," he said, returning. "You want to press charges, miss?"

"Yes," Echo said staunchly.

"Let's see your ID, buddy," Wyatt told Willand.

Grumbling, Willand fished out his wallet, extracted a driver's license.

"Expired," Wyatt said.

"The shit-luck just keeps on comin'," Jesse philosophized.

Willand was handcuffed and hustled to the end of the alley.

The sweet sound of Miranda rights trailed back to Echo, Jesse and Keegan.

"Phew," Echo said.

Jesse and Keegan walked back with her, Snowball trotting along in front as cheerfully as though dog-napping and subsequent heroic rescue were a regular part of her experience.

"She's not really my dog, you know," Echo confessed when they were all inside.

Jesse and Keegan exchanged glances.

"She belongs to some people named Ademoye. Herb and Marge. They're on their way to get her right now." Tears welled in Echo's eyes, and she blinked them away.

"What's with the redneck?" Jesse asked, cocking his thumb in the direction Bud Willand and Wyatt had gone.

"He tried to claim Snowball once before," Echo explained, still a little dazed. "He was really quite intimidating. But Rance made him leave."

Rance. Just thinking of him opened a trap door in the pit of Echo's soul, and she thought she might retract to a speck and fall right through, into oblivion.

By then, Keegan was examining what passed for a padlock. "Hell," he said. "My ten-year-old daughter could have broken this thing."

Snowball/Avalon gave Echo's hand a lick, then

went off to climb the stairs, no doubt headed for her airbed.

Jesse proceeded to the front of the store. "This one isn't much better," he called back to Keegan, while Echo stood in between, like a net at a tennis match.

"Hardware store," Keegan decided.

"Big time," Jesse agreed.

"I probably should go over to the police station and sign a complaint," Echo said, just to be part of the conversation.

Jesse nodded.

"You hold down the fort," Keegan told his cousin, talking over Echo's head. "I'll go get the locks and a few tools."

"Tools," Jesse said, with a deliberately idiotic grin, and made a Tim Allen, *Home Improvement* kind of sound, which Keegan dutifully returned.

Echo went upstairs, told Snowball she'd be safe with Jesse, downed two glasses of water to rehydrate herself, and headed for the cop shop.

Bud Willand sat in the front office, his greasy head down, hands still cuffed behind him.

"You're not really going to do this, are you?" he asked plaintively when Echo appeared.

"You'd better believe I am," she answered.

He narrowed his eyes at her.

"Please," she said, straightening her spine and lifting her chin.

Wyatt Terp, watching the whole exchange from the water cooler, smiled and approached.

"Look," Willand pleaded. "I'm not a criminal. Just an ordinary guy, trying to make his way."

"You know what?" Echo responded. "That's what the loser who tried to mug me said one night in Chicago, when a passerby turned out to be a plainclothes detective. I think a forensic scientist could still scrape bits of his DNA up off that particular sidewalk—the mugger's, I mean. He's doing three to five at Joliet."

"I guess that means you're going to press charges?" Willand ventured.

Echo widened her eyes. "And I thought you were terminally stupid," she said.

Wyatt laid a form on the desk. The pertinent details were already filled in.

Echo found the appropriate line and signed with a flourish.

Willand groaned. Then, a beat too late, his gaze turned shrewd. "I'll be out on bail, you know," he said. "Most likely before morning."

Wyatt leaned in. "Are you threatening a citizen of my town?" he asked very quietly.

"Who are you kidding?" Willand retaliated, but he shrunk a little inside his filthy, wife-beater T-shirt. "This is the *McKettricks'* town—everybody knows that."

The lawman smiled and beckoned to a passing deputy. "Mr. Willand is weary of our company," he said to the other officer. "Why don't you tuck him away in a nice, quiet cell."

The deputy nodded and hoisted Bud to his feet. Shuffled him through a rear door that whooshed hydraulically and closed with an authoritative snap.

Some of Echo's bravado drained away. "Do you think he'll bother me?" she asked, looking not at Wyatt but at the door through which Willand and the deputy had disappeared. "He's probably right about making bail before morning, you know."

Wyatt smiled again. "He's right about something else, too," he said.

"What?" Echo asked, turning to go.

"This *is* the McKettricks' town."

Echo wondered, as she left the police station, if Wyatt had meant that statement to be reassuring.

RANCE WAS IN AN AFTERNOON meeting when his cell phone vibrated in his shirt pocket. Frowning, he extracted it, looked at the caller ID panel, recognized Keegan's mobile number, and just about had a heart attack.

Stateside calls were routine, of course, but they always came from the San Antonio offices, the Indian Rock branch, or one of the houses on the Triple M.

A series of possible tragedies reeled through Rance's mind, and he broke out in a cold sweat. He excused himself with the obligatory bows of the head, and made for the corridor.

"Rance," he barked into the cell phone, bracing himself.

Maeve. Rianna.

Echo.

"Everybody's okay," Keegan said immediately.

Rance nearly collapsed against the corridor wall. "*Damn* it," he rasped, shoving his free hand through his hair. "It must be the middle of the night over there—I thought—"

"I know what you thought," Keegan answered, "and I'm sorry. It's not 'the middle of the night,' it's ten o'clock. I thought you'd want to know there was some trouble at Echo's place earlier in the evening."

Rance's gut seized, hard. "What kind of trouble?"

"Take it easy," Keegan counseled. "Jesse and I handled it, with some help from Wyatt. Some yahoo broke in the back way, while the three of us were having dinner at the Roadhouse, and took her dog."

Rance felt the blood drain from his face. Hell, from his whole body. He wouldn't have been surprised to look down and see the stuff lapping at his shoes. "Is she all right?"

"I said we handled it, didn't I?"

"What about the dog?"

Keegan chuckled. "No damage," he said.

Rance ran a hand over his face. He needed a shave. "You said Wyatt was involved?"

"He made the bust. The guy's in jail. Jesse and I replaced the locks on the shop doors, front and back."

Rance was both relieved and a little annoyed that his cousins, not him, had been there for Echo when the proverbial chips were down. "Thanks," he said.

Keegan chuckled again. "I can tell you're thrilled."

"So the three of you had dinner together," Rance said.

"Yeah," Keegan answered, a little smugly, and there was a smile in his voice as big as the ranch. "I don't mind telling you, if you're not inter-ested—"

"Stop right there," Rance warned.

Keegan laughed. A couple of Taiwanese busi-nessmen came out of the conference room, gave Rance sidelong glances of polite curiosity and headed for the men's room. "According to the lovely Ms. Wells, there's nothing going on between the two of you."

Rance remembered the way the headboard had slammed against the wall while he and Echo were making love. He'd be lucky if he didn't have to spackle and repaint, just to hide the evidence. "That's right," he said, biting the words off as if they were chunks of beef jerky well past the sell-by date.

"You are *so* full of shit," Keegan said.

"Did you call me to say that?" Rance snapped.

"Hallmark didn't have a card, so I had to relay the sentiment via satellite," Keegan answered. He paused, the way he always did when he was about to deliver a zinger. "Listen," he said at last, "if *she* says there's nothing going on between you, and *you* say there's nothing going on between you, what's to stop me from turning on the charm?"

"My fist," Rance said, serious as the heart attack

he'd fully expected to have in the conference room a few minutes before.

"We may have to settle this behind the barn," Keegan answered mildly. And then, just like that, he rang off, leaving Rance standing in a foreign corridor, holding a cell phone suspended in midair and blowing fire from his nostrils.

He shrugged, bowed to the next executive escaping the conference room, and calmly keyed in another number.

"McKettrickCo, San Antonio," said a smiling female voice from halfway around the world.

"This is Rance," he said. "I want the jet."

THE SHOP TELEPHONE RANG first thing the next morning, before Echo had even opened for business. She'd slept with one eyelid raised, terrified that Bud Willand would make bail and come straight for her, and now she felt frazzled, so she might have been just a *touch* on the snappish side when she said, "Good morning. Echo's Books and Gifts."

There was a moment of silence.

"This is Marge Ademoye," Snowball's true owner said tentatively.

"Marge," Echo said, sighing the name. "Hello." She looked down at Snowball, who gazed up at her with the usual fathomless devotion. Then she swallowed a lump. "Hello," she repeated.

"How is Snowball?" Marge asked, sounding relieved.

"She's fine," Echo answered, because Snowball *was* fine, thanks to Jesse and Keegan. No sense in worrying the Ademoyes with the Bud Willand story, when they were still on the road and helpless to protect their dog.

"We made it as far as Boise," Marge said. "Then Herb had a little incident with his pacemaker. It might be a few more days before we can get there. I could send you something for taking care of Snowball—"

"That won't be necessary," Echo broke in gently, ashamed of the surge of relief that made her lean against the counter's edge and lower her head. Poor Herb had pacemaker problems in Boise and she was *relieved?* "She's no trouble at all."

"You've become attached to her, haven't you?" Marge asked, with a tenderness and perception that took Echo completely by surprise. After all, the woman was a complete stranger, hundreds of miles away, and they weren't on picture phones.

"Yes," Echo admitted.

"It would be impossible not to be," Marge said. "That dog is a saint. When Herb came home from the hospital, after his prostate surgery, she wouldn't leave his side for a week."

Echo looked down at Snowball, whose ears were perked, as though she could hear Marge's voice, and maybe she could. *Yes,* Echo thought, *it would be impossible not to become attached to this dog—unless you were somebody like Bud Willand.*

She shook off the image of that odious man and

fuel-injected a smile into her voice. "Would you like to say hello to Snowball?" she asked.

"I'd love to," Marge said, and she sounded choked up.

"Give me a second," Echo replied, and lowered the receiver to Snowball's ear.

Marge spoke, and Snowball gave a little yelp, swishing her tail hard from side to side.

Echo crouched beside Snowball, stroking her.

Marge was just finishing when Echo put the phone back to her own ear. "And we'll be so glad to see our sweet puppy—"

Echo waited a moment or two, then said, "She'll be waiting for you, Marge."

"Thank you," Marge said, and promptly burst into tears. After a little recovery time, she apologized. "I'm sorry. It's just that we've been so worried, and now there's Herb's pacemaker—"

"Take your time," Echo told her. "Snowball misses you, but she's fine, really."

"We'll be there as soon as we can," Marge said after one last sniffle.

There was a jiggling sound at the front door, and Echo's gaze darted in that direction—she fully expected to see Bud Willand looming on the other side. Instead, it was Ayanna, with her key in hand, looking baffled.

Echo waved, said goodbye to Marge, hung up and hurried over to let her friend into the shop.

Burdened with two lattes, Ayanna stepped past her.

"I know I'm not on the schedule for this morning," she said, "but this love-spell thing is heating up, and I thought you might need help."

"Heating up?" Echo echoed, frowning. What with all that had happened the night before, and then the call from Marge, she was having trouble getting up to speed with current events.

"There could be a riot," Ayanna confided, handing over one of the lattes.

Echo thanked her, breathed in the heady aroma of strong coffee, foaming with full-fat milk, and parroted stupidly, "A riot?"

She definitely needed a serious jolt of caffeine.

"I was at the post office, not twenty minutes ago," Ayanna told her, turning to peer through the display window like a private eye suspecting a tail, "and I almost didn't dare stop for this coffee." She faced Echo again. "Jessica Borger's mother was there. At the post office, I mean. Three boys asked Jessica to the dance before supper was on the table last night. *Three* of them. The kid's probably at her computer right now, composing a testimonial."

Echo beamed. "But that's wonderful!" Her smile faded, as the possible implications struck home. "Isn't it?"

"If you're up for a stampede," Ayanna answered, checking the sidewalk and street again. "Half the high school will probably be in here, demanding love-spells, once they wake up."

Echo put a hand to her mouth.

"Then there are the old maids and the divorcées," Ayanna went on. "*They* don't sleep in, the way teenagers do."

"Yikes," Echo said, resisting an urge to fling herself bodily against the door. "What am I going to do?"

"I'd be for stuffing a boxcar-load of those little velvet bags," Ayanna said.

Before Echo could answer, Cora bustled in.

"Whoop-de-do," she cried jubilantly. "Nothing this big has hit Indian Rock since that time in the eighties, when we accidentally got a shipment of Cabbage Patch Kids bound for a Wal-Mart in Flagstaff!"

Echo could almost hear the hordes, thundering toward her. She'd be trampled. And, once these people came to their senses, run out of town on a rail. Maybe even thrown into Wyatt Terp's jail for fraud. In the cell adjacent to Bud Willand's.

She spilled her guts. "I get the bags from a wholesaler in Hoboken!"

Snowball whimpered, sensing disaster. Or perhaps, Echo thought wildly, with her superior canine hearing, she'd already caught the pounding of approaching feet.

"Lock the door!" Echo cried.

Cora stared at her. "Are you out of your mind, girl? They'd break it down. Besides—you're in business. You've got to think about the bottom line!"

"We'd better start stuffing," Ayanna said.

Echo dragged out the box of supplies from

behind the counter, and the three women were on their knees around it in a heartbeat, jamming prayers, stones and feathers into little bags.

Maeve and Rianna soon arrived from next door and immediately started helping.

The first onslaught came fifteen minutes later.

"I wonder what kept them?" Cora muttered, when no less than fourteen women blew in like a desert whirlwind, waving twenty dollar bills.

Ayanna manned the cash register, while Cora, Echo, Maeve and Rianna kept on stuffing.

They'd sold forty-seven, by Ayanna's count, when the rush ended.

"Thank God that's over," Echo said.

"Over?" Cora challenged, still on her knees, amid piles of tiny velvet bags bulging with promises only Cinderella's fairy godmother could keep. "By now they've called and e-mailed all their friends. Folks are probably hitting the road as far away as Phoenix!"

Echo paled. "No," she whispered.

The first tour bus arrived at two-fifteen that afternoon.

At three-thirty, they closed the store to regroup.

"How could a tour bus…?" Echo began, shaking her head.

Cora gave her a congratulatory slap on the back, nearly sending her face first into the box of supplies, which was rapidly emptying. "What are you fretting about?" she asked. "You're making a fortune!"

Echo sat back on her heels, utterly exhausted.

She hadn't even had a chance to walk Snowball, or call the jail and find out if Bud Willand was on the loose. "What's going to happen when all those people decide they've been taken, and storm in here demanding their money back?"

"They won't," Cora said.

"Not all of them are going to find love before supper," Echo reasoned.

"No," Cora answered, "but they'll be too embarrassed to ask for a refund."

Since Maeve and Rianna were upstairs by then, watching fuzzy TV with Snowball, Echo felt safe in whispering, "Cora Tellington, that is *devious*."

"Business," Cora said, "is business. Keep on stuffing, ladies. That was just the first wave."

THE COMPANY JET WAS TIED UP in New York, where Meg and her mother, Eve, were doing something vital to the corporation's future, like *shopping*.

First class was booked solid on every airline flying out of Taiwan, so Rance sat in coach, on a red-eye, wedged between two women who kept passing a cookbook back and forth across his tray table. He couldn't move his elbows, and the old rodeo injury to his right knee, dormant for years, chose then to kick in.

He was crazy, putting himself through this.

Plum loco, as old Angus might have said.

In two days, he could have had the McKettrickCo jet.

In *one* day, there would have been a first-class seat available.

But he couldn't wait even that long.

Oh, no.

Because he, Rance McKettrick, was certifiable.

He rubbed his chin, not an easy thing, since his seatmates overlapped their assigned space on both sides. He was bristly as a pissed-off porcupine in mating season. He'd showered and changed before leaving his plush hotel suite, but shaving had slipped his mind. Unless he wanted to lather up and scrape in a restroom the size of a laundry chute, he'd just have to endure the itching—not to mention the way the cookbook women kept looking at him as though he'd just been released from a maximum security prison—all the way across the Pacific.

All because of Echo Wells.

Because Keegan might consider her fair game.

Because Bud Willand might have made bail.

Rance shifted until he managed to turn sideways and catch hold of the onboard phone imbedded in the back of the seat in front of his. More maneuvering followed, because he needed a credit card, and that meant getting his wallet out of his back pocket.

The cookbook women became thoroughly disgruntled.

Rance gave them both a Shawshank glare, no redemption included.

His wallet wasn't in his back pocket. It was in his

suit coat, which was wadded up and stuffed between a lot of carry-ons in the overhead compartment.

Honest to God, the stuff people brought on airplanes.

Since when did a bulging suitcase on wheels qualify as a "small personal item?"

The gourmet on the aisle wouldn't let him out.

In desperation, he finally pressed the call button. When the flight attendant condescended to answer, he asked for his jacket, very graciously, too, if you overlooked his clenched teeth.

At last, he produced a credit card.

Snatched the phone from its holder, and went through the protracted and painful process of dialing in every number from his collar size to his great-aunt Nellie's age on her last birthday.

The line rang on the other end.

"McKettrickCo," Myrna Terp chimed.

"I want to talk to Keegan," Rance said, trying to unclamp his jaws.

"Who's calling, please?"

"Myrna," Rance replied carefully, "you know *damn well* who's calling." This earned him more disparaging glances from the cookbook women. "Put Keegan on *now*."

"Keegan McKettrick," Keegan said a couple of moments later.

Rance resisted an urge to spread his elbows into flab territory. "Stay away from Echo," he said.

CHAPTER  13

THE POUNDING AWAKENED ECHO from a sound sleep, simultaneously eliciting a low growl from Snowball.

Another tour bus? Echo wondered, rummy even in a state of rising panic.

She raised herself onto her elbows, blinking, and as the pounding intensified, so did the anxiety.

Bud Willand. Who else could it be, at that hour?

She looked around for her cell phone, having no extension in the apartment, and realized she'd plugged it in behind the counter in the shop to charge.

Snowball barked and cannon-balled for the stairs, nails clicking on the hardwood floor.

Echo, clad in boxers and an old T-shirt, had no choice but to follow.

She was midway down when it came to her that Snowball had quit barking.

Had Willand gotten past the new locks somehow? Harmed the dog?

But, no, Echo reasoned, still foggy. He couldn't have, because the pounding hadn't stopped.

At the bottom of the steps, Echo paused, considered flipping on the inside lights, decided it was a bad idea. She'd be illuminated, in her boxers and T-shirt, like an actress on a stage, and thus at a distinct disadvantage.

She squinted.

Snowball sat in front of the door, tail whisking back and forth.

A man's shape was framed against the glass center of that door, and Echo automatically yelped. She was sidestepping toward the counter, and the shop telephone, when the visitor's identity finally registered.

"Rance?"

Snowball's tail accelerated.

Rance.

A surge of jubilant fury sent Echo hotfooting it across the floor. Closer inspection confirmed her theory.

Rance McKettrick stood on the other side of the door, grinning.

She worked the locks, turned the knob and wrenched.

"Do you realize it's the middle of the night?" she demanded.

Rance came as far as the threshold, leaned one shoulder against the doorjamb and took in everything from her bare feet to the top of her head before engaging her eyeball to eyeball.

His white shirt was hopelessly wrinkled and open at the throat, leaving his tie askew. The lower half of his face was blue-black with beard, and his eyes were bloodshot.

"Have you been drinking?" Echo asked.

"No," he said. "I've been *flying*. In *economy*."

"Poor you," Echo said, because she didn't want him to know how glad she was to see him. Conversely, she could have strangled him—that part, she didn't care if he knew.

"Can I come in?" he asked.

Echo stepped back, nearly stumbled over Snowball, who scrambled to get out of the way and then stood to one side, panting.

Distractedly, Rance leaned down to ruffle the dog's ears in the time-honored man-canine greeting ritual.

"What are you doing here?" Echo inquired, shutting the door behind Rance and wishing she had shades to pull down. As if Rance hadn't roused half the town with all that pounding.

Talk about shutting the barn door after the horse escaped.

"I'm not sure," Rance said, with endearing confusion and a silly grin.

Echo leaned in a little, sniffed. No alcohol. Just

a faint but enticing blend of laundry starch, expensive cologne and pure hombre.

Rance chuckled at her expression. "I need coffee," he said. "Or, maybe, sex." He paused, pondering. "Sex would be good."

Every nerve in Echo's treacherous body turned itself into a little rocket and lifted right off the launch pad. "Not a chance," she retorted, taking a step back precisely because she wanted to jump him on the spot, get him in a scissor-lock with both legs. "What are you *doing here?*" she asked for the second time.

He laid his hands on either side of her waist, and Echo had to close her eyes for a moment, in order to focus on fighting down another elemental urge.

"Obviously, I came to see you," he said in a gruff, wheedling voice that wouldn't have worked for anyone else on the face of the earth but him.

"It will be morning in a couple of hours," she pointed out, going for irony and missing by a mile, wanting to pull away but not quite able to rise to the occasion.

Rance, she suspected, from the heat he was radiating, was having no such difficulty. She used all her determination to keep from looking down to find out.

"We need to talk," he said.

"Another thing we could do in the morning," Echo replied, melting inside because the pads of his thumbs were making little circles just beyond the curves of her hip bones. She drew a deep, shaky breath. "I'm not having sex with you, Rance. Not after what happened last time."

"Funny," Rance said. "I remember last time as—well—nuclear."

"I meant afterward," Echo answered quickly, because other, far less sensible words wanted to tumble off her tongue, like *yes* and *now.* "You said things were happening too fast—"

"I've revised my opinion."

"Good for you. It just so happens, though, that I *haven't* revised mine."

Liar.

"Okay," Rance said, sounding affably resigned. "Can I spend the night?"

Echo blinked, stunned by his off-the-charts audacity and, at the same time, all too ready to share her bed. "Spend the…?"

"Night," Rance finished.

"I just told you, I do not want to have sex with you."

He frowned. "Is there somebody you *do* want to have sex with?"

"No!" Echo cried on a burst of frustration.

"Good," he said with a deep sigh. His thumbs continued their minimassage, awakening parts of her that had been safely asleep until five minutes before, when she'd been foolish enough to let him in.

"Rance," Echo said, "go home."

"I can't."

"Why not?"

"Because I'm jet-lagged. What if I went off the road on one of those curves between here and the ranch?"

Echo paled, realized a second too late that she'd taken the bait. "You could stay at Cora's. Sleep in your car. Rent a motel room—"

Rance lifted his hands from her hips and raised them to chest level, palms out, like a cornered fugitive proving he was unarmed. "I promise I won't make love to you," he said. "Just let me use your shower and crash beside you for the rest of the night. That's all I ask."

"Great idea!" Echo mocked, a little too quickly. "Then, when the town of Indian Rock wakes up— if they haven't already, thanks to you trying to break down my door—your SUV will be parked in front of my shop…"

He cupped her chin in one hand. More thumb-work, this time on the curve of her cheek. "I'll be gone before the sun comes up," he said.

"Why do you want to do this?" Echo asked, ter-rified he would kiss her, and pretty sure she'd collapse with disappointment if he didn't. The air was thin—any second now, she expected yellow oxygen masks to drop from the ceiling.

"I wish I could give you an intelligent answer," he replied. "All I can tell you is, I came from the other side of the planet because I need to be close to you."

"Damn," she said. "You're good."

He grinned, gave her a nibble-kiss, then yawned. Awaited her answer with sleepy eyes, luminous with mischief.

Echo caved.

She'd never claimed to be a woman of steel.

"Okay," she said.

"Okay?" Another yawn. How could a man manage to contort his face like that and still look sexy as hell?

"Quit while you're ahead, Rance," Echo told him.

"I'll just get my shaving kit."

Echo's gaze darted from his face to the display window, beyond which his SUV loomed like some vehicular Darth Vader. "Give me the keys," she said, holding out one hand. "I'll get it."

Another grin. "No need," he said. "It's on the sidewalk, just outside the door."

"You *knew* I'd say yes!"

He laughed. "Nope," he told her. "But I'm a gamblin' man, like my cousin Jesse. I'll admit to hedging my bets a little."

A few minutes later, they were upstairs—Snowball snoozing on her beloved airbed, Rance in the shower, Echo lying stiffly on one narrow slice of the bed, wishing there was a suit of armor in her wardrobe.

Suddenly, Snowball growled again, low and fierce.

"Shhh," Echo said.

Snowball didn't shhh.

The pipes rattled in the bathroom.

Echo tried to stretch her hearing beyond that and the spray of the shower.

The soft closing of a car door in the alley behind the shop.

Frowning, she rolled off the bed, padded to the back window and looked out, but she couldn't see anything but the neighbor's moonlit garage, because of the roof slanting over her storeroom.

Snowball bared her teeth, snarled.

A soft, metallic jiggle teased Echo's ears, more of a prickle at the edge of her senses than a sound.

"Hush!" she whispered to the dog.

A faint pop, then the creak of hinges.

So much for Keegan and Jesse's locksmithing skills. Somebody had just jimmied open the back door.

Echo scampered to the bathroom and practically dived through the shower curtain to get to Rance. He stared at her, half his face shaved, the other half lathered, then grinned.

"Somebody's breaking in the back way!" she whispered.

He frowned, reached for a towel, wrapped it around his middle. He put a finger to his lips as he passed, and a low "Stay here" trailed in his wake.

Echo *wanted* to do just that, but her legs were already moving. Carrying her out of the steamy bathroom. She caught Snowball by the collar, just as Rance disappeared down the stairs, and crouched beside the dog, trying to muzzle her with one hand.

Today, she decided, she was *definitely* plugging in an upstairs phone.

Her heart hammered in her throat; she strained to hold on to Snowball and hear something—anything—from the first floor.

An instant later, her effort was rewarded by a crash that actually reverberated through the old walls of the building and threatened to bring the plaster crashing down from the ceiling.

Rance.

She launched herself from that crouch, like a runner on a block, and Snowball, freed from the five-finger muzzle, streaked ahead of her.

"Rance!" Echo cried from the middle of the stairs.

"Call Wyatt," Rance answered. "Tell him we need an ambulance."

Sheer terror sent her not to the phone, but into the back room, where the action was.

The light was on.

Rance was still standing, apparently unharmed. He hadn't even lost the towel.

Bud Willand sat on the floor, lolling against the wall, blood streaming from his flattened nose.

"This sucks," he said, aggrieved.

Echo glanced at Rance again, to make doubly sure there were no visible knife or bullet wounds, then turned and ran for the front of the shop.

Wyatt arrived, sleep-disheveled, before ten

minutes had passed. His deputy screeched to a halt out front just as he was stepping over the threshold, and the ambulance wasn't far behind.

"This way," Echo said, beckoning toward the back room, where neither Rance nor Willand had moved from their original positions.

Out of the corner of her eye, she saw Wyatt take notice of Rance's presence, the towel and her own skimpy sleepwear. It was a relief when his attention shifted to the intruder.

Wyatt sighed. "Bud," he said, "you are one stupid SOB, but I'll give you one thing. You're persistent."

"I didn't think *he'd* be here," Bud answered peevishly, proving at least one part of Wyatt's thumbnail personality profile. He glowered indignantly up at Rance.

"That's obvious, Bud," Wyatt said, stepping aside to let the paramedics through. "Rance, you want to tell me what happened here?"

Up until that moment, Rance hadn't looked away from Willand's battered face. It was as though he'd been keeping the man pinned to the wall with his gaze. "Not much," he told Wyatt.

Willand groaned as an EMT tried to examine his nose. *"Not much?"* He pointed an accusing, and bloody, finger at Rance. "He knocked me clear from that doorway there to this wall. I never saw it comin'. It's freakin' *assault,* that's what it is. I could be maimed for life. I might even lawyer up."

Wyatt shook his head and sighed deeply. "You all right, Rance?"

Rance nodded.

"Is *he* all right?" Willand whined. "Look what he *did* to me!"

"Mr. Willand," Wyatt said patiently, "you are under arrest. You have the right to remain silent, and unless you are an even dimmer bulb than I think you are, you will take full advantage of that right. You have the right—"

Echo began to tremble. The back room was getting crowded, and now that the immediate crisis was over and she knew Rance hadn't been hurt, throwing up rose to the top of her personal agenda.

She rushed to the shop restroom and did so, and when she came out, Rance and Snowball were standing right there, waiting for her.

Bud Willand passed behind them on a gurney, handcuffed to one of the rails.

Rance opened his arms.

Echo went into them, and clung.

"You can make a report in the morning," Wyatt told them. "Mike," he added, addressing the deputy, "you secure the back door as best you can, then head for the station and get the paperwork started. I'll hold Mr. Willand's hand in the ER."

Echo began to cry. Her home had been broken into. She'd inadvertently become the grand maven of love-spells. And on top of all that, her breath had to be terrible.

Snowball whimpered sympathetically.

And Rance tightened his hold on her, chuckled into her hair and whispered, "You know, of course, that we might as well go ahead and have sex, because once this story hits the streets, our reputations are toast, anyway?"

Echo laughed through her tears, and punched him in the chest with the heel of one palm. "Don't you ever quit?"

"I'm a McKettrick," he answered. "We have a dictionary all our own, and *quit* isn't in it."

Deputy Mike wandered through, pretending not to notice that Rance was all but naked and Echo bought her nightwear in the men's department. "I wedged a chair under the knob in the back," the officer said. "I figure the world is safe for democracy, tonight, anyhow."

Rance steadied Echo by briefly gripping her shoulders, then turned and followed Deputy Mike to the front door. The two men shook hands, the cop left, and Rance turned the locks behind him.

Echo's knees wobbled. "What if you hadn't been here?"

Rance came back, lifted her off her feet and carried her toward the stairs. Rhett Butler in a terry loincloth.

"I *was* here," he told her. "That's what matters."

She rested her head against his bare shoulder. "Don't kiss me," she said.

He laughed, starting up the steps, Snowball following dutifully behind. "Why not?"

"Because I—was sick."

"I'm guessing you own a toothbrush. Maybe even a bottle of mouthwash."

"Very funny."

Upstairs, Snowball settled onto the airbed again, sighed and immediately drifted off to sleep.

Echo dashed for the bathroom, shut the door and scrubbed her teeth and her tongue until her mouth stung. When that was done, she stared sternly at her reflection in the mirror, silently listing all the reasons why she should *not* have sex with Rance McKettrick.

He was emotionally unavailable.

The *last* time it happened, he'd dumped her and flown to Taiwan.

Indian Rock was a small town, and when this thing ended, provided it ever actually got started in the first place, they wouldn't be able to avoid each other.

She could live a celibate life. Other women had done it. Mystics in the Middle Ages, for instance.

That was the list.

"You," she whispered to her image, "would make a lousy lawyer."

Rance rapped lightly at the bathroom door. "You're not heaving up your socks again, right?"

Mr. Romance.

Echo turned the knob and peeked out through the tiny crack. "I'm not really dressed for sex," she confided solemnly.

He laughed. "I didn't know there was a uniform," he replied. "Anyway, you look good in skin."

She kept her voice down. *Way* down. "You probably didn't bring any protection," she said, "and I certainly don't keep anything like that on hand."

"Who are you afraid will hear you?" Rance whispered back. "The dog?"

"I'm *serious*, Rance."

"So am I. Look in my shaving kit. It's on the back of the sink."

Echo retreated, leaving the door only slightly ajar, and peered into the black zippered bag. A razor. Deodorant. A toothbrush and paste.

And condoms. The man carried condoms.

"What do you do?" Echo asked, annoyed out of all proportion to the situation. "Sleep with somebody every time you shave?"

When she looked up, he was standing directly behind her.

Echo watched their reflections in the glass over the sink as he slowly raised her T-shirt up over her belly, until her breasts were bared.

She groaned.

He played with her nipples.

"It's just adrenaline," Echo said. "We'll— ooooh—come to our senses in the morning...."

Rance pulled the T-shirt off over her head and tossed it aside. Then he cupped her breasts in his hands again, chafing the nipples with the sides of his thumbs. He rested his chin on top of her head, pressed closer from behind.

She groaned again. Serious erection at twelve o'clock. Or was it six?

"You're beautiful," he said.

"I bet you—say that—to everybody…."

He chuckled, bent his head to nibble at her right earlobe. While his left hand continued to fondle her breast, his right slid slowly down over her stomach and then under the waistband of her boxers.

She gasped when his fingers found their target, tilted her head back and closed her eyes.

He told her to open them.

She did.

He teased her with his fingertips.

She squirmed as heat suffused her whole system.

Rance worked her harder, brought her to the brink, and then lightened his touch until she bit her lower lip to hold back a plea.

He grinned at her. Left off caressing her breast long enough to moisten the tips of his fingers with his tongue. Then he rubbed her nipple until it was so hard and wet, she tried to turn in his arms, wanting his mouth on her.

But he didn't allow her to turn around.

The pressure began to build, and still Rance played between her legs.

She moved against him, unable to help herself, her breath fast and shallow. "Oh—Rance—please…"

He eased her back from the sink, just far enough

to kneel in front of her, and then he parted her with his fingers. She gripped the edges of the counter, felt his tongue flick lightly across her clitoris. A searing tremor snaked out from the epicenter.

"Do...not...close...your...eyes," he told her.

The climax had already begun, a soft shattering, starting deep, building slowly but inexorably toward a flash-point of cosmic scale.

"Rance," she whispered, her voice ragged. *"Rance."*

He suckled.

Echo stood, supported by Rance's hands, now clasping her bare buttocks, staring at her reflection in the mirror and watching herself come. Her body moved to its own ancient rhythm, swaying and supple, seeking release from something it craved.

When it was over, she slid to her knees, spent.

Rance had long since lost the towel, and he reached back over one shoulder, fumbling for his shaving kit, even as Echo sought a sweet vengeance all her own.

The black bag tumbled to the floor, and the contents scattered.

"Echo," Rance rasped. "The con—"

She looked up at him, saw that his head was thrown back, and the cords in his neck stood out with the effort to restrain a force as natural, and as inviolable, as gravity.

Later, she would wonder what possessed her.

In the moment, she simply shifted, until she was

astride Rance, and claimed him in one sure motion of her hips.

He said her name again, and might have lifted her off, except that it was already too late. She rode him unmercifully, faster and faster, until they both splintered into fragments.

"I CAN'T BELIEVE WE DID IT ON the bathroom floor," Echo said an hour later, lying flat on her back in the middle of the bed, while Rance rested with his head on her stomach.

"Believe it," he said.

"Are you going to fly to Taiwan again?"

He planted a circle of kisses around the circumference of her navel. "No," he answered. "Are you?"

The truth was, a part of Echo wanted to load Snowball and a couple of suitcases in the Volkswagen and boogie for parts unknown.

"I'm a nervous flier," she said. "Is there a bridge?" She tried to laugh at her own joke, but it came out sounding more like a sob.

Rance moved up beside her, took her in his arms. Brushed his lips across her temple. "Hey," he said.

"Hey," she answered.

"I'm not leaving," he told her.

"Me, neither," she replied. "But not because I'm not scared."

He raised himself onto one elbow. "I'm sorry, Echo," he said.

The words froze her blood. Not an easy thing,

since it had been molten only minutes before. "You're…sorry?"

"Not about the lovemaking."

"What then?"

He widened his eyes at her, circled one of her nipples with an idle motion of his fingertip. "Taiwan," he said.

She bolted upright. "You did something in Taiwan? *That's* why you had condoms in your shaving kit—"

Rance laughed, eased her back onto the pillows. *"No,"* he said. "But I like knowing it would matter if I had."

She giggled, snorted and cried harder. "Of all the—"

He kissed her, deeply.

"What now?" she asked, with her heart, as well as her lips, when she could breathe again.

"I was going to ask you the same question," Rance admitted.

She wished she could blow her nose. Tears might be romantic, but boogers were over the line. "Any suggestions?" she asked.

He grinned, stretched to pluck a wad of tissues from the box on the table next to the bed, and handed them to her.

She reminded herself of the mirror session, and the fact that she'd thrown up earlier. Dignity was a faint memory.

She sat up and blew.

Rance watched with a sort of amused tenderness. "I guess I'd suggest that we agree not to panic," he said. "We're going to have to find our way through this thing, whatever it is. Figure it out."

"Are we dating?"

He laughed again. "After what happened on the bathroom floor? God, I hope so."

Echo remembered a pivotal moment and slapped a hand over her mouth.

"What?" Rance asked.

"That one time—we didn't—I didn't…"

He'd reached for a condom. Echo hadn't given him a chance to open the packet, let alone put the thing on.

"How's the timing?"

"The timing?"

"Echo? Don't echo."

She blushed. "My cycle? Is that what you're asking about?"

"That's what I'm asking about."

"I'm irregular," she said.

"Then I guess we have to play that part by ear."

"You're not…mad at me?"

He took her hand, kissed the backs of her knuckles. "Do I look mad?"

"No."

"My turn to ask a question."

Echo waited, building up her courage, watching him, memorizing his face. What she had with Rance was half again too good to last. She'd survived being jilted at the altar, because that was Justin, and a part of her had been relieved. Yes, she'd cried when she realized her groom wasn't going to show up. Yes, she'd gone back to her solitary hotel room and thrown pillows, the phone book, and everything in the desk drawer against the walls.

And then she'd done a victory dance and consumed a little bottle of champagne from the minibar.

"What's your real name?"

"I'm not ready to tell you."

"Why not?"

"Because she's not me. Not yet."

"How can she not be you?"

"She just isn't."

"Hortense," Rance guessed.

Echo laughed.

"Minerva?"

She hit him with a pillow.

"Wilhelmina?"

"Please."

"Please?" He bent, tasted her nipple. "Your name is 'Please'? Or are you making another scandalous request?"

Echo stretched, deliciously ready to make love again.

"Guess," she said.

He rolled on top of her, gently parted her legs with one knee. "I'm thinking it's the scandalous request."

"Umm," she purred. But she reached for one of the packets on the nightstand and handed it to him.

A few moments later, he was inside her, and this time, their lovemaking was slow, tender, and sweet enough to break Echo's heart.

CHAPTER 14

"Dad?"

"Hey, Rance," his father responded easily. God knew where he was, but he could always be trusted to keep his cell phone charged.

"There's a woman." Rance leaned back against the counter in his kitchen, closest to the coffeepot, waiting for the java to perk. He'd been as good as his word to Echo earlier—before the sun rose over the hills east of Indian Rock, he was long gone.

He'd locked the shop door behind him, using Echo's spare key, stopped by Wyatt's office to make sure Bud Willand was still in custody, and now he was home. Alone. Maeve and Rianna were at Cora's.

After the night with Echo, the place felt bigger and emptier than ever before.

"Well, hallelujah," Wade McKettrick answered. "It's about time."

"You don't understand."

"Try me."

"Where are you?"

"Beside the point."

"Dad."

"Tahiti, surrounded by beautiful women in grass skirts. Where are you?"

It was a reasonable question, given Rance's travel history. "The ranch."

"How are the girls?"

"Fine."

"So tell me about the woman."

"I don't know her real name."

"Is she a secret agent or something?"

"No. She's some kind of wood nymph." Rance smiled. Did wood nymphs wear boxer shorts and T-shirts? He took a mug down from a shelf and poured coffee. Slurped some up. "She calls herself Echo."

"You're sleeping with her."

"Yeah."

"This is a healthy thing, Rance. So why the panicked phone call?"

"I'm not panicking."

"Aren't you? I haven't heard from you in six months."

Rance sighed. "Sorry about that. Of course, I haven't heard from *you,* either."

"Semantics. What's up?" Wade paused. Chuckled. "As if I didn't know."

"Dad? You aren't helping."

Wade echoed the sigh Rance had just given. "You're scared."

"I'm not."

"Don't bullshit me, boy. I've been down this trail before, and a mapful of others you haven't gotten to yet. Are you in love with her?"

"No," Rance said. "I feel something, that's a given. But love? Hell, I'm not even sure what that is."

"She's not Julie," Wade said, after a few moments of pregnant silence.

"That's the problem," Rance replied.

"No," Wade answered, "it's the solution."

"Thanks for that pearl of wisdom, Dad."

Wade laughed. "Think about it."

"I can't *stop* thinking about it."

"Well, that ought to tell you something, right there. You know what's getting in your way, Rance? That McKettrick pride of yours. You're scared of making a fool of yourself. I've been down that road, too. Take it from me, it's a dead end." Another pause followed, then, "Is your mother coming home for Jesse's wedding?"

In the back of Rance's harried, jet-lagged mind, two boxcars shifted onto the same spur and connected with a clang. "Don't know," he said. "Probably."

"Do me a favor," Wade said. "Find out. And whatever you do, don't mention that I plan to be there, too."

Rance frowned. "Dad—"

"We'll talk more when I get home. In the meantime, don't do anything stupid."

Rance laughed, even though there was a strange thickness in the back of his throat, and the space behind his eyes burned. "Too late," he said.

"You taking good care of Cassidy's horse?"

Rance took another slug of coffee. That way, if his voice caught, he could blame his gag reflex. "Soon as I feed the cattle, I'm going to saddle old Snowball up for a ride."

"Good," Wade answered, and from the sound of it, he'd just swallowed something, too. "What cattle?"

Rance filled his dad in on the gentlemen-rancher angle. He'd hired the old man on the next place to dump hay out of the back of a pickup while he was away, but he didn't feel good about it.

They were his cattle, after all. His responsibility.

The next leap was easy. Maeve and Rianna were *his* daughters. As much as Cora loved those girls, it wasn't her job to take care of them.

Wade chuckled. "Damn. The McKettricks ride again. Just like the old days."

"Just like the old days," Rance replied, wishing it was true.

Jesse was the real thing. He'd never sold out. Himself and Keegan? Now, that was another matter.

They'd traded in their saddles for seats on a company jet. Abandoned the land. Left their kids for other people to raise.

And for what? More money?

Prestige?

The thrill of the chase?

What?

Something shifted in Rance as he pondered those questions and stood, unflinching, before the obvious answers.

"I'll get a room ready for you," he told his dad.

"And call your mother?"

"And call my mother. Right after I feed the cattle."

"Rance? Call her *now*."

"Why don't *you* call her?"

"Because you came by that pride of yours honestly, that's why. Do this for me, Rance. You know better than anybody how hard it is to ask."

"I'll get right back to you."

"I'll be waiting."

Rance looked up his mother's number and placed the call.

She answered on the first ring. "Rance! How are you? Is everybody all right?"

"Everybody's fine, Mom," Rance said, rubbing his eyes. "I'm just checking to see if you're coming back for Jesse's wedding."

"I wouldn't miss it," Katherine McKettrick replied. "It'll be good to see you."

"And you, sweetheart. You tell Cora I'm muscling in on some of the grandmother action."

Rance laughed. "I'll tell her."

They chatted for a few more minutes, then rang off.

Rance immediately called his dad back.

"Well?" Wade demanded.

"She'll be here," Rance said.

"Hot damn," Wade replied, and hung up in Rance's ear.

Rance finished his coffee and went out to feed the cattle.

When that was done, he saddled Snowball and mounted up. Rode to the top of Jesse's ridge and looked back over the Triple M, the sprawling range land, the creek, the copses of trees. It seemed, though he knew it was crazy, that Cassidy had made the trip with him, and stood now, at his elbow, the way she'd always done.

His eyes smarted.

"I miss you, Cass," he said aloud. "If I could take back even one of those times I told you to get lost, I would."

And he thought he heard her answer, with his heart, not his ears.

Just ride Snowball, she said.

Rance ran a sleeve across his face. And when he lowered his arm, he blinked, because he'd have sworn he saw five riders in the long coats of another time, traveling single file along the far side of the creek.

They were gone again, in an instant, but the

memory was fixed on Rance's brain in images as clear as if he'd been riding beside those men.

Old Angus, in the lead, followed by Holt, his elder son, then Rafe, Kade and Jeb.

His dad's words, spoken just that morning over a cell phone, echoed in his mind.

The McKettricks ride again.

Rance laughed right out loud, and if he'd been wearing a hat, he'd have thrown it in the air.

"MORE LOCKS," ECHO TOLD Eddie, the handyman, when she got back from filing a second complaint against Bud Willand, who was at that moment being transported to jail in Flagstaff. "Bigger locks. Lots and lots of locks."

Ayanna, who had admitted Eddie, sighed. "Crime comes to Indian Rock," she said.

Echo glanced at the almost-empty box of love-spell supplies sitting on one end of the counter. "Yeah," she reflected.

"Were you scared?" Ayanna asked. It was a rhetorical question, of course, and because Echo liked the woman so much, she let it pass without remarking on the inanity of it.

"Yes," Echo said.

"Good thing old Rance was around," Eddie put in. Echo blushed.

Ayanna twinkled. "The whole town knows," she said out of the side of her mouth.

Rance had predicted just that, of course, but Echo

had still cherished a forlorn and flickering hope that word wouldn't get around.

Before she could think of anything to say, Cora zipped in, waggling a yellow flyer in one hand. "Came to tape this up in your window," she announced, beaming at Echo. "It's your civic duty to let me."

Echo blushed again. Someone had probably awakened Cora out of a sound sleep the night before, with the news that her son-in-law happened to be present, wearing nothing but a towel, when Bud Willand broke into the bookshop by the back way and got himself punched in the nose.

"What is it?" she asked, not really caring.

"Summer Dance," Cora said, as if Echo should have known. Maybe, given Jessica's visit and the subsequent rush on love-spells, she should have. She'd just assumed it was a high school affair, that was all.

"You got a date, Cora?" Eddie teased. He was kneeling just to one side of the door, laying out tools and taking the new locks out of their packaging.

Cora grinned, taped the poster to the glass, facing the street, and gave back as good as she got. "You asking, Eddie?"

He turned bright crimson.

Cora dropped her tape into the pocket of her cotton vest, leaned slightly and mussed his hair. Then she waltzed over to the counter, reached into the love-spell box and plucked out a bag.

"Put it on my tab," she said.

Echo laughed. "On the house," she answered.

"I wouldn't mind one myself," Ayanna mused.

"Help yourself," Echo told her, with a grand gesture of one hand.

"What about you?" Ayanna asked Echo, twinkling again.

"She doesn't need one," Cora said happily, just before she sailed out the door again, probably intent on hanging more flyers in more windows.

Echo turned as red as Eddie had a few moments before.

Then she went outside, stood on the sidewalk and read the flyer.

Oh, for a pair of glass slippers, she thought.

Size eight-and-a-half, medium.

DOC SWANN HIMSELF UNLOCKED the front door of his office to let Cora in.

She felt the familiar flutter in her heart.

He'd been widowed three years before, and folks said he still visited his late wife's grave at all hours of the night. Cora had seen his study light on, in the wee-smalls, plenty of times, when she got restless herself and went out to drive around town. Doc always had bags under his eyes, and even when he smiled, there was an air of sadness about him.

"What's this?" he asked, taking a flyer from the stack she'd brought in from the truck and reading the print. "The Summer Dance. Is it that time again?"

"It *is* June," Cora said, glancing around. The reception area was empty, except for the two of them. "Where is everybody?"

"I sent Cindy up to Flagstaff to pick up a software program and some equipment so we can read those lost-pet microchips without having to extract the thing and send it to a lab," he answered, but he was still looking at the flyer. "Time we dragged this practice into the twenty-first century."

"I guess I'll just tape that flyer up and be on my way," Cora said.

"I hear there was some excitement down at the bookstore last night," Doc Swann remarked, looking up from the flyer at last.

"Rance took care of it."

Doc chuckled. "So I'm told. I had breakfast out at the Roadhouse this morning, as usual, and the story was hotter than the grill back in the kitchen. No harm done, then?"

"Everything's fine," Cora confirmed, coloring up a little.

Doc's tired blue eyes sparkled. "I love a good romance," he said.

Cora almost choked. She'd known this man all her life, but she'd never once heard the R-word come out of his mouth. She managed a nod.

"They out of the woods, Rance and Echo?"

It was Cora's turn to chuckle. "Not by a long shot," she said, shaking her head. "But if they stick together, they might make it."

Doc nodded. "That's good," he said.

Cora turned, reached into her vest pocket for the roll of tape.

"Cora?"

She looked back.

"You own a pair of dancing shoes?"

Cora blinked. "Now, why would you ask a question like that?"

Doc cleared his throat. Looked away. "Never mind."

"Oh, no, you don't, Walter Swann," Cora burst out, poking him in the chest with her roll of tape. "I want to know what you meant."

More throat clearing, and just the slightest shuffling of his feet. "I thought…maybe…it was just a crazy idea—"

"Walter."

"I was going to ask you to the Summer Dance."

"Did you decide not to?"

"Not to what?"

"Not to ask me to the Summer Dance, Walter."

He smiled. "Will you, Cora? Be my date for Saturday night?"

Cora blinked.

"Well?" Walter prompted.

"Yes. If—if you really meant to ask, I mean."

"I meant to ask," he said.

"Okay, then," Cora said, feeling flustered.

"Pick you up at seven? We could have dinner at the Roadhouse. Fortify ourselves before we go tripping the light fantastic."

"Seven," Cora agreed.

"What color is your dress?"

"I don't know," Cora replied. "I haven't bought it yet."

Walter laughed. "I've seen you go six months without wearing the same outfit. Are you telling me you don't own a dress?"

She smiled. "No," she said. "I'm telling you I don't own *the* dress." With that, she left. She'd gone in there an old woman and come out feeling like she was eighteen again.

When she glanced back, Walter was taping the flyer to the inside of his front window. He grinned and waggled his fingers in farewell.

Cora waited until she was behind the wheel of her truck. Then she took Echo's love-spell out of her vest pocket, held it in the palm of her hand and wondered.

JESSE WAS IN FRONT OF the barn when Rance and Snowball got back from their ride, leaning against his truck and chewing on a blade of good high-country grass.

"I don't even own a cell phone," he said, as Rance swung down from the saddle, "and I already know where you spent the night."

Rance grinned, patted Snowball's neck and hooked one of the stirrups over the horn so he could unbuckle the cinch. "That so," he replied, in his own good time.

"Saturday's her birthday," Jesse said.

Rance went still. Turned to look at his cousin.

"Saturday," Jesse repeated. "Echo's birthday."

"How the hell do you know that?"

Jesse laughed. "Keeg and I ran a background check on her." He slapped Rance on the shoulder, then tugged Snowball's saddle down off her back.

"You did *what?*"

"Hey, she turned up out of nowhere. You're a decent catch. We were looking out for your best interests, man."

"You'd better not know her real name," Rance said.

Jesse looked puzzled. "Legally, she's Echo Wells. What else would she call herself?"

Rance wrenched the saddle out of his cousin's arms and headed for the barn. Jesse followed, leading Snowball by her reins.

"Rance?"

"Forget it."

"I'm not going to forget it."

"Tell me what you dug up on her, since you've already checked her out behind my back." Rance put the saddle in its customary place.

"She'll be thirty this Saturday. She's an only child, orphaned young, raised by an aunt and uncle. Put herself through college, worked in an art gallery until she came here. Never married, no rap sheet."

"What are you, an FBI mole?"

Jesse put Snowball in her stall, slipped the bridle

off over her head and stroked her side. Something in the slant of his shoulders told Rance he was thinking about Cassidy, not the conversation at hand.

A gap of silence opened.

"Nice to see you riding this horse," Jesse said when they got to the other side. "Out of all the things we could do in her memory, I guess Cass would have wanted that most."

Rance swallowed hard. Looked away.

Jesse gave him another slap on the shoulder as he passed.

"You remember how I used to tell her to get lost?" Rance asked.

Jesse stopped in the barn doorway, but he didn't turn around. "I remember," he said.

Rance gave Snowball some extra hay and followed Jesse outside.

With a little distance between them and the subject of Cassidy and the horse she'd loved more than just about anything else, it was easier to talk.

"Saturday, huh?" Echo hadn't mentioned that her birthday was coming up, but, then, they'd never gotten past the sex. He knew what she liked in bed, but not much else.

"Saturday," Jesse confirmed, climbing into his truck and starting the engine.

"I don't want to hurt her," Rance heard himself say.

"Then don't," Jesse replied. With that, he put the truck in gear, turned it around and drove away.

RIANNA'S FACE LIT UP WHEN Rance walked through the front door at the Curl and Twirl. "Daddy!" she whooped, and flew at him. "You're back from Taiwan!"

"Sure am." He lifted her up, swung her around once and gave her a smack on the cheek. "How's my girl?" he asked.

"Bored," Rianna said. "Granny's putting up posters all over town, and Maeve spent the night at her friend Suzie's. They got to have pizza and stay up all night and watch DVDs."

"Your grandmother is putting up posters?"

"For the dance," Rianna informed him.

"What dance?"

"The *Summer* one. It's this Saturday."

"Oh," Rance said. Now that he had the information, he didn't know what to do with it. Not an uncommon experience when it came to things that interested those of the female persuasion.

He set Rianna back on her feet.

"Are you going to invite Echo?" she asked.

"I hadn't thought about it," Rance admitted. It was true. He'd thought about plenty else, though.

"Do you like her, Daddy?"

Three women with goop on their heads peered around the portable wall separating the waiting room from the main part of the shop.

Rance felt his neck heat up. "Yes," he said. "Of course I like her."

"Then *ask her to the dance,*" one of the women said.

Rance glared at her.

The trio retreated, but he knew they hadn't gone far.

"I'll go with you if you're scared," Rianna offered, looking up at him with huge, hopeful eyes.

Rance put out a hand to his daughter. "Okay," he said.

The portable wall wiggled.

He shook his head.

Rianna pulled him out the door, onto the sidewalk. "Ready?" she asked.

Rance stifled a grin. "Yeah. Any last-minute pointers?"

"Tell her she's pretty."

"Got it."

Rianna tugged him into Echo's shop. The bell tinkled over the door.

Echo, busy unpacking a box of books, looked up and then looked down again.

"My daddy wants to ask you to the Summer Dance," Rianna announced.

"Thanks, coach," Rance said.

"I was afraid you'd chicken out," Rianna replied in a stage whisper.

Echo turned roughly the same color as her car, then smiled.

Ayanna, watching the whole exchange, beckoned to Rianna. "We just got a new shipment of pop-ups," she said. "Wanna see?"

Whatever "pop-ups" were, Rianna seemed delighted by the prospect.

They disappeared into the back room.

"I'd understand if you said no," Rance told Echo when she didn't jump right in there with a yes.

She studied him. "Okay," she said.

"Okay 'yes,' or okay 'no'?"

She grinned. "Okay, 'yes.'"

Rance felt ridiculously happy, and his tongue had tied itself up in a knot. Since he couldn't speak, he nodded.

"Was there something else?" Echo asked.

"Jesse and Keegan ran a background check on you," he said, half expecting her to throw something.

"I know," she said.

"You know?"

"Rance? Don't echo."

He laughed, and it felt almost as good as making love to her on the bathroom floor.

"They told me. Keegan and Jesse, I mean."

"Oh."

Most of what he knew about Echo, he'd gotten secondhand, either from Cora or his cousins. It was amazing how much that bothered him. He wanted to know everything all of the sudden. If she'd been lonely as a kid, for instance, and how her aunt and uncle had treated her.

He couldn't ask, because things like that had to be offered. So he just stood there, like a fool, wondering what to do next.

She tried to let him off the hook. "See you Saturday, then?"

"Saturday," he agreed hoarsely. He'd hoped to see her a lot sooner than that. Like tonight, and tomorrow night, and the night after that, but it was probably better to take things slowly.

She took in his boots, jeans and work shirt. "Looks like you're back to ranching," she said.

He nodded, stuck where he was as surely as if he'd planted the soles of his boots in a spill of superglue.

Rianna saved him by bursting out of the back, carrying a book. She held it up to him, opened the covers with a flourish and laughed with delight when a fully formed paper horse jumped to life right before his eyes.

"Can I have it, Daddy? Can I? Please?"

Rance studied the horse, fascinated. At the same time, he reached for his wallet.

Rianna relayed the money to Echo, who rang up the purchase and sent back change.

"Pretty amazing, huh?" Echo asked, resting her forearms on the counter and leaning a little, so her plump breasts pushed together under the fabric of her frothy sundress.

Rance shifted, pulled his feet loose from the invisible superglue. "Pretty amazing," he replied.

A knowing look sparked in her eyes. "I meant the pop-up book," she said.

"That, too," he responded.

She laughed.

"Wait till Maeve sees this!" Rianna cried, in little-sister triumph. She dashed out the door, waving the book in the air.

"I'd better make sure she doesn't run all the way to Suzie's place," Rance said, and turned to follow his daughter.

Echo laughed again.

Or was it the little bell over the door?

THE PACKAGE WAS BULKY, and it had been forwarded at least once. The wrapping was coming undone, the return address was smudged, and the handwriting, though vaguely familiar, didn't bring any names to mind.

Echo set it on the counter and stood back from it, frowning.

"Do you think it's going to explode?" Ayanna asked, only half joking.

Snowball rose on her hind legs and sniffed the wrapping.

"No," Echo said, after biting her lower lip for a few moments. "It's just weird, that's all."

"You get packages all the time," Ayanna reasoned.

"From companies," Echo told her. "This looks—personal."

Snowball dropped back to all fours and strolled away.

"Well," Ayanna said, "the bomb dog doesn't seem alarmed."

Echo gave her a nervous glance, approached the package again and tried to make out the return address. There was no name, just a post office box and a Chicago zip code.

That eliminated one possibility—that Justin had found some of her stuff at his place, tucked away and forgotten in a box or a drawer, and decided to send it back. He still lived in New York.

"Open it," Ayanna urged.

Echo's hands trembled slightly as she tore away the ruined paper.

Whatever it was, it was gift-wrapped. Little bears and balloons, something the worse for wear, but determinedly cheerful. A card was taped to the top, with her name printed in block letters.

A birthday present?

Her palms grew moist.

Ayanna appeared at her side. Elbowed her lightly.

Echo pulled the envelop free, opened it. The card was cheap, the kind that comes twenty to a box, and it looked as forlorn as the bears and balloons.

There were flowers on the front, along with a generic "Happy Birthday."

Holding her breath, Echo opened the card.

"I'm sorry if this is a little scruffy," the inside read. "I found it on eBay. Hope you're okay. Uncle Joe." A phone number was scrawled beneath.

Gently, Echo tore away the wrapping paper, and there, looking tired and tattered from her long journey, still smiling and holding her wand with the star at the top, was the doll she'd been waiting for since she was seven years old.

CHAPTER  15

ECHO DIDN'T MOVE. She simply stared at the doll, speechless.

Ayanna elbowed her gently. "Echo?"

"How could he possibly have remembered?" she whispered, putting one hand to her throat.

"Who?" Ayanna asked. When she didn't receive an answer, she reached for the card, opened it. "Your Uncle Joe?"

Echo nodded.

"There's a number here. Why don't you call him?"

Echo nodded again. And stayed right where she was.

"What a pretty doll," Ayanna said, probably trying to resuscitate the conversation.

"Her name is Margaret," Echo said. Tears stung her eyes.

"Maybe you should sit down," Ayanna suggested kindly.

"I'm all right," Echo lied.

Ayanna took Echo's elbow in one hand and the unexpected birthday gift in the other, and walked her to the steps. Echo plopped down.

Snowball approached, sniffing the box again.

"What does this mean?" Echo asked, very softly.

"I haven't a clue," Ayanna answered. "That's why I think you should call your uncle."

"I wouldn't know what to say," Echo lamented. "We haven't spoken since the day I left for college." Once or twice, she'd asked a friend to drive her past the house where she'd grown up, and, later, when she had a car of her own, she'd made the pilgrimage herself, every Thanksgiving and Christmas. She'd never stopped, and the last time she'd gone, the place had changed hands. A strange man had been in the driveway, scraping the windshield of a strange car.

Ayanna sat down on the step below Echo's, wrapped her arms around her knees. "Hello might be a good start," she said. "Followed by, thanks for the doll." She paused. "Unless this isn't the kind of gift I think it is."

Echo drew up her own knees, rested her forehead on them, and drew several slow, deep breaths. "I can't believe he remembered," she murmured.

"Odd things stick in people's minds," Ayanna said. "Tell me about the doll, Echo."

Echo lifted her head. Sighed. Explained, as best she could, how she'd gone to live with her aunt and uncle after her parents were killed, how she'd seen the doll and worked up the courage to say she wanted it for Christmas. When she looked at Ayanna, she saw that her friend was crying.

"It's his way of saying he's sorry, Echo. Your uncle's, I mean."

Echo swallowed. "My parents had a small life insurance policy," she said. "A lawyer sent me the check, out of the blue, right after I turned eighteen. Just before I got on the bus to leave for college, my uncle told me I was ungrateful. That I should give him the money, to make up for all the expense they'd gone to, raising me like one of their own."

"There must have been social security payments for that," Ayanna said.

"There were," Echo said. "And they certainly didn't raise me 'like one of their own.' But I still felt guilty, turning my back on him and getting on that bus. I knew if I didn't, I'd never get out of the neighborhood."

Ayanna patted her hand. "You did the right thing, sweetie."

"Did I?" Echo asked softly. "They weren't much of a family, but they were all I had."

"You need to call home," Ayanna reiterated

firmly. "Tell you what. I'll take Snowball out for a walk. You lock up behind us, get on the phone and find out what's what."

"I'm not sure I want to open this can of worms," Echo said. "Maybe, at this late date, a relationship—"

"It's not a relationship, Echo. It's a phone call. Nobody's saying you have to go back there and fall into their arms."

Echo nodded. "You're right."

Five minutes later, Echo was alone in the storeroom, with her cell phone in hand, thumbing in the numbers written at the bottom of her birthday card.

"Hospice," a woman answered on the fourth ring.

Hospice? Echo's heart stopped, started again. "I must have the wrong number," she said. "I'm sorry—"

"Who are you looking for?" the woman broke in gently, as though she was accustomed to calls from confused people.

"Joe Wells." Suddenly, she knew she *didn't* have the wrong number. "This is Echo Wells. I'm his niece."

"He's been hoping you'd call," the woman replied.

Echo squeezed her eyes shut. "Is he…? I mean, if you're a hospice—"

"I'll let him tell you, Miss Wells. I will say that Joe has been hoping you'd call. Hold on a moment, please."

Echo nodded miserably and waited.

"Echo?" Her uncle's voice sounded just the same. "Is that you?"

"It's me, Uncle Joe," Echo said. "H-how are you?"

"Not so great," he answered. "I have good days, and bad ones. This is a good one."

"I'm glad."

"You got the package?"

Echo nodded, remembered he couldn't see her and croaked out, "Yes." Stopped to clear her throat. "Yes. How could you possibly have remembered?"

Joe Wells chuckled, but it was a sad sound, used-up and broken. "I've still got a few brain cells working," he replied. "This cancer ate up a lot of them, though." He paused, and a soft stillness trembled between them. Then he went on. "I went back for the doll, honey. They were all gone. You were so little, and you still believed in Santa Claus, so I figured it was better not to mention it to you. Put it right out of my mind. Didn't think of it again, until you went away to college. Then it started bothering me."

"It's okay," she whispered.

"No," he insisted. "It's not okay. You were my baby sister's little girl. She wanted a doll once, when we were kids, and our dad was out of work, so we got charity stuff for Christmas that year. Maureen never got over wanting that doll—"

Maureen. When was the last time Echo had heard someone say her mother's name out loud?

"So I figured maybe you didn't get over wanting yours, either."

"She's beautiful, Uncle Joe," Echo said. "Thank you. H-how is everyone else?"

"Laura and I got divorced a long time ago," Joe Wells answered. His words were coming harder now; he was getting tired. "The kids took her side, and I don't see much of them."

"I'm sorry," Echo told him. Brain cancer. The man was dying of brain cancer, but he'd still managed to track down both her and the doll. "D-do you need anything?"

"I got good insurance," Joe said. "You married, honey? Got any kids?"

"No husband, no kids," Echo said. "But I'm happy enough."

"Good." The word was gruff.

"You're sure there's nothing I can do?"

"Nothing anybody can do," Joe answered, with a complete lack of self-pity. "I'm not suffering, Echo. Just fading away."

Echo's face was wet. "I guess you're probably getting tired," she said.

"Tired," Joe said, "isn't the word. I wish I'd done better by you, honey. My baby sister's baby girl. But the plain truth is, back in those days, I had all I could do to keep the rent paid and put food on the table. If you'd say you understand, even if you don't, well, that would mean the world to me."

"I do understand," Echo said. "I do."

"That's good, honey. You have a nice life, now. Time for me to get off this phone and rest a while."

You have a nice life, now.

"Goodbye, Uncle Joe."

"Goodbye, honey."

There was a clunking sound on the other end of the line, then a dial tone.

Echo hung up, set her cell phone on the step, grabbed the doll and went upstairs. There, she lay down on the bed and cried in earnest.

"I SHOULD HAVE ASKED FOR a key," Ayanna told Rance, watching as he unlocked the door of Echo's shop. She and Snowball preceded him, and the dog headed straight for the stairs as soon as Ayanna unhooked her leash.

Rance followed. Ayanna had gone to Cora when she couldn't raise Echo either by knocking or calling, and Cora had called him. He'd driven in from the ranch at top speed, called Wyatt on the way, just to make sure Willand was still in police custody. He'd imagined all sorts of possible scenarios, even after he knew old Bud wasn't a factor.

Maybe she'd fallen and hit her head.

Maybe she was sick.

He took the stairs three at a time.

Echo was curled in a ball in the middle of the bed, with her shoes on and her dress in a twisted fluff around her thighs. Snowball, having made the jump from the floor, was trying to lick her face.

"Hey," Rance said when Echo opened her eyes.

"Hey," she answered.

He approached, sat down on the edge of the bed, resisting the urge to gather her up and hold her the way he would have held Rianna or Maeve. Instead, he touched her forehead.

"He sent me the doll," Echo told him. She didn't move, otherwise.

"Who sent you a doll?" Rance asked quietly.

"My uncle. He's dying of brain cancer. He said, 'Have yourself a nice life.'"

Rance decided not to stand on ceremony and drew her onto his lap. She sighed and rested her head against his shoulder. He felt a slight shudder go through her. "Brain cancer," he repeated.

She nodded.

"You want to talk about this, or shall I just hold you?"

Echo nestled closer. "Just hold me," she said. Then, in that peculiar, paradoxical way of women, she went right on talking. She told him about her folks dying, and going to live with her aunt and uncle, and wanting the doll so badly that she waited for it for five Christmases before she finally gave up.

Rance listened, absorbing it all, his eyes hot with sympathy.

It would have been easy to judge Joe Wells, but on another level, Rance couldn't help drawing a few parallels. Sure, he gave Maeve and Rianna the best of everything—at least, everything money could buy. But what secret hopes were *they* harboring? What, when his time came, and it was too late, would he wish to God he could go back and do over again?

"I should be downstairs taking care of the shop," Echo said when she'd poured it all out.

"Ayanna's got it handled." He tugged off her shoes, tossed them aside. Then he, Echo and the dog stretched out full-length on the bed. He kept his arms around Echo, loved the way her soft hair tickled the underside of his chin. "You going back there? To see your uncle?"

She shook her head. "I want to call the hospice people back, though. He told me he didn't need anything, but—well—I just want to make sure."

"I'll take you to see him," Rance said. "If you want to go, I can have the jet here within a few hours."

Again, she shook her head. "Probably not a good idea." She drew back far enough to look into Rance's face. "It's just a feeling I got when we were talking," she said, "but I think he wanted the doll and the phone call to be enough." She sniffled, then smiled in a way that made Rance's heart hurt. "What are you doing here, cowboy?"

He nuzzled her neck. "I figured I'd take the scandal up another notch," he said. "Come up here and lie in bed with you in the middle of the day."

She laughed, but it was a moist, fractured sound. "Nothing in Chicago," she said, "prepared me for this particular element of small-town life."

He kissed her forehead. "You're sure you don't want a ride in my jet, little lady?" he teased.

Her eyes, though puffy and red-rimmed, were as beautiful as ever. "Is that a double entendre?" she asked.

He grinned. "If you want to interpret it that way, I guess there isn't much I can do to stop you," he said. If they'd been alone in the bed, he might have eased her sundress up and off, and made her forget all the heartache, if only for a little while. But Snowball was right there, keeping a vigil of her own, and Rance didn't have the heart to send her away.

Besides, Ayanna was right downstairs, and technically, the shop was open for business.

"Thanks, Rance," Echo whispered, tracing the outline of his mouth with one fingertip.

"For what?"

"For being here. For holding me."

"You're welcome."

"Don't you have to herd cattle or something?"

He chuckled. Kissed her again. "No," he said. "The fences are sound, so they'll be pretty much where I left them when I get back to the ranch."

She sighed, closed her eyes and fell asleep.

When he was sure she was settled, Rance eased out of her arms, got off the bed and stood looking down at her for a long time. Finally, he shook out the quilt folded at the end of the mattress, draped it over both Echo and the dog, and left.

ECHO AWOKE, BLINKING, to find herself alone on the bed, except, of course, for Snowball. The room was shadowy, though it was still light outside, and she felt starved.

She got up, padded into the bathroom, recalling the gentle way Rance had taken off her shoes before taking her into his arms.

Or had she dreamed that part?

She yawned, splashed her face with cold water and headed downstairs, followed by Snowball.

Ayanna was just closing the shop.

"Feeling better?" she asked.

Echo nodded sheepishly. "I'm sorry, Ayanna. For leaving you to run the place on your own and everything."

"I was fine," Ayanna said, watching her closely. "Can I do anything, Echo? Maybe heat up some soup?"

"I can do that," Echo answered.

"I don't like leaving you alone. Is Rance coming back?"

Is Rance coming back?

So he *had* been there. She hadn't been dreaming, then.

"I don't think so," Echo said. "He was just— being a friend."

"Nothing wrong with that."

Once, in Chicago, Echo had caught the flu. Justin had taken a commuter flight, come to the apartment and shoved a take-out carton of won-ton soup at her.

She'd been charmed, until she found out why he'd made the trip.

"You're not pregnant, are you?" he'd asked anxiously. "Because I'm really not ready for you to be pregnant."

"Echo?"

She came back to the here and now, and noticed the look of concern in Ayanna's eyes. "Sorry," she said. "Just one of those little mental side trips."

"You've had a hard day," Ayanna said. "Maybe I'll just go pick up something to eat and stick around for a while."

"I'm really all right," Echo insisted. She'd been alone most of her life, and she'd done okay, even during the rough times. But something had changed; she was fragile in a new and scary way. Secretly, she wished Ayanna *would* stay, or better yet, that Rance would come back. "Please, Ayanna, go home. You've done enough."

She put a hand to her forehead, pushed back her hair.

Ayanna hesitated, then went to fetch her purse from behind the counter. "You have to promise to call me if you need anything."

Echo nodded. Once Ayanna had left, she went upstairs, changed into jeans and a tank top, and found Snowball's leash. After their walk, they shared a peanut butter and jelly sandwich upstairs, and watched the one staticky channel Echo's TV managed to drag out of the ether.

When she couldn't bear the boredom any longer, Echo shut off the television set, dug through boxes until she found a telephone and plugged it into the jack beside the bed.

Sitting cross-legged in the center of the mattress, she called the number her uncle had written on the bottom of her birthday card and asked to speak to his nurse.

The woman was cautious at first, but she warmed up when Echo's name finally registered. "You're Joe's niece. The one he bought the doll for."

"That's me," Echo said after swallowing a couple of times. Margaret, still in her original carton, was propped on the nightstand, the glitter in her blue ruffled dress dulled by time, but winking faintly in the light of the lamp.

"He was on the Internet day and night, looking for that thing," the nurse said. "The rest of us helped when we could, but we didn't really know what we were looking for. When he found that doll, I'll tell you, the angels sang. Ordered it right up with his credit card. Then he didn't know where to send it, and the search was on again." A faint note of disapproval entered the woman's voice. "It wasn't easy tracking you down."

"My uncle and I weren't close," Echo said.

"So I gathered," the nurse replied.

"Is there anything I can do for him? He implied that he'd rather I didn't visit."

"He's not up to a visit," said the nurse. She sounded sad, and Echo wondered what it would be like to work with patients who were never going to get better and go home. "If you want to make things a little easier for him, you send him some pictures of yourself, and maybe a nice card."

Echo didn't have any pictures, not recent ones, anyway, but she'd buy a card in the morning, along with a disposable camera, and have someone snap a few shots. Maybe she'd enclose the clipping from the Indian Rock *Gazette*—her and Snowball and the cake.

"I'll do that," she said quietly. "If—if something happens, would you mind calling me?"

"Not at all," the nurse answered. "But there isn't going to be a funeral. Joe doesn't want any fuss made, and his family has already said their goodbyes."

How sad, Echo thought. When a person died, shouldn't there be some kind of service? Shouldn't there be people gathering in a church or a hospice chapel, sorry to see him go?

But, she realized, her uncle hadn't led that kind of life.

He was divorced, and apparently he'd never re-married.

He wasn't close to his children.

His sole remaining relative, a niece, was as much a stranger to him as he was to her.

Echo took down the address for the care center, thanked the nurse and hung up.

Snowball was lying at her feet, watching her.

It was only a matter of time before Marge and Herb would roll in, in their RV, and take the dog away, too.

Echo bit down hard on her lower lip.

There was Rance, of course, but she couldn't expect him to fill the empty spaces in her life. He had his daughters, cousins who cared enough about him to run background checks on prospective girlfriends. He had a ranch to run.

Sure, they'd made love on two different occasions, and it was better than good. He'd saved her from Bud Willand the night before, and today he'd held her until she fell asleep.

But that didn't make her his problem.

If she wanted to fill in emotional gaps, she was going to have to do it herself. Get to know people, make more friends. Maybe get herself another dog, after the Ademoyes came for Snowball. God knew, there were plenty of strays out there needing a good home.

She'd make one—for herself, first.

Rent a little house with a backyard. Plant some flowers. Serve supper at a picnic table, the way Cora did.

She looked around at the tiny apartment. It was cozy, and living there was a good economic move, given that her business wasn't established. But it was never going to be a home.

For once in her life, Echo wanted one, with all the trimmings.

The thought kept her eyes dry until she fell asleep.

RANCE SADDLED SNOWBALL, right after the evening chores were done, along with his own gelding. Maeve didn't wait for him to help her, she mounted up all by herself. For a moment, sitting there on the white mare's back, she looked like Cassidy had at her age.

He and Rianna rode the gelding, Rianna perched in front, as easy on that horse as a jockey on a favorite Thoroughbred.

"Let's run!" she cried.

Rance reached around her to take the reins. "No running," he said. "Snowball's a little out of shape."

"Can we go to the graveyard?" Maeve asked, taking him by surprise.

"Too far," Rance said. "It'll be dark in an hour or two."

"Can we go tomorrow?"

Rance studied his daughter, thinking of all the things he didn't know about her, would never know. "Why the sudden interest?" he asked.

"It isn't sudden," Maeve informed him. "Granny takes us all the time. We put flowers on Mom's grave."

Rance tried to remember the last time he'd done that, and couldn't.

"Tomorrow," he agreed.

They rode alongside the creek, as McKettricks had done for generations, Maeve leading the way. She was good on a horse, just as her mother had been. And Cassidy, too.

"Is there anything you wanted for Christmas that you never got?" Rance asked, after trying the words out a dozen different ways in his head and never managing to get them right.

Rianna turned to look up at him. "Daddy," she said. "It's *June.*"

He laughed.

But Maeve's expression was solemn.

Rance sobered. "What about you, Annie Oakley?"

"You," Maeve said.

He frowned. "I've been around every Christmas of your life, kiddo."

"Not just at Christmas," Maeve told him. "When we have a recital at the Curl and Twirl. Uncle Jesse always comes, but it isn't the same."

The thought of Jesse at a baton-and-tutu extravaganza would have made Rance smile, under any other circumstances. As it was, he didn't trust himself to say anything, so he rode alongside Maeve, reached across and held her against his side for a moment. It was a teasing gesture, the kind of thing he did when he was trying to jolly her out of some preadolescent mood, but for some reason, it choked him up.

"You work too much, Daddy," Rianna told him, looking back over her little shoulder and squinting against the dazzle of the sinking sun. "We don't need the money, do we?"

Rance cleared his throat. "No, short stop, we don't need the money."

"Is it because we're girls?" Maeve asked.

"What the he—heck kind of question is that?"

"Maybe if we were boys," Rianna said, "you'd like us more."

Rance was poleaxed. He stopped the horse,

because even though he'd ridden even before he could walk, he wasn't sure he could stay in the saddle and talk, both at the same time.

"What?" he rasped.

Maeve stiffened her spine, McKettrick style. "We can do anything a boy can do."

"Except pee standing up," Rianna put in.

Maeve rolled her eyes. "Like *that's* important," she said.

"Hold it," Rance cut in. "I wouldn't trade either one of you for a *boatload* of boys. And I don't just like you, I *love* you."

When had he last told them that?

They'd said it to him, a thousand times.

He was thunderstruck by the realization that he'd invariably replied, *Me, too,* or, *Back at you, kiddo.*

"You do?" Rianna asked.

"Really?" Maeve asked.

"Of *course* I do."

"You're always gone," Maeve reasoned.

"To Taiwan or someplace faraway like that," Rianna added.

"Hey," Rance said. "Listen up, both of you. I'm your *father.* And whether I'm here on the Triple M or in Timbuktu, nobody matters more to me than you two. *Nobody.*"

Rianna believed first. Maeve was a slightly harder sell.

"Until some big deal comes up," she said. "Then it's see you later, alligator."

The horses were impatient, wanted to keep moving. Rance held the gelding's reins in one hand and leaned to catch hold of Snowball's bridle with the other. "There might be times when I have to go away," he told Maeve quietly. "Things happen that have to be handled—you're old enough to understand that. I'll admit I had a little trouble breaking the McKettrickCo habit, but from now on, I'm going to be a rancher. And a father. You have my word on that."

"How can you break the habit of being a McKettrick?" Rianna wondered aloud.

Rance laughed.

So did Maeve.

Finally, probably because she was a good sport, not because she understood what was funny, Rianna joined in.

"You can't quit being a McKettrick, silly," Maeve informed her sister, as they turned, by tacit agreement, to ride back to the barn. "Even when you get married, you'll still be one."

"I'm never getting married," Rianna announced, with the certainty of a seven-year-old. "I want to be like Echo when I grow up. I'm going to have a pink car and a white dog and sell pop-up books with horses in them."

Rance's throat felt raw. All too soon, he knew, his daughters would grow up. They'd be women, not little girls, picking out wedding dresses and leaving on honeymoons. Yes, they'd still be McKettricks.

But, like Jesse's older sisters and Meg, they'd leave the Triple M. It would be a place they visited once in a while, when their busy schedules allowed.

They'd have husbands, and kids of their own. Careers, too, probably.

And even though all that was natural and good and right, a bleak feeling settled over Rance.

Time was precious, and it slipped away faster than greased rope with a spooked cow at the other end. He'd acted as though Maeve and Rianna would always be little—next week, next month, he'd spend more time with them. But never now, when they were small, and still coping with the fact that they didn't have a mother.

Back at the barn, the girls got underfoot while Rance put the horses away, but he didn't mind. They were there. They were seven and ten. And he was still the most important man in their lives.

When the work was done, they went inside, switched on all the lights and ate cold cereal for supper, laughing because they knew Cora would have a fit if she found out.

The night was good, and only one thing could have made it better.

Having Echo there, too.

CHAPTER 16

THE NEXT MORNING, RANCE watched in silence, and from a slight distance, as his daughters stood solemnly at the foot of their mother's grave. They had gathered wildflowers, outside the iron gate of the private cemetery, dandelions and bluebells and little pink things he couldn't identify, and laid them beneath Julie's headstone.

He'd brought no such offering himself. Nothing could have matched those colorful weeds, clenched in sweaty little palms, and released with the kind of unself-conscious love only a child can manage.

Within a few minutes, there was a shift. Children know little of death; they are too alive for that.

Maeve and Rianna scampered away to play among the statues and less spectacular markers of other McKettricks, long gone.

Rance stood alone. The wad of paper, folded and stuffed into his shirt pocket, burned right through fabric to flesh, and beyond flesh to the heart of his pride.

During the night, when the girls were enjoying the untroubled sleep of the profoundly innocent, he'd finally bitten the bullet, gone to Julie's computer, and opened the file he'd known was there. Maybe she'd wanted him to find it, one day— or maybe she'd thought she had all the time in the world to delete it.

It didn't matter now.

He touched the pocket. "I'm sorry, Julie," he said in a raspy whisper.

A fierce ache swelled behind his eyes, jammed up his throat.

He heard Cora's truck rattling up the winding dirt road. Saw her get out of it and come toward him, but he couldn't speak. Couldn't acknowledge her presence in any way.

Reaching his side, she touched his arm.

"It's all right, Rance," she said gently.

He shook his head.

Cora bent to lay a supermarket bouquet next to Maeve and Rianna's wildflowers. When she straightened again, he felt her gaze burning like an August sun against his face.

"Rianna called and told me you were coming up here this morning," she said to him. "She also mentioned that you were on the computer all night, in Julie's office. I may be all wet here, but my guess is, you finally read those e-mails."

Rance could only nod.

"She didn't love him, Rance," Cora went on. "She was trying to get your attention. That's why she didn't delete the files."

At last, Rance found his voice, but it was ragged, and he wouldn't have recognized it if it hadn't come from his own mouth. "I know," he said. And he *did* know, but his eyes burned, just the same. "I guess I've got nobody to blame but myself."

Cora's eyes flashed. "What Julie did was flat wrong, and I told her so at the time. She never betrayed you physically, Rance, and I hope you never betrayed her. But she had no business visiting those chat rooms in the first place, let alone striking up an intimate friendship with a stranger. Julie's not here to ask your forgiveness, so I'm asking for her. You've got to erase those files, Rance, so your daughters never see them."

"Already done," Rance said. He took the crumpled printouts from his pocket, handed them to Cora. She took them with a shaky hand and stuffed them into her purse. "She threw it up to me a couple of times, Cora," he went on, after a decent interval. "She *wanted* me to read what she'd written to that guy, and what he'd written to her. And until last night, I couldn't do it."

Cora rested a hand on his back. "You do understand, don't you, that Julie was really writing to
you, not that man in California?"

He nodded. "That's the hardest thing of all," he
said. "Knowing it was my fault. She tried to tell me,
so many times, how she felt. I thought she ought to
be content with two amazing children, a big house,
and all the money she cared to spend. I didn't *listen*
to her, Cora."

"He wanted to meet her. She said no. Do you
know why, Rance?"

He waited.

"Because she loved you. Not him. *You.*"

He managed another nod.

"Let this all go," Cora pleaded softly. "Let it be
over, Rance. For your own sake, and for the girls'.
I don't know what's developing between you and
Echo—I have my hopes, but it's not my call. All I'm
asking is that you set aside that damn pride of yours
long enough to give it a chance."

"You're an amazing woman, Cora," he told her.
For the first time since she'd arrived, he was able to
look her straight in the eye.

Maeve and Rianna's voices rang on the soft
breeze of the morning, and the sound made him
smile, albeit sadly.

Cora grinned, though there were tears standing
in her eyes. "Sometimes I even amaze myself," she
said. "I've got a date for the Summer Dance.
Imagine that! An old fogey like me."

Rance slipped an arm around Cora's waist, held her close for a moment. "Half the widowers in town lust after you," he teased. "Didn't you know that?"

Cora sighed. There was a new peace about her, as though she'd taken her own advice and let go of something. Laid down some heavy burden, never to pick it up again. "For a long time," she said, "I hated myself for outliving Julie. It just didn't seem right."

"I imagine my folks could identify. Neither one of them ever got over losing Cassidy. I'm pretty sure that's what broke up their marriage."

"Isn't it peculiar," Cora mused, after a nod of agreement, "that the things that ought to bind a man and woman at the heart can drive them apart instead?"

Before Rance had to frame an answer to that one, Maeve and Rianna rushed up, whooping with delight and enfolding their grandmother in little-girl hugs.

"Mind if I take these yahoos to Flagstaff with me for the day?" Cora asked Rance. "I'm shopping for a new dress to wear to the dance, and I could use the moral support."

"Can we go to the dance, too?" Rianna immediately asked.

"Can we get new dresses?" Maeve asked, the words tumbling right over the top of her sister's.

Rance looked down into the eager, upturned faces of his daughters. "You can go to Flagstaff. You can have new dresses if you want them. But I'm not too sure about the rest. You'll be running off to dances soon enough, to my way of thinking."

"Every kid in town will be there, Rance," Cora said, but softly.

Three beautiful women, one man. Rance knew the odds were against him, so he relented. "Okay," he said reluctantly.

Maeve and Rianna jumped up and down, whooping like Apaches around a campfire.

Cora smiled and herded them toward the truck, parked just outside the cemetery gates, next to his rig. He watched them till they were out of sight, and when they were gone, he tipped his hat to Julie, turned and walked away.

He'd said what he had to say to his late wife, and now he could leave her to rest in peace.

Carrying his hat in one hand, he approached Cassidy's grave.

It was a day for setting aside his pride, and saying what was in his heart instead.

THE WOMAN, dRESSED IN OLD jeans and a faded T-shirt, slipped furtively into the shop, as though she expected to be thrown out at any moment. Her hair was a nondescript brown, worn in a style at least a decade out of date, and a tiny rose tattoo marked her right forearm. Her skin was muddy, her eyes at once defiant and resigned.

Echo knew instantly who she was.

She could only guess at what she wanted.

Snowball whimpered and low-crawled behind the counter to hunker down.

"Hello, Mrs. Willand," Echo said, grateful there was no one else in the store and, at the same time, wishing Ayanna would appear. Although the day had started out sunny, there were already dark clouds rolling in from the west, and Echo couldn't help drawing certain parallels.

"Della," the woman answered, pausing just inside the door. "My name is Della."

"Echo Wells," Echo replied, stepping over Snowball to come out from behind the counter and extend her hand.

Della hesitated, then took Echo's hand briefly in her own. "I guess you know I'm here about Bud," she said.

Echo *hadn't* known that, not for sure, anyway, but she didn't say anything. She just waited.

"He done a stupid thing," Della said, blushing a little. "Coming here like he did. Breaking in. Once Bud gets an idea in his head, seems like it takes a stick of dynamite to blast it out again."

"What do you want me to do, Mrs. Willand?"

"Della."

Echo suppressed a sigh, along with a badly timed desire to recommend an exfoliant. "Della, then," she said.

"I come to ask you to drop the charges against Bud."

"He broke into my store. My *home*."

Della Willand might have been a con artist, but the pain in her eyes was real. "Bud's been out of work awhile," she said. "It did something to his brain. Last night, he got a call from his foreman, Bob Walker. He can start a new job Monday morning if he gets out." She pried a scrap of paper from the hip pocket of her tight jeans, shoved it at Echo. "Here's Bob's number. He'll tell you it's true."

Echo looked at the name and number scrawled on the corner of an old envelope. "How do I know this isn't one of your friends, just pretending to be a foreman?" she asked.

Della shrugged wearily. "I guess you don't. Bud's never been in trouble before, Miss Wells, and that's something you can check up on easily enough. Anyhow, it's partly my doing—that he was so all-fired determined to get that dog back, I mean. We bred her to our friend Clovis's dog, and we had most of the pups already sold. We had some fancy plans for the money."

Echo considered. On the one hand, she was no great judge of character—she'd trusted Justin, and several other people she shouldn't have. On the other, some part of her truly believed Della Willand and wanted to offer a second chance.

"I'll need to think about this," she finally said. "I'm not sure it's in my power to get the charges dropped, even if I decide that's what I want to do."

Della started to say something, stopped herself and swallowed visibly. Then she nodded. "Thanks," she said at last. "I'm really sorry for what Bud done."

With that, Della left the shop, and Echo trailed her as far as the front door, where she stood watching as the other woman got into a battered compact and drove away.

Thoughtfully, Echo tapped her chin with the tip of one index finger.

Then she went back to the counter, got out the phone book and looked up the nonemergency number for the local police.

Wyatt Terp answered.

Echo gave her name and told him about Della Willand's visit.

Wyatt was quiet for a long time. "I've already run some checks on Bud," he said. "He's a loser, all right. But as far as I can tell, he's never been in trouble with the law."

"If I were to drop the charges against him, would they let him go?"

"That's up to the prosecutor. What Willand did was pretty serious, any way you look at it, and we don't have any real assurance that he won't come after you again."

Echo looked down at the phone number Della had given her. "He's got a chance for a job, according to his wife. She gave me a number."

"I'll run it down, if you'd like. Speak to somebody at the prosecutor's office, too. It might take a while, though."

Echo sighed gratefully. "I'd appreciate it. I just have a feeling—"

The shop bell tinkled above the door and Ayanna came in.

"I don't know as anything can be done," Wyatt said. "I'll see what I can find out, though, and get back to you as soon as I can."

Echo thanked him, said goodbye and hung up.

"It's the darnedest thing," Ayanna said, bright-eyed and breathless. Tiny diamonds of rain twinkled in her dark hair, with its lovely streaks of silver. "I ran into Virgil Terp at the gas station this morning, and he asked me to the Summer Dance."

Echo had never met Virgil, but she knew, via Cora, that he was brother to Morgan and Wyatt, whom she'd just been talking to. "Did you say yes?" she asked, smiling at Ayanna's flushed cheeks.

"Sure I did," Ayanna answered. "I like Virgil. He's pretty shy, but he's nice enough."

Echo smiled again. "You wouldn't happen to know of a house for rent, would you?"

"Not right off the top of my head," Ayanna said, looking intrigued. "Why?"

"I think I'd like a little more room," Echo replied. "A yard, too. So I can raise flowers."

"Cora'd be the one to ask," Ayanna told her. "She knows everybody in Indian Rock. Or you could call Elaine, over at the real estate office."

Echo nodded.

"It's nice to know you plan on staying here, Echo," Ayanna said. She came around to put her purse in its usual place, under the counter. A mischievous look came into her eyes. "Does it have anything to do with Rance McKettrick?"

"Everything and nothing," Echo said.

Ayanna chuckled. "I know what you mean," she answered. "Speaking of houses, I see somebody's moving into the old Lindsay place."

Echo frowned, not recognizing the name.

"It's that old three-story pile of brick on the corner of Maple and Red River Drive. The only genuine mansion in Indian Rock."

"I'm surprised it doesn't belong to a McKettrick," Echo said, and then could have bitten off her tongue because Ayanna's daughter, Cheyenne, was about to *become* a McKettrick. "I didn't mean to sound flip," she added hastily.

Ayanna chuckled. "No offense taken. Actually, it did belong to them, once. Doss McKettrick, one of Holt's sons, built it for his bride, Hannah, back in the 1920s, because she had a hankering to live in town. Eventually, they moved back out to the ranch, though. Sierra and Meg's place was theirs, back then. Sold the mansion to a banker for a chunk of change."

Echo shook her head. "I envy them all that history. The McKettricks, I mean."

Ayanna eyed her curiously. "Don't you have a history, Echo?"

The question took Echo aback. With one fingertip, she spelled out the letters of her real name on the countertop, where they left no trace at all. "Not like they do," she said.

"But the doll, and your Uncle Joe—"

"Hardly a legacy," Echo said without rancor.

"Then maybe it's time to *start* one. So things will be different for the ones who come after you."

Echo wasn't entirely sure anyone *would* come after her. She'd be thirty on Saturday, with no prospect of marriage on the radar. Sure, there was something going on with Rance, but she was afraid to trust it—or him. It would simply hurt too much to fall in love and then fall out again.

No, she intended to live the best life she could. She wanted a house, a yard full of flowers, a dog or two. For the moment, she didn't dare plan beyond those things.

"Echo?" Ayanna prompted when she didn't say anything.

A tour bus rolled up outside.

"Showtime," Echo said, with a forced smile.

MAEVE NEVER INTENDED TO read the papers. It was just that Granny sent her back to the truck for her purse when they got home from Flagstaff late that dark and windy afternoon, and everything had tumbled out of the bag, onto the floor.

She was stuffing things inside when she accidentally turned back the corner of what looked like a thick, folded letter, and saw her mom's name.

After that, even though she knew better, knew it was wrong, reading private things other people had written, she couldn't help looking.

She didn't read it all, and she didn't understand a lot of what she *did* read. But it was clear enough, from the beginning, that these were e-mails. There were love words in them, too—and her mom had been writing to some guy named Steve, not her dad.

Not her dad.

Carefully, Maeve refolded the pages and tucked them into Granny's purse. Her hands trembled and her skin felt clammy. She got that taste in her mouth, like she was going to throw up.

She desperately wanted to tell somebody what she'd discovered, so they could say it didn't mean what she thought it did, or it happened before her mom and dad were married. But who could she tell?

Granny?

No. Granny already knew, if the e-mails were in her purse. Of course she hadn't said anything, because Maeve was a kid, and grown-ups didn't tell kids stuff like this.

Her dad?

Double no. He might hate her mom forever, if he found out. And, besides, she knew her parents had gone steady practically since they were little kids. There was no time when it would have been all right for her mom to say things like that to another man.

Maeve closed her eyes and drew a couple of deep breaths, trying to get her balance. She had to be McKettrick tough. The only problem with that was, being tough was harder when you were only ten, whether you were a McKettrick or not.

"Maeve!" Rianna yelled from Granny's front porch. "Hurry up! We're going to put on our new dresses and have a fashion show—you and me and Granny!"

"Coming," Maeve called back, after swallowing some burny stuff that rose into the back of her throat.

Uncle Jesse. That was it, Maeve decided, wildly relieved—she could tell Uncle Jesse. He'd probably say it was all a mistake. He'd say her mom and dad loved each other, and those e-mails belonged to somebody else, some other Julie.

Gathering Granny's purse tight in both arms, she turned and headed back up the walk, big drops of rain splatting down on her like tears.

RANCE WOULD HAVE LIKED to stop by the bookshop, just to spend a few minutes looking at Echo, but by the time he got to town, there was a storm gathering. He had to pick up the girls, then get back out to the ranch, because cattle tended to spook when there was weather, and he'd already heard a few long, low rolls of thunder, between brief downpours.

He used his cell phone to call Jesse, then Keegan.

The way things were shaping up, he was going to need help.

Warm rain hammered the ground as Maeve and Rianna rushed out to jump into the truck, Rianna giggling, Maeve looking unusually somber.

"We had a fashion show," Rianna told him, once she'd bounded up into the seat.

Maeve didn't speak. She just climbed in, clutching a shopping bag and fastened her sister and then herself into the seat belts.

The air smelled of wet dust.

"You okay, Maeve?" Rance asked, concerned.

She gave him a determined smile. "I'm okay," she said.

"I'm going to have to herd cattle when we get back to the ranch," he told his daughters. "You girls want to stay here with your granny?"

"We're old enough to be alone in the house, Dad," Maeve said.

Rianna could barely contain her excitement. She kicked her little sandaled feet and smoothed her rain-dampened hair. "Maybe we can have another *fashion show!*"

"Like I want to put on this stupid dress again," Maeve said, with a sniff. She turned her head away then and stared out the window as if she'd never seen Indian Rock before.

"You didn't think it was stupid when we bought it," Rianna pointed out.

"Well, I think it's stupid now," Maeve countered, without turning around.

Rance put the truck in gear and laid rubber.

He was a rancher now. He had to keep those cattle as calm as he could.

He covered the miles between town and the

Triple M as fast as he dared with his children in the truck. When he got to the ranch, Jesse was already there, saddling up out in front of the barn.

"Go inside and stay there," Rance said to Maeve and Rianna.

Maeve gave Jesse an odd look when she got out of the rig, and even took a step toward him. Then, because it was raining harder than it had been in town, she grabbed Rianna's hand and the two of them raced for the house, leaving the shopping bag behind.

"Keeg's on his way," Jesse said with a grin. "This ought to be fun. Just like the old days, when the Triple M was a real cattle ranch."

"Fun?" Rance mocked, irritated. He was worried about Maeve, but the cattle were already restless, bawling and churning in a mass of confusion out there in the pasture. One good clap of thunder, and they'd probably trample one another or stampede through one of the fence lines. "We'll be lucky if none of us gets struck by lightning!"

"I'm always lucky," Jesse told him, with an easy grin. Then he swung up into the saddle and tugged at the brim of his hat.

Rance hurried inside the barn to saddle the gelding, and one of the other horses for Keegan. Snowball was itching to go, but she wasn't up to a job like this one.

When he rode out of the barn, Keegan was just driving up. He'd stopped at his place, evidently, to exchange his customary suit for jeans, a work shirt and boots. They'd all be wet through next time the clouds opened, but Rance didn't give a damn.

By then, he was thinking about one thing, and one thing only—keeping two hundred head of cattle from killing themselves.

Jesse leaned to open the gate, gave a whoop and rode for the herd.

Rance and Keegan followed.

It felt good, all of them being together on horseback like that, but for Rance the sentiment was short-lived. The thunder was deafening, and a streak of lightning snaked down out of the sky and came within sizzling distance of Jesse.

His horse reared, and Jesse let out another yeehaw and grinned like an idiot.

They made a good team, and they were containing the cattle, when Keegan suddenly gave a shrill whistle and pointed toward the house. Maeve was over the fence and bounding straight toward them, like the devil himself was on her tail.

At least twenty head of cattle turned in her direction, barely slowed by the wet, slippery ground.

Both Rance and Keegan rode hard to reach her, but Jesse got there first, moving like fire along a ground fuse. He leaned down, grabbed her by one arm and hauled her up into the saddle seconds before the cattle would have trampled her to death.

He sat like a statue, Jesse did, controlling his horse with one arm and holding Maeve with the other, while those beeves cascaded around him. Ran on past.

Rance scanned the fence line, to make sure Rianna hadn't followed, then heeled his horse up alongside Jesse's.

Maeve scrambled into his arms and clung.

Rance closed his eyes, holding her as tightly as he dared.

She buried her head in his neck, sobbing.

He stroked her back. Waited. Later, he'd give her what-for for pulling a damn fool stunt like that, but for the moment, he was just glad she was alive.

"Rianna!" she finally cried. "I told her about the e-mails—I had to tell somebody. And then I went to my room and cried for a while, and when I g-got back, she was gone—and I couldn't find her s-stupid pink car—"

Rance's heart, just now beginning to beat again, seized up once more. He turned to Jesse and Keegan—they'd been close enough to hear, but with the cattle bawling and thunder shaking the ground, he couldn't be sure.

"Rianna's taken off in that toy car of hers!" he shouted.

"Damn," Jesse said grimly.

"Let's go find her," Keegan added.

Rance nodded. They rode back to the yard, where Rance let Maeve down off the horse with strict orders to go in the house and stay there. The cattle would have to fend for themselves; he had one little girl lost, and he wasn't about to put the other at risk.

"It's my fault!" Maeve wailed.

"Go in the house!" Rance yelled.

She turned and dashed through the rain, disappearing into a sheet of gray.

ECHO DROVE SLOWLY ALONG the road to the Triple M, squinting through the windshield. Snowball panted in the passenger seat next to her, fogging up the windows, giving a little anxious yelp every once in a while.

Echo'd gotten a frantic call from Maeve, twenty minutes before. Sobbing, the little girl had babbled something about e-mails, and said she thought Rianna might be on her way to town, alone. When Echo had asked where Rance was, Maeve had said he was herding cattle, with Jesse and Keegan.

Terrified, Echo had left the shop in Ayanna's care, loaded Snowball, who insisted on going along, into the Volkswagen, and started for the ranch.

Maeve thought Rianna was driving her Barbie car. If so, she couldn't have gotten very far—could she?

And what was Rance thinking, leaving his daughters alone in that big house while he played cowboy?

Suddenly, Snowball gave a loud woof, then turned backward in the seat and tried to claw her way over it.

Echo brought the car to a stop at the side of the road.

The dog pawed at the passenger door and yelped frantically, frenzied.

Praying there were no cars coming the other way,

Echo leaned across, unsnapped Snowball's seat belt and pushed open the door. The dog shot out into the rain, baying now.

Echo struggled to open her own seat belt, got out of the car and was immediately blinded by a curtain of rain. When she caught her breath, and wiped the water from her eyes, she saw Snowball running back in the direction they'd come, heedless of the storm.

Echo sped after her, slipping and sliding in the mud, barely able to see. The wet wind buffeted the breath from her lungs, more than once, and she was gasping by the time she found the little car, over-turned on the side of the road.

Fear surged through her. She looked all around her, but there was no sign of Rianna, or of Snowball. Then, from over the steep, grassy bank, she heard the dog howling.

Praying, half aloud and half under her breath, Echo kicked off her shoes and followed the sound, shouting, "Rianna! Snowball!" as she slithered and stumbled down over that bank.

The creek, the same one she and Rance had ridden beside on horseback that day, lay below, swollen and angry with rainwater and debris of all kinds.

"Rianna!" Echo shrieked.

She fell, got up, fell again.

Snowball yowled.

Forget the Universe, Echo thought. *Put me straight through to God.*

"Echo!" The voice was thin and small, and

very frightened. And it was Rianna's. "Echo, help me—"

Flailing blindly through brush and over logs, Echo reached the creek's edge. Rianna, having tumbled into the stream, clung to a bare tree root, and Snowball gripped the back of the child's T-shirt in her teeth, hind legs scrabbling for purchase as the furious water washed over the little girl's face.

Echo didn't think.

She didn't pray.

She just jumped right into that ice-cold creek and grabbed until she got a firm hold on Rianna. She dragged her up onto the bank, and the two of them were lying there, trembling with exhaustion, when Rance, Jesse and Keegan came down from the road, on foot, a blur of wet denim and muddy boots.

Both arms wrapped around Rianna, Echo wept with relief.

CHAPTER 17

RANCE TORE OFF HIS LINED denim jacket, soaked on the outside but relatively dry on the inside, and, dropping to one knee, bundled the garment around Rianna's small, shivering form. Her teeth chattered, and her lips were blue. She had a few visible cuts and scratches, but at least she was conscious.

Echo, lying on her side in the grass and stones and mud, rolled onto her back and stared up at the sky. Between the pounding rain and the roar of the storm-swollen creek, it was no use talking, but her gaze found Rance's and locked on.

"Are you hurt?" he mouthed.

She shook her head, raised herself onto her

elbows and promptly collapsed again. Rance yearned to gather her up, but he had Rianna.

Keegan crouched, lifted Echo into his arms and started up the bank toward the road. Jesse did the same with the dog, falling in behind Rance, still carrying Rianna, trying to will his own strength into his daughter.

Once they reached high ground, they stopped for a brief conference.

"It's too far to town, especially in this weather," Keegan yelled, over the rain. He opened the door of the pink car and set Echo gently in the passenger seat. Rance placed Rianna on her lap and buckled them in together, while Jesse maneuvered the sodden dog into the back, from the driver's side.

"You're going to be all right," Rance told Echo, Rianna and the dog, hoping to God it was true.

Echo nodded, holding Rianna close.

"We'll take care of the horses," Jesse said, catching hold of Rance's gelding's reins before getting back on his own. Keegan nodded and mounted up, too.

And Rance squeezed behind the wheel of the Volkswagen.

Echo stared out through the windshield, which was practically opaque with steam and rain. Rianna rested her head against Echo's chest and closed her eyes, then gave a slight, shuddering sigh.

Back at the ranch house, Rance parked as close

to the back door as he could, flipped the seat forward so the dog could get out, and rounded the car for Rianna.

"Sit right here till I come back for you," he told Echo.

Of course she didn't. She'd lost her shoes somewhere, and picked her way barefoot over the dirt, keeping pace with Rance as he sprinted for the kitchen door, where Maeve stood waiting, framed by the light behind her.

Once they were inside, Echo spoke for the first time since Rance had found her down there by the creek, clasping his daughter in her arms. "Get her out of those wet clothes," she said, with a nod to Rianna.

Rance nodded. "You'll be okay here for a few minutes?"

Echo returned his nod.

"I'll get you a bathrobe," Maeve told Echo.

"Thanks," Echo answered, dropping into a chair at the kitchen table. The dog slumped down at her feet, in a pool of water, and sighed.

Rance took Rianna upstairs, stripped her to the skin and wrapped her in a blanket.

"You hurt anywhere, honey?" he asked her. His voice sounded gruff.

Rianna started to cry. "No," she said. "I thought I was going to get drowneded, Daddy. Then Snowball came and she bit my shirt. Then Echo—"

Rance drew her close for a moment, held her

tightly. "You rest," he told her, silently thanking the good Lord for big favors. "I'm going downstairs to make sure Echo's okay and call the doctor."

Rianna lunged for his neck with both arms. "Take me with you, Daddy," she pleaded.

He blinked his eyes dry and lifted her off the bed. "No problem, short stop," he said.

When the two of them reached the kitchen, Jesse and Keegan were there. Jesse crouched in front of Echo's chair, chafing her hands between his, while Keegan built a fire in the old wood stove they used on winter mornings, more for atmosphere than heat. A fresh pot of coffee chugged away on the countertop.

Maeve watched the whole scene from a little distance, as though longing to be part of it and, at the same time, afraid of being swept away in some invisible current.

Rance squeezed her shoulder lightly as he passed, then set Rianna in the antique rocking chair over by the stove.

Echo, swathed in one of his old bathrobes, looked up at him.

"I called the clinic," Jesse told Rance, rising and stepping back. "Doc says it's better to stay put, if everybody's breathing and nobody's bleeding. He'll get here was soon as he can."

Keegan turned from the stove, bent to ruffle Rianna's hair and straightened. "Jesse, we ought to go out and see to those cattle," he said.

Jesse nodded, and in the next moment, they were gone again.

"I never thought I'd drive a pink car," Rance said, just to get the conversation started.

Echo smiled, then a laugh bubbled from her throat. "I won't tell anybody if you don't," she said.

He grinned, paused to cup the curve of her cheek in one hand. He'd hardly known this woman any time at all, but she'd changed everything. When he'd seen her on that creek bank, wet and bedraggled because, with the help of her dog, she'd just saved his daughter's life, a lot of rusted cogs and gears had suddenly ground into motion.

"What's your name?" he asked.

She beckoned, and he leaned down to listen. Whispered the name she'd kept from him up to then.

He grinned.

"I like it," he said.

"Tell us!" Rianna pleaded from the rocking chair. The fire in the stove was snapping behind its murky glass door, brightening the room.

Echo put a finger to her lips and smiled.

"Not yet," Rance told his daughter.

He poured coffee for Echo, when the pot stopped perking, and started a batch of hot chocolate for Maeve and Rianna.

Rianna accepted her cup eagerly, and slurped, but Maeve, busy towel-drying the dog, shook her head when he brought her the mug and wouldn't look at him.

He put the cup on the table and dropped to his haunches beside her. "Maeve," he said. "Talk to me."

"It's my fault that Rianna and Echo and Snowball almost drowned in the creek," she told him, still averting her eyes.

He caught her chin in one hand, made her look at him.

Rianna got out of her rocking chair, trundled over and climbed into Echo's lap, wanting to be held.

"Mommy wrote love letters to another man," the child announced.

Echo caught Rance's eye, but she didn't say anything.

"Not letters, e-mails," Maeve corrected, a stickler for facts even in her current state of almost unbearable guilt.

"I know about the e-mails," Rance said. "It's not what you think."

Maeve's eyes widened with bruised hope. "I didn't mean to look at them," she said. "They fell out of Granny's purse—"

"It's okay," Rance told her. He hooked an arm around his daughter's neck and pulled her close so he could plant a kiss on top of her head.

"How can it be okay?" Maeve asked.

"It just is," Rance said, glancing at Echo again.

"Was my mommy bad, like one of those ladies on the soap operas?" Rianna inquired, and she looked really worried about the answer.

"No," Rance replied. "Your mommy wasn't bad. Just lonely sometimes."

"I wish I hadn't told Rianna," Maeve confided, as though Echo and Rianna had suddenly vanished and they had the room to themselves. "She's just a little kid."

"But you had to tell somebody, didn't you?" Rance asked gently.

Maeve bit her lower lip, nodded.

Rance got to his feet, went into the pantry and brought out a big can of chicken noodle soup. By the time he'd heated the stuff on the stove, and Rianna, Maeve, Echo and the dog had all had some, Doc arrived.

He examined Rianna, pronounced her fit, gave her a shot and ordered her to bed.

She was asleep before Rance left her bedroom.

Echo came under Doc's attention next, but she preferred to stay in the kitchen, in Rance's bathrobe, with her feet curled beneath her.

Maeve went upstairs to look in on her sister.

Doc, meanwhile, checked out the dog. "Looks like we've got a third patient here," he said, feeling Snowball's belly.

Echo instantly tensed. "Is she hurt?"

"No," Doc answered. "She's fixing to spring a few puppies on us, though." The older man looked up at Rance. "You got an old blanket around here?"

Rance went upstairs and plundered the linen closets until he found one.

Maeve followed him back down.

The first pup was born five minutes later. A second followed, then a third. There were four by the time Doc said the whole thing was over.

Rance, feeling as though he'd just witnessed the birth of quadruplets, sank onto the bench lining one side of the kitchen table.

Echo had been kneeling on the floor the entire time, across from Doc, stroking Snowball and whispering words of encouragement. Her eyes shone with tears when she looked up at Rance.

"Aren't they beautiful?" she asked.

Rance could hardly bear the naked emotion in her face. She was going to have to give this dog up one day soon, and all the puppies with it. She grieved, and yet she seemed suffused with joy.

"Shouldn't there be more than four?" Maeve asked, frowning. "I thought dogs always had big litters."

"Not necessarily," Doc said. Rising, with a creak of old bones, he went to the sink and scrubbed his hands.

Snowball licked her babies and gave Echo a grateful glance as she helped them nestle against the dog's belly.

Rance almost had to turn away, because it was a powerful thing to see.

"Best I get back to the clinic," Doc told them, reaching for his bag. "On the other hand, on a day like this, only the hypochondriacs make it in."

"The roads are pretty bad," Rance said, and though he was talking to the doctor, he was looking at Echo. "Maybe you ought to stay the night."

Doc shook his head. "Can't do it," he said. "If I were you, Rance, I'd call Cora. She hears about this through the grapevine, there'll be hell to pay."

Grimly, Rance nodded.

He saw Doc out to his car, then came back inside and made the call to Cora. He had to talk fast to keep her from jumping into her truck and wheeling it on out there, and by the time he hung up, Echo was back in the rocking chair and Maeve was sound asleep in her lap.

Gently, Rance lifted Maeve into his arms, carried her upstairs and tucked her into bed.

She opened her eyes once, while he was still standing over her, yawned and said, "I'm sorry, Dad."

He bent, kissed her forehead. "I love you, little girl."

She hugged his neck for a long moment. Then she went back to sleep.

ECHO WATCHED AS THE puppies nursed and Snowball snoozed.

Rance came back, refilled Echo's coffee cup, this time adding a dollop of Southern Comfort, and drew the chair from the end of the table over next to hers.

"Thanks," he said.

"All in a day's work," Echo joked.

"I should never have bought Rianna that damn pink car," Rance mused.

Echo reached over, took his hand. Squeezed.

"How did you happen to be traveling that road just when my daughter needed your help?"

She knew she ought to let go of his hand, but she couldn't quite do it. Their fingers interlaced. "Maeve called me at the shop," she said.

He kissed the backs of her knuckles. Closed his eyes for a moment.

"Don't, Rance," Echo whispered. "Don't imagine what would have happened if we hadn't found her in time."

He stared at her, clearly confounded.

She grinned. "I'm psychic," she teased. She wasn't psychic, but she was a woman, and that was enough.

He pulled her out of the chair and onto his lap. She snuggled up against him, just the way the girls had done earlier, when she held them.

"I suppose it's too soon to ask you to move in here with us," he said, after a very long time.

Echo's heart fluttered, and she tugged at his collar. Kissed the cleft in his strong McKettrick chin. "Way too soon," she said.

"I love you," he told her.

She sat bolt upright, stunned.

"I know, I know," Rance said, before she could get a word out. "It's too soon for that, too. But I'm in love with you, just the same."

"Rance," she said reasonably, "you're just overwrought. So much has happened and—"

He laid a finger against her lips. "No," he said. "It isn't what happened down there by the creek, or the puppies being born, or any of that. *I love you*, woman."

Echo's heart picked up speed, hammered at the base of her throat. "Are you trying to seduce me?" she asked.

He grinned, and the flash rivaled the lightning bolts still ripping the dark sky over their heads. "I wasn't, but that's not such a bad idea, either."

"Rance McKettrick, your *children* are in this house."

"They're asleep. Zonked. Out like lights."

"Still," Echo said, ashamed of how much she wanted to lie in Rance's bed while the storm raged, and give herself up to his lovemaking.

He put his hands on either side of her face. "Do you love me?" he asked.

She swallowed hard. "Of course I do," she said.

"You do?"

"Yes."

"When did you know?"

"When I saw you coming down over that bank a little while ago. I thought to myself, 'Everything's going to be all right now, because Rance is here.'"

He smiled, shifted beneath her, gave her a nibbling kiss on the mouth. "If you're planning to hold out until we're married," he told her, "it's going to seem like a really lo-o-ong engagement."

Her eyes widened. "Married?"

"When I love a woman," Rance said, still grinning, "I like to marry her."

"Just how many women have you loved?"

"Two."

"You want to get married—now?"

"Well, that depends on whether or not you're willing to sleep with me in the meantime."

She punched him in the chest, but not very hard. That was when she realized that he was still wearing wet clothes. He'd been so busy looking after Maeve, Rianna and her—not to mention Snowball—that he hadn't gotten around to changing.

"You're going to catch your death," she said.

"I guess I *could* use a hot shower." He paused, wriggled his eyebrows. "In the bathroom by the pool. Long way from the girls' rooms. Long, *long* way."

"Are you suggesting…?"

"That you join me? Yeah. That's what I'm suggesting. Among other things."

Echo squirmed. Except for a breath of air, when she'd been struggling to get hold of Rianna in the creek and the water kept splashing her face, she'd never wanted anything so much as she wanted to get into a shower with Rance.

He slipped a hand inside the bathrobe, cupped her breast. Chafed the nipple with the side of his thumb.

"Jesse and Keegan will probably be back any minute," Echo fretted, with a little shiver.

"They'll figure it out."

"That's what I'm afraid of," Echo said.

Rance laughed. And then he stood, lifting Echo with him as he rose.

Ten minutes later, making love with Rance under a blessedly hot spray of water, Echo stepped into her real name.

Stepped into her real self.

And it was a strange and wonderful place to be.

SATURDAY MORNING, ECHO awakened to the mewling of puppies.

Smiling, she got up, stretched and bent over the airbed to watch as Snowball nursed her babies.

"I'm thirty," she told the dogs.

Snowball eyed her with the usual adoration.

Echo patted the dog's head, caressed each of the puppies in turn and went to the sink to wash her hands and get the morning coffee started. She stood at the front window while she waited for it to brew.

The streets were quiet, and as Echo looked out over the town, she speculated that everybody must be sleeping in that day, resting up for tonight's dance.

The telephone rang, and she hurried to answer it. If it was a last-minute order for a love-spell, she'd provide one, but it would be a gift. She'd already closed down the Web site, and when the last of her supplies were gone, that was it.

She was out of the spell-casting business. It seemed there was magic under way in Indian Rock, but she didn't want to be responsible for so many hearts. She had enough trouble managing her own.

"Echo's Books and Gifts," she said, even though she was upstairs and still in her pajamas. It was just easier that way. "May I help you?"

Rance's low chuckle rumbled in her ear. "I hope so," he said. "It's been a couple of days."

She blushed and laughed at the same time. After she and Rance had made love in the shower, they'd gone to bed and made love again.

In the morning, they'd tried to pretend it was normal for Echo to be in the ranch kitchen making pancakes and still clad in Rance's bathrobe, and while Rianna had seemed to buy the story, Maeve was thoughtful.

Rance and Echo had agreed to give the dust a few days to settle.

"Still in love with me?" Rance asked now.

"Ridiculously," Echo answered. "How about you?"

"Ready to buy a ring and round up a preacher," Rance said. "I'm taking you to breakfast, so get dressed. Maeve and Rianna are going to Cora's to spend the whole day getting ready for the dance."

"I'm supposed to open the shop in less than—"

"It can wait," Rance said. "Can't it?"

She smiled. "I guess so."

"Good."

They said their goodbyes, and Echo hurried to shower and get dressed. After fortifying herself with fresh coffee, she went downstairs to see if there were any customers waiting on the sidewalk.

Ayanna was just letting herself in.

"I'm going out to breakfast with Rance," Echo said. "Can you hold down the fort for an hour or so?"

Ayanna smiled. "Sure," she replied. "How's the new mama?"

Snowball and her puppies had made the front page of the Indian Rock *Gazette* a few days before, with a full account of Rianna's rescue in the article beneath, and they'd been holding court ever since. Echo usually moved the airbed downstairs every morning, then carefully carried the puppies down, too, one by one. Snowball, of course, followed. Today, they'd been resting so comfortably that she hadn't wanted to disturb them.

"She's bouncing back," Echo said.

"How about you?" Ayanna asked. "Are *you* bouncing back?" She was referring, of course, to Echo's plunge into the water to get Rianna.

"Couldn't be better," she said, but before the words were out of her mouth, a giant RV pulled up in front of the shop.

She knew, even before the door opened on the passenger side and an older, balding man climbed down, that the Ademoyes had finally arrived to reclaim their lost dog.

Tears sprang to Echo's eyes.

"Echo?" Ayanna said, giving her a concerned look before glancing back to see the RV.

The man hurried toward the front door of the shop, beaming with anticipation. Echo stood rooted to the floor, wondering how a person could be happy at the same time as their heart was breaking.

Herb was on the threshold when Marge appeared, a plump, middle-aged woman in pastel pedal-pushers, espadrilles and a ruffled blouse. Her smile was even broader than Herb's.

"Is she here?" Marge asked breathlessly when they were both inside.

Upstairs, Snowball gave an uncertain woof.

"Snowball!" Herb whooped.

The dog barked joyously and shot down the stairs and across the shop.

Herb and Marge, on their knees a few feet inside the open door, enfolded Snowball in their arms, while she wriggled and lapped at their faces, making a soft, happy whining sound.

Behind them, Rance stepped in. His gaze went straight to Echo's face.

She nodded, because she couldn't speak. She surely looked like a crazy woman, she thought, smiling while tears wet her cheeks.

"You must be Echo," Herb said, when he'd recovered enough to notice her. Marge was still on the floor, her face buried in Snowball's neck, weeping with relief.

Echo nodded, swallowed. Put out her hand.

"We can't thank you enough," Herb told her.

"It was a pleasure," Echo said, and she meant it.

Snowball had come along when Echo needed a friend, and they'd made a journey together that had little to do with the miles they'd covered getting from Tucson to Indian Rock. As reluctant as she was to part with the dog, she knew the time had come, and that it was right.

Rance cleared his throat. "Did you tell them about the puppies?"

Marge, swabbing at her face with a handkerchief, brightened.

Herb's smile widened.

"Puppies?" the two of them chorused.

"Four of them," Echo confirmed. "All healthy and beautiful."

Snowball, as if on cue, started for the stairs. Paused and looked back at Marge and Herb.

"It's all right," Echo told them. "Go ahead. Snowball wants to show you her babies."

Herb and Marge followed Snowball upstairs.

"I wish I'd made the bed," Echo lamented.

Rance crossed the room, took her in his arms and propped his chin on top of her head.

"I think I'll go out and buy a newspaper," Ayanna announced, even though one had already been delivered, and vanished.

"You okay?" Rance asked Echo.

"Yes," she said, burying her face in his shoulder. "And no."

Presently, the Ademoyes came back down from

upstairs, into the shop, each carrying two tiny white puppies. Snowball was at their heels.

"You'll need the airbed," Echo said. "Snowball loves the airbed."

Tears filled Marge's eyes. "I'd give you one of these puppies," she said, "but they're too little to be away from Snowball."

Rance went upstairs to get the airbed.

"I know," Echo said, stroking one warm little ball of fur, then another.

"We'll come through next spring," Herb said, his voice hoarse all of the sudden. "We'll bring you a pup then, if you want one."

"I want one," Echo replied.

Snowball went to the door, turned and came back. Looked up at Echo with what she would have sworn was a smile.

Echo sat on her heels, ran her hands lightly over Snowball's ears. "Goodbye, sweet dog," she said. "Thank you for everything."

Snowball licked her face, gave a yearning little whimper.

"You have to go now, huh?"

Snowball whimpered again. Went back to the door. Echo stood.

Rance returned with the airbed, went outside with Herb to put it in the back of the RV. Snowball followed eagerly and didn't once look back.

Marge lingered, still cradling two of the puppies in her arms. "I know it's hard," she said.

Echo nodded.

"We'd be glad to pay you a reward of some kind."

"One puppy," Echo said. "Come spring."

"Come spring," Marge agreed. Then she crossed to Echo and gave her a motherly kiss on the cheek. "We've got two daughters, Herb and I," she said. "They'll each want one of the puppies. We'll keep one for ourselves and Snowball, and bring one to you. I promise you that."

"Thank you," Echo told her.

She followed Marge outside. Watched as the other woman handed the puppies through the open door at the side of the RV. Rance came out, stood on the sidewalk with Echo, one arm around her shoulders.

The Ademoyes drove away.

Echo trembled.

Rance gave Echo a light squeeze.

Echo lifted her hand and waved.

Marge honked the horn in farewell.

And then the big RV rounded the corner and disappeared.

"Still want breakfast?" Rance asked quietly, after a long time had passed.

People going by in cars glanced curiously their way.

"Yes," Echo said with a sniffle, because life went on. Because Snowball was back with her people, where she belonged, and because, despite it all, she was ravenously hungry.

After they'd eaten pancake specials at the Roadhouse, Rance drove Echo back to the shop and returned to the ranch. Both of them had work to do, after all.

The store was busy that day, which helped, but there was a hollow place in Echo's heart, just the same.

At six o'clock, just as she was about to close and force herself upstairs to dress for the dance, Rance's SUV whipped up to the curb out front.

Maeve and Rianna spilled out, wearing their pretty new dresses.

Cora came over from next door, along with Ayanna, who had told Echo she was going home to get ready for her date with Virgil Terp.

Echo smiled.

"Happy birthday to you!" Rianna crowed, flying into her arms for a hug.

Echo embraced the child, looked up again.

And there was Rance, standing in the doorway, with a sizable white box in one arm and a small, squirming dog in the other.

Echo gasped and put a hand to her mouth.

"He's an ugly little critter," Rance said, of the dog, who was gray and short-haired, a mixed breed of some kind, and sporting a red neckerchief for the occasion. "But the folks at the pound said he really needed a home."

Echo laughed and cried, both at the same time.

"You do want Scrappers, don't you?" Maeve asked, looking worried.

"I want him, all right," Echo said.

Rance set the dog down, then put the box on the counter. "Open it," he said.

Echo crossed the shop, lifted the top of the box and looked inside.

It was a cake, and there was writing on top.

Echo gazed at Rance, loving him more than she'd ever believed she could love any man. Scrappers, meanwhile, sniffed at her shoes and licked her ankles.

She lowered the sides of the box.

There were candles, a 3 and an 0, but it was the words, scripted in blue frosting, that almost made Echo's heart stop.

Happy Birthday, Emma.

"Emma," she said. "My name is Emma."

Maeve and Rianna were delighted to have the mystery solved, but Scrappers quickly distracted them.

"Darned if I didn't forget the plates for the cake over at the Curl and Twirl," Cora said, her eyes gleaming with happy tears.

"I'll help," Ayanna told her.

They both rushed out.

Rance took her hand.

"Will you marry me, Emma Wells?"

She nodded, too stricken to speak.

He lifted the 3-candle off the cake, and Echo—now Emma—gasped.

An engagement ring lay beneath it.

Rance slipped it onto her finger, frosting and all.

"Whenever you're ready," he said, and then he kissed her.

When their lips parted, Emma dabbed a bit of frosting onto Rance's mouth, and kissed it off again.

Some things, like wonderful white dogs found outside a truck stop in the rain, were meant to be loved for a while, and then given up with as much grace as humanly possible. Other things, like the land that made up the Triple M, and like Rance McKettrick's love, were made to last forever.

Whenever you're ready, Rance had told her.

Well, Emma was ready.

She was ready to love and be loved.

She was ready to trust.

She was ready to raise two beautiful little girls, now watching her with shining eyes.

"You'll be our stepmom, right?" Rianna asked hopefully.

"We promise to be good," Maeve added.

Echo-now-Emma embraced both girls, leaned to kiss the tops of their heads. "I'll be proud to have you two for stepdaughters," she said. Then, knowing her heart was shining in her eyes, she looked up at Rance. "What do you say we make some history, cowboy?" she asked.

Rance grinned, jutted out his elbow. "Don't we have a dance to go to?"

She laughed. "We do," she agreed.

The gym at Indian Rock High was decorated to

the hilt, with streamers and balloons dangling from the ceiling, and a live band on stage. It was, Emma thought, like going back in time, like attending all the proms she'd missed, rolled into one.

Rance led her to the middle of the dance floor, turned and opened his arms. Emma moved into them.

And it was a perfect fit.

EPILOGUE

June 29
Jesse's Ridge

THE CLEARING ON TOP OF the mountain was jammed with people in wedding-going clothes. Some had ridden up in SUVs, others in horse-drawn buggies and carriages. A few had even traveled on horseback.

Jesse and his lovely bride, Cheyenne, stood with their backs to the assembly, facing the minister, a long-time family friend of the McKettricks.

"Dearly beloved," the preacher began. "We are gathered here…"

Rance and Keegan stood proudly at Jesse's left

side, looking wonderfully out of place and breathtakingly handsome in their tuxedos. Rance glanced back at Emma, who was standing with Cora, Dr. Swann, Rianna and Maeve, and winked.

She smiled, and her face warmed.

Rance's diamond glinted on her left hand, and she took a moment to admire it.

A soft breeze ruffled the branches of the ancient pines lining the clearing, and the sky overhead was a heartbreaking shade of blue.

The ceremony passed in a blur—Emma heard little of it.

She thought of her estranged uncle, who had passed away peacefully in his sleep a few days before, at the care center, and been buried without any fanfare at all.

And then there were Della and Bud Willand. The prosecutor had decided to give Bud a second chance, and according to Della, he'd started his new job as a welder and was behaving himself.

The Ademoyes called regularly, with updates on the puppies. All was well with Snowball.

Scrappers was proving to be a challenge, but he was Emma's dog. Nobody could come and take him away.

The bookstore was thriving.

Emma loved Rance McKettrick, and he loved her.

A person couldn't ask for more.

"…I now pronounce you man and wife," the minister said. "Jesse, you may kiss your bride."

Jesse kissed Cheyenne, and gave a whoop of joy afterward.

The wedding guests laughed and applauded, and the sounds echoed off the surrounding hills, hills that had witnessed the births, marriages and deaths of countless McKettricks.

Emma closed her eyes for a moment and breathed in the sweet mountain air. Jesse and Cheyenne would add to the family history, and so in time, would she and Rance. Eventually, Rianna and Maeve would, too.

The story would go on, weaving like a bright, strong ribbon through the present and into the future.

* * * * *

Turn the page for a preview of
McKettrick's Heart, the conclusion to
Linda Lael Miller's McKettrick Men trilogy,
available in April from HQN.

KEEGAN MCKETTRICK STOOD impatiently beside his black Jaguar, waiting for the tank to fill and pondering the pile of designer luggage resting between the newspaper box and the display of propane tanks near the entrance to the town's only gas station/convenience store. Even from a distance, he could tell the bags weren't knockoffs, and whoever owned them had most likely come in on the four o'clock bus from Phoenix. He pondered the discrepancy between the fancy bags and their modest location while his car guzzled liquid money.

He was replacing the hose when the familiar station wagon bounced off the highway and rolled by with Florence Washington at the wheel.

Keegan wanted to duck into the Jag and drive off, pretend he hadn't seen her, but that would have gone against his personal code, so he didn't. He'd known Psyche Lindsay, née Ryan, was back in town, that she'd come home, with her adopted son, to die.

He'd geared himself up to go by and see her several times since her return to Indian Rock, but he'd been reluctant to call or knock on the door, in case he disturbed her. If she was as sick as he'd heard she was, she was practically bedridden.

The station wagon rolled to a stop, over by the propane tanks and the Louis Vuitton bags.

As Keegan squared his shoulders, he saw Florence turn in his direction, gazing balefully through the driver's-side window.

He reminded himself that he was a McKettrick, born and bred, and approached, assembling a smile as he did.

Meanwhile, the door on the driver's side sprang open, and a slight woman with shoulder-length blond hair got out.

Keegan glanced at her, looked away, registered who she was and looked back. He felt the smile evaporate from his mouth, and forgot all about his plan to ask Florence if Psyche was up to receiving visitors.

His jaw clamped as he rounded the back of the wagon to confront Thayer Ryan's mistress.

"What the hell are you doing here?" he growled. He couldn't recall her name, but he remembered running into her at a swanky restaurant up in Flag one night. She'd been sitting with Ryan, that scumball, at a secluded table, clad in a slinky black cocktail dress and dripping diamonds—gifts, no doubt, from her married lover, and almost certainly charged to Psyche, since Ryan had never had a pot to piss in.

The blonde blinked, startled. A pink flush glowed on her cheekbones, and her green eyes flickered with affronted guilt. Still, her gaze was steady, and more defiant than ashamed.

"Keegan McKettrick," she said. Then she tried to go around him.

He blocked her way. "You have a good memory for names," he told her. "Yours slips my mind."

Florence, meanwhile, opened the back of the station wagon, presumably to stow the bags. "I'm not doing this all by myself," she said.

Keegan remembered his manners—at least partially—and waved Florence back from the luggage. "There's another bus tonight," he told the woman, whose face and body he recalled so well.

"Molly Shields," she said, and raised her chin a notch to let him know she wasn't intimidated. "And I'm not going anywhere. Kindly get out of my way, Mr. McKettrick."

Keegan leaned in a little. Ms. Shields was a head shorter than he was, and he must have outweighed her by fifty pounds, but she didn't' shrink back, and he had to accord her a certain grudging respect for that. "Psyche's sick," he said, in a grinding undertone. "Just about the last thing she needs is a visit from her dead husband's girlfriend."

The flush deepened, but the green eyes flashed. "Step aside," she said.

Keegan was still getting over the brass-balls audacity of her attitude when Florence interceded, poking at him with a finger.

"Keegan McKettrick," the old woman said, "either make yourself useful and load up those bags, or be on your way. And if you can take time out of your busy schedule, you might stop by the house one of these days soon and say hello to Psyche. She'd like to see you."

Keegan deliberately softened his direction. "How is she?" he asked.

Molly Shields took the opportunity to slip around him and grab one of the suitcases.

"She's bad sick," Florence answered, and tears glistened in her eyes. "She asked Molly to come here, and I'm not any happier about it than you are, but she must have a good reason, and I'd appreciate some cooperation on your part."

Keegan was both confounded and chagrined. He nodded to Florence, lifted two of the five suitcases by their fancy handles, and hurled them unceremoniously into the back of the station wagon, doing his best to ignore Molly Shields, who sidestepped him.

"You tell Psyche," he said to Florence, "that I'll be by as soon as she feels up to company."

"She usually holds up pretty well until around two in the afternoon," Florence replied. "You come over tomorrow, around noon, and I'll set out a nice lunch for the two of you, on the sunporch."

Keegan didn't miss the phrase "for the two of you," and neither, he saw, from the corner of his eye, did Molly, who was wrestling with the largest of the bags. "That sounds fine," he said, and jerked the handle from Molly's grasp to throw the suitcase in with the others.

She glared at him.

He went right on ignoring her.

"I'd best pick up some bread and milk while we're here," Florence said, addressing Molly this time. With that, she disappeared into the convenience store.

"Does Psyche know you were boinking her husband?" Keegan asked in a furious whisper, the moment he and Molly were alone.

Molly gasped.

"Does she know?" he repeated.

She bit her lower lip. "Yes," she said very quietly, when he'd just about given up on getting an answer.

"If you're trying to pull some kind of scam—"

Molly's shoulders had been stooped a moment before. Now she rallied and looked as though she might be about to slap him. "You heard Mrs. Washington," she said. "Psyche *asked* me to come."

"Not without a lot of setting up on your part, I'll bet," Keegan argued. "What the hell are you up to?"

"I'm not 'up to' anything," Molly answered, after

an obvious struggle to retain her composure, such as it was. "I'm here because Psyche—needs my help."

"Psyche," Keegan rasped, leaning in again until his nose was almost touching Molly's, "needs her *friends.* She needs to be home, in the house where she grew up. What she *does not* need, Ms. Shields, is *you.* Whatever you're trying to pull, you'd better rethink it. Psyche's too weak to fight back, but, I assure you, I'm not!"

"Is that a threat?" Molly countered, narrowing her marvelous green eyes.

"Yes," Keegan retorted, "and not an idle one."

Two unforgettable classics from
New York Times bestselling author

DIANA PALMER

Get swept away once again by these vintage tales
celebrating two Diana Palmer heroes we dare
you to forget...

Rediscover HUNTER and MAN IN CONTROL
in HARD TO HANDLE.

"The ever-popular and prolific Palmer has penned
another sure hit."
—*Booklist* on *Before Sunrise*

*Available wherever
trade paperbacks are sold.*

HQN™

We *are* romance™

www.HQNBooks.com

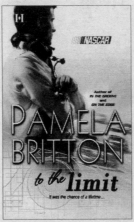

REQUEST YOUR FREE BOOKS!

2 FREE NOVELS FROM THE ROMANCE/SUSPENSE COLLECTION PLUS 2 FREE GIFTS!

YES! Please send me 2 FREE novels from the Romance/Suspense Collection and my 2 FREE gifts. After receiving them, if I don't wish to receive any more books, I can return the shipping statement marked "cancel." If I don't cancel, I will receive 4 brand-new novels every month and be billed just $5.49 per book in the U.S., or $5.99 per book in Canada, plus 25¢ shipping and handling per book plus applicable taxes, if any*. That's a savings of at least 20% off the cover price! I understand that accepting the 2 free books and gifts places me under no obligation to buy anything. I can always return a shipment and cancel at any time. Even if I never buy another book from the Reader Service, the two free books and gifts are mine to keep forever.

185 MDN EF5Y   385 MDN EF6C

Name	(PLEASE PRINT)
Address	Apt. #
City	State/Prov. Zip/Postal Code

Signature (if under 18, a parent or guardian must sign)

Mail to The Reader Service:

IN U.S.A.: P.O. Box 1867, Buffalo, NY 14240-1867
IN CANADA: P.O. Box 609, Fort Erie, Ontario L2A 5X3

Not valid to current subscribers to the Romance Collection,
the Suspense Collection or the Romance/Suspense Collection.

Want to try two free books from another line?
Call 1-800-873-8635 or visit www.morefreebooks.com.

* Terms and prices subject to change without notice. NY residents add applicable sales tax. Canadian residents will be charged applicable provincial taxes and GST. This offer is limited to one order per household. All orders subject to approval. Credit or debit balances in a customer's account(s) may be offset by any other outstanding balance owed by or to the customer. Please allow 4 to 6 weeks for delivery.

Your Privacy: Harlequin is committed to protecting your privacy. Our Privacy Policy is available online at www.eHarlequin.com or upon request from the Reader Service. From time to time we make our lists of customers available to reputable firms who may have a product or service of interest to you. If you would prefer we not share your name and address, please check here. ☐

BOB07

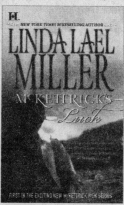